Crash – The Comp

CRASH
MIRANDA DAWSON

Part One

Chapter One

I took a peak into the conference hall to look at our audience. There were hundreds or people out there. Mainly men, but with a token scattering of women in power suits. Soon they would all have their attention fixed on me. Was I ready for that? I'd never been the subject of attention like this before.

"Do you think we should do one more run through of the presentation?" I asked John. "We did slip up a little in the middle when talking about the historic financial data."

John smiled at me. "Relax, Emily. We've got this. That slip up was entirely my fault and it won't happen again. The more we stress about every little detail, the more likely we are to make a mistake."

"I can't help it," I said. "You do realize that everyone out there is going to be waiting for me to screw up?

"Not this again, Emily," John sighed. "No one in the audience even knows about your leg."

"Actually, smartass, I was referring to the fact that I am a woman. I've checked out the list of speakers for this conference, and only three women are scheduled to speak. And the other two look like they could be part-time supermodels."

John sighed again, but he didn't argue. He couldn't disagree with me on this one; Silicon Valley was still a boys club, and the vast majority of women who did make it here were attractive or had other connections. I had neither.

"The fact that you are a woman gives you an advantage, not a disadvantage," John said. "Besides, I guarantee you that most of the men in this audience would do anything to get you in the sack."

"Oh, please," I said. "I'm hardly beating men off with a stick."

"That's because you won't even let them get that close. I'll let you in on a little secret, Emily—when men think about what they like in a woman, the lower half of one leg features pretty low on the list. Now stop sulking and get ready for this presentation."

John was right. I needed to get my head in the game and stop worrying about things that were out of my control. This presentation could make or break our startup, so it had to be a good one. My paranoia about having a prosthetic leg would have to wait.

John was on fire. He spoke with a confidence I had not seen in him before as he wowed the audience of investors with the business plan for our start-up venture. LimbAnalytics had started as just an idea—something I had dabbled with in my spare time while pursuing my biology major at Stanford—but with John's help, I had made it into a business.

With the right investors, LimbAnalytics might revolutionize life for people with artificial limbs like me. To say I was excited would have been an understatement.

I scanned the room and picked out a few faces I recognized. Silicon Valley was a close-knit community, so the same people appeared at most of these events. Every face in the crowd represented cash, the lifeblood of my business.

But one face stood out from the crowd. A man stood at the back of the room whispering into a woman's ear. I saw her giggle as he handed her a business card. Based on her body language, they would be having more than a networking lunch.

I kept an eye on him as he pulled his mouth away from the woman's ear. He was captivating. I was standing on stage next to my business partner as he gave a presentation and yet all I could do was stare at this man. He wore a fitted, light gray suit that hugged his muscular arms and bulging chest. I'd never mentally undressed a man before—heck, I'd never undressed a man period—but I already had him shirtless and was unbuckling his belt in my mind.

My eyes followed him as he left the room. His tight trousers left me with a detailed view of his rear and I couldn't help but imagine sinking my teeth into it. The man was a walking Greek God—an Adonis. I ached with longing and found myself eager to get back to my hotel room and spend some time between the sheets.

"Emily?" John said next to me, sounding a little agitated.

I looked toward him and could hear the crowd murmuring and snickering at me as I stood there under the lights. I looked at our presentation and realized it was my turn to speak. Judging by the sweat glistening on John's forehead, he had been trying to get my attention for some time.

"Uh, sorry. Um..." I muttered, kicking myself for daydreaming at the worst possible time. "As John has explained the business plan, please now let me explain a little more about how LimbAnalytics works and how it will revolutionize medical treatment for people with—"

As I spoke, my fake leg hit the back of my other calf and I went flying into the podium. I tried to grab hold of it, but only succeeded in pushing it over on my way down to meet the floor. My knee took the brunt of the fall, but that wasn't my concern right now. My trouser leg had crept up and my prosthetic limb was showing to all and sundry. The gasp from the audience washed over me as John picked me up.

"At least now I have your attention," I said, rearranging my clothing. It was a bad joke, but the audience gave a polite laugh.

The rest of the presentation went surprisingly well, given that little incident. I did have to apologize to John for leaving him hanging. Apparently he had called my name at least five times with no response. I gave him some excuse about seeing an old college friend in the audience and he seemed to buy that.

It didn't matter anyway. After the presentation we were inundated with people who wanted to speak to us about our product. Intriguing people had never been a problem, though; it was getting them to invest that had caused many sleepless nights. LimbAnalytics had a great business model, but we required huge capital investment with little chance of return for five years. I had every belief we would succeed, but I couldn't blame potential investors for getting cold feet after looking at our accounts.

John and I spent the rest of the afternoon and into the early evening networking with nondescript men who all started to look alike after a while. They were all white, middle-aged, and dressed in a suit, but without the tie, which was about as formal as it got in the Valley.

The only way I could tell them apart was the way they acted with me. There was Niles, the skinny guy who kept trying to peer through the gap in my blouse. Preston kept putting his hand on my knee or on my arm whenever he made a bad joke. Richard and Wilson treated me like an idiot and assumed I wouldn't understand any of the financial aspects of investment.

None of them were ideal investors, but at least they retained my vision for the company. They were not the real problem. The problem that kept me up at night was PharmaTech, the world's largest pharmaceutical firm that had been sniffing around our company for months. They would make an offer sometime in the next few months, that much I knew. It would be an offer that would make us millionaires overnight and likely mean we would never have to work again for the rest of our lives. But they would also destroy my dream.

PharmaTech would buy the company and then immediately dismantle it because our product threatened their profits. PharmaTech made big money under the existing system and we worried them. I couldn't let them buy the company. I started LimbAnalytics to help people, not to make a rich company even richer.

"You going to call it a night, Emily?" John asked when he had finally managed to shake off the last hanger-on.

"I'm going to grab a bite to eat at the bar," I said. "I haven't eaten since breakfast and my stomach is growling. Want to join me?"

"No, better not. I promised Tom I would give him a call. He always worries that these networking trips are just orgies in disguise."

I smiled and said goodbye. John's boyfriend was a little clingy, but it was nice to see John settling down in a serious relationship. He'd spent all of college sleeping around, so a boyfriend was a big lifestyle change for him.

The hotel restaurant was small and all the tables were taken. I considered heading out into the city for food when a few people got up from the bar and vacated their seats. I grabbed a stool and skimmed the menu before settling on a large burger. It was hardly an original choice, but I needed comfort food right now.

The burger arrived quickly and I immediately set about destroying it. I didn't look entirely ladylike, but at that point I couldn't have cared less; it'd been a long day. Not a lot could have taken my attention from my dinner right then, but someone walked into my line of vision and stopped me mid-bite.

In through the hotel entrance walked the man I had seen earlier while I gave my presentation. He strolled through the door in the same gray suit, although I would never have guessed he had spent the day in it. The only change to his appearance from earlier was the rough stubble around his face. Other than that, he looked immaculate.

The man stopped to finish up a phone conversation, giving me a great opportunity to take him all in and store him in my memory for later. He held the phone in his hand; elbow bent to reveal a large bicep that seemed eager to escape his suit. His tailored shirt did not leave a lot to the imagination either, and if I had to guess, I would have imagined he had the beginning of a six-pack on his stomach.

He put the phone down and I quickly looked away to avoid getting caught, then went back to picking at my food. Just a few moments later, someone pulled out the stool next to me and took a seat.

My peripheral vision took in a gray suit. I chanced a quick look to the side as he picked up the menu. It was him. He was sitting right next to me. I could smell a faint whiff of subtle aftershave and it sent my hormones into overdrive. Suddenly I felt drunk and giddy like a schoolgirl.

The bar had emptied out somewhat while I had been eating, and there were now plenty of tables free. He did not have to sit next to me, and yet here he was. If I were to move slightly to my right, my arm would brush against his.

Why had he sat next to me? Surely he wasn't planning to hit on me? One-night stands were hardly unusual in hotels, but that sort of thing didn't happen to me. Just a few seats to my left a stunningly gorgeous woman in a red dress was drinking alone, practically screaming for a guy to buy her a drink, and yet this man, this god in human form, had chosen to sit next to me.

Maybe he had a thing for broken women? Or he could detect my innocence and wanted to teach someone "pure?" I wasn't technically a virgin, but I felt like one and I was sure I gave off that vibe.

I made an effort to eat slowly and finish my drink. Hopefully he would take note of the empty glass and decide it might need a refill.

"Hi," came a soft voice from the seat next to me. "Can I buy you a drink?"

Oh my God, it had worked. It was really happening. No one like this had ever hit on me before except at college, and that was usually as a joke.

I tried to act cool. "Sure. I'll have a vodka tonic," I said, turning my head to smile at him. But he had his back toward me. He turned and looked at me over his shoulder, staring into my eyes and looking confused. My heart sank as I saw a stick-thin, beautiful woman in a silver dress on the other side of him. It was the same woman he had been talking to during my presentation. He wasn't asking me for a drink; he was asking her. The woman snickered and made little effort to hide her amusement.

"Oh, I'm sorry," the man said, looking at me with pity. "I was asking this lady. But please, allow me to buy you a drink anyway."

I quickly rummaged around in my purse for some cash, then threw it down on the bar and ran as fast as I could with only one working leg. A few strangers cast worried looks in my direction, but I ignored them and headed straight for the elevators. Unfortunately, they were all on their way up to other floors.

I looked back over and saw them both still looking at me. The elevator took an eternity to arrive and by the time I arrived back in my room I was a hot, sweaty mess. What a fool I had been. Men like that did not buy drinks for women like me. I lay on the bed and cried myself to sleep.

Chapter Two

I couldn't face going downstairs to breakfast the next morning. It took me nearly an hour to shower and make myself look presentable, and by the time I was done, the breakfast buffet was probably just down to the dregs anyway.

My phone had a few missed calls from my mom. I'd promised to update her on how the day went and she tended to panic when I forgot to call. I contemplated just sending her a text, but I really needed to speak to a comforting voice right now.

Mom always answered the phone with a generic, "Hello?" as if she didn't know exactly who was on the other end. It usually drove me nuts, but right now I found it kind of endearing.

"Hi, Mom."

"Oh, hello, dear. How are you? How did the big day go?"

"I'm fine, mom. Sorry for not calling last night. John and I were networking into the early hours, and by the time I got back to my room I was just exhausted. I fell right to sleep." I could never outright lie to my mother, so I just kept to statements that were technically true.

"Networking?" Mom said. "I am impressed, dear."

Mom was impressed with most of what I did. I was the first in the family to go to college, so when I graduated Stanford University with a major in human biology, it was a pretty big deal. Mom didn't entirely understand my business or the amounts of money that were being bandied around, but that was probably for the best.

"It's not as exciting as it sounds, I'm afraid," I said. "Just talking to lots of rich men about money."

"Sounds exciting to me dear. I wouldn't mind spending my evenings talking to rich men who want to give me money."

"Mom!"

"What? I'm just saying that perhaps things aren't all that bad. Any chance one of these rich men wants to buy you dinner?"

"Hardly, Mother," I said. "I doubt I'm their type."

I heard my mother sigh on the other end. "Not this again, darling. You are a beautiful young woman, and when you project a little confidence, I doubt any man can resist you. No man worth having is going to care about your leg."

"I know, I know," I said, just to keep Mother happy. I didn't want to get into that discussion right now. "This is just not a good place to meet men, that's all."

"I thought it was a sausage-fest over there," Mom said. "You should be able to have your pick."

I cringed at Mom's choice of words. No one wanted to hear their mother talk about "sausage-fests." Her and Dad had started drifting apart after my brother died and Mom seemed determined to regain her lost youth. That meant talking to me like she was still twenty, and it was painful.

"I'm trying to keep it all business while I'm out here," I said. That should keep her happy. She wanted me to find a man, but she also wanted me to be successful, so work had to come first sometimes.

"Anyway, can we talk about that on your birthday? I assume you can still make it over for that weekend? I've booked a restaurant for us." It wasn't a cheap one either, but then it wasn't every year your mother turned fifty. With Dad unable to get out of work this weekend, she would only end up spending it with other couples. She hated that, so we'd arranged for her to come and spend the weekend with me in the city.

"Oh, yes," Mom said. "I'll be there. Can't wait to get out of this place, actually. The weather is getting up into the hundreds, so it's too hot to even go outside."

16

"All right, well, I'm going to buy your plane ticket when I get home tonight. I've got to dash now. I have one final bit of networking to do."

"Okay, dear. Do see if you can snare a man while you're at it."

"I've told you, Mom. I'm not interested in these guys."

"Not for you. For me. Have a good day."

Mothers. I checked myself in the mirror and decided to try and take Mom's words to heart. I was the founder of a popular start-up company and people were interested in me. I wasn't unattractive. When I wore trousers or a long skirt to hide my leg, I attracted a lot of glances. Bigger tits would have been nice, but the ones I had were pert and went well with my slender frame.

I pulled on a professional pair of trousers and paired it with a blouse that opened low, revealing a hint of bosom. I didn't have a lot to work with, but I was damn sure going to make the best of it. Time to go charm some investors.

Chapter Three

After two days of mingling with investors, I actually found it rather challenging to return to work. Whereas I usually leapt out of bed in the morning ready to change the world, I now found myself lingering between the sheets and reluctant to even switch on my computer.

I spent Saturday at home, but it was not exactly productive. I answered some emails and made a few minor tweaks to the code, but nothing exciting. John didn't like it when I fiddled around too much with his code, because more often than not, I broke it and he would spend days fixing it. Still, given that only a year ago I had known nothing about computer coding, the fact that I could do anything at all was an achievement.

Unfortunately I made the mistake of streaming TV shows on Netflix, and from that point, the day was over in terms of productivity.

John apparently had the same problem. "Want to work at the SF Station tomorrow?" he asked in a message. "Can't work at home with Tom around."

"Sure. See you there at 10 am."

The SF Station was our go-to coffee shop located roughly equidistant between John and me. They served excellent coffee but were criminally underrated, which meant John and I could always find a table to sit down and work.

"Usual, Emily?" Jane asked as I approached the counter.

"Yes, please, but could you drop a second shot of espresso in there today?"

"One of those days, is it?" Jane asked with a smile.

"Something like that."

John had already claimed a table in the corner that was big enough for four people. Or it was until we pulled out laptops and chargers and spread ourselves out.

"Morning," I said, sitting down adjacent to him.

"Hey," John replied. "Thanks for coming here today. I was just getting so much grief from Tom for working at the weekend. I had to get out."

"But he doesn't mind you working at the coffee shop?" I asked.

"He might," John said. "But I told him I was visiting my brother down in Palo Alto."

"Ah. Well, I would likely have come here anyway. I barely got a thing done yesterday."

"*How I Met Your Mother*?" John asked.

"*Frasier*, actually," I replied. "Haven't watched it in years, and you know what it's like once you get started."

"Only too well," John said.

We had a quick catch up on where we were with the business and then divided up a couple of important tasks. LimbAnalytics had started with us working like this in the coffee shop, so being back here with John helped me forget about the investors and really knuckle down to work.

"I'm going to need another coffee," John said after we had worked in silence for at least two hours. "You want one?"

"Oh, yes," I replied. "Soy milk latte, please."

John left the table and headed over to order the drinks. I should have asked him to grab me a snack as well. As soon as I stopped working I realized how hungry I was.

"Do you mind if I join you?" asked a man with a strong accent. Was he English?

I hated sharing a table, but the two of us could hardly justify taking up a large table if the place was busy.

Except it wasn't busy. I looked up and saw a number of empty tables in front of me. It was too late to say anything now; the stranger was taking a seat opposite me and next to John.

"Thank you," the man said.

"No problem," I muttered and took a quick look up at the man.

It was him; the guy from the bar at the conference, the man in front of whom I had completely embarrassed myself.

"Hi," he said with a grin. "Remember me?"

How could I forget him? In shock, my lungs expelled the air from my body and I saw a tiny bit of spittle escape from my mouth and land directly in front of him. He pretended not to notice. His appearance was different from the night before. The stubble had gone and a polo shirt and jeans had replaced the tailored, slim-fit suit, but his face was not one I was likely to forget in a hurry.

"Yes," I said, finally able to form a word. "I'm sorry about what happened. I hope I didn't spoil your evening."

The man looked puzzled. "Why are you sorry? That was all just a misunderstanding. These things happen."

He kept staring at me, his eyes looking deep into mine as if he were trying to read my mind. What should I say next?

The silence stretched on while he waited for me to speak. With impeccable timing, John returned to the table with my coffee.

"Oh, hello," John said to the stranger, assuming I knew him from the way we were looking at each other. "I'm John, Emily's business partner." John held out his hand to the man while I looked on, still not entirely sure what was happening.

"Hello, John. I'm Carter. Pleasure to meet you."

"Is that an English accent?" John asked, his eyes lighting up. He was a sucker for an English accent almost as much as I was. Knowing my luck, the two of them would be talking about *Doctor Who* any minute now.

"Yes," Carter replied, glancing back at me. "I'm from Winchester. It's near London," he added when John glanced at him with a confused look on his face.

"I met Carter at the conference the other night," I said, trying to take some control over the situation.

"Ah, you want to invest in LimbAnalytics?" John asked.

Carter lifted his cup to his lips, his bicep flexing under the tight shirt as he did so. God, this guy was a dream. Better, in fact. Even the men in my dreams were grounded in reality. This guy should not have been real.

Two Chinese girls at the table next to us were clearly talking about him. I didn't need to know Mandarin to recognize sexual desire when it was that obvious.

"No, no," Carter said. "I'm afraid I know nothing of technology. Not my thing at all. I just popped by to ask Emily for a favor."

It all fell into place. The other night was no doubt an illicit liaison that needed to stay secret. He had come here to ask me to keep my mouth shut. How romantic.

"How can I help you, Carter?" I asked.

Carter smiled. "You can accompany me to dinner on Friday."

Chapter Four

I saw John mouth the words, "holy crap!" He looked as excited as I should have felt.

"I, uh, I've just remembered I need to make a call outside," John said, standing up from the table so quickly he banged his knees and nearly tripped over the power cord connected to his laptop. I thought he mouthed, "go for it," as he left, but I couldn't be sure.

"You want to take me to dinner?" I asked.

"Yes, if you would be so kind." Carter leaned back in his chair and crossed one leg over the other, never losing eye contact with me.

"Look, I get that the other night was embarrassing for all concerned, but you don't need to make it up to me."

"I know," Carter said. "I'm not trying to make it up to you. I just want to buy you dinner."

"Why?" I asked. "I'm not exactly your type, am I?"

I caught a hint of confusion in Carter's face, but he did a good job of hiding his emotions.

"What is my type, exactly? I wasn't aware I had one."

"I saw the woman you were with the other night. She was stunning. Don't tell me you are interested in someone like me."

"You don't really think a lot of me, do you?" Carter asked, each word coming out soft in his English accent. "I don't have a type. I just like beautiful women, and you, Emily, are very beautiful."

He must have been lying, but what for? Did he just want to sleep with a disabled girl for a laugh? Maybe he hadn't noticed my leg? I'd assumed he'd noticed as I tripped on my way out of the restaurant, but it was possible he'd been too fixated on Miss Big Tits to notice.

"Why are you in the US?" I asked, changing the subject.

"On business," Carter replied.

"So you are only here for a week or so?"

"A couple of months, actually."

"And then you go home. I'm not looking for a short fling, I'm afraid. I suggest you stick to women who are only looking for a night of fun."

"Ouch," Carter said. He looked genuinely offended. "All I want to do is take you for dinner this Friday. Is that really so much to ask? I think I could show you a good time, and if you don't want anything else to happen, then it doesn't have to."

Carter wasn't used to people telling him no, and I must have been crazy to be doing that. I could see John staring through the window and egging me on. Was I mad to be turning him down? Carter looked genuine enough, but something didn't quite fit in this situation, and there was no way I could let myself fall for someone like him. In a few months he would head home and leave me here where no man could ever measure up.

"I don't mean to sound rude," I said. "I'm sorry. I just don't like jumping into things so quickly, and knowing that you're going home in a few months just makes this the sensible decision. Besides, I have a disability that isn't exactly conducive to having passionate flings."

Carter smiled. Was that a nice smile or a condescending one? I couldn't decide.

"You have an artificial leg, Emily. That hardly makes you incapable of going to dinner with me. Do you always do the sensible thing? Because life would be a lot more fun if you let your hair down once in a while."

"Unfortunately, yes," I replied. Every decision in my life was based on being sensible. "Anyway, it's

26

my mom's birthday on Friday and I'm taking her for dinner."

"Okay," Carter said, standing up. "I'm not going to try and force you to do something you don't want to do. It's a shame, though, because you seem like a remarkable woman."

"Wait," I called out as Carter walked away. "How did you know I would be here?"

"Easy," Carter replied. "I saw your company name on your name badge at the convention. That company has an office nearby, according to public records. I assume it's just a PO box, or something like that?"

I nodded.

"You're a start-up. Start-ups like to work in coffee shops. I looked in a few ones nearby and bingo, here you are."

"Impressive," I said.

"Like I said, I really want to take you to dinner, and I always get what I want. Goodbye, Emily. I will see you again soon."

I gave a weak wave as he left the coffee shop. He had gone through all that effort to find me. Why would he do that for a girl who made a fool of herself in front of him?

"Are you crazy?" John yelled at me as he sat back down. "You turned him down? Are you blind?"

Everyone in the coffee shop was staring at us now.

"He just wanted a one-night stand," I said. "And yes, I know he is attractive—"

"No, he's not attractive," John said. "Brad Pitt is attractive. Carter looks like he was personally sculpted by God and then given an English accent. What were you thinking?"

"Come on, John. Doesn't this all sound a bit weird to you? He could have anyone he wants, but he decides to invite me out to dinner? He just wants to have a bit of fun with a cripple and then ditch me. Maybe he just wants to brag to his friends that he slept with a one-legged girl."

"Don't be ridiculous," John scolded. "Anyway, so what if he just does want a bit of fun? What's wrong with that? I don't mean to sound rude, Emily, but you really need to let someone in one day. And not just in your heart, if you get my meaning."

"He's not my type, John, okay? Now just leave it."

John dropped it and we got back to work, but he looked baffled and acted a little off for the rest of the day. I kept typing away, but couldn't get Carter out of my mind. Those eyes. Those arms. I just couldn't shake them.

As soon as I got home, I took some time to myself between the sheets. I shuddered to a climax imagining Carter's strong arms lifting me up and throwing me onto the bed before making me into a woman.

Every time I masturbated, I told myself that I would loosen up and get a man for real. I'd allow him to breach my sex and fill my insides with flesh in a way that my fingers just couldn't do. But then I would meet men and clam up; all the negative possibilities would take over my mind.

What if he freaked out when he saw my leg? What if I was crap in bed? Logically, I knew thinking this way was stupid, but that didn't help. I couldn't change the way I was, but didn't seem to be able to accept it either. Until I did, men like Carter would only be fucking me in my fantasies.

Chapter Five

Mom insisted on staying in a hotel even though I offered her my bed. She said she didn't want to cramp my style, but I had a horrible feeling she just didn't want me to cramp hers. My mother made no secret of her newfound lust for life, and I dreaded to think of the ways she might occupy herself with a hotel room in a big city.

On Friday night, we met at the expensive restaurant I'd picked for her meal—La Table. John and I ate here the night we first got some seed funding for the company. It was a reckless way to blow through a couple of hundred bucks, but we'd both been living on noodles for months and John convinced me that we deserved a treat.

The business was generating a bit of cash now, but this night would still represent a noticeable blow to my bank balance. Still, my mom wouldn't be turning fifty every year, and without Dad around I felt like I had to make an effort.

The restaurant was one of the few places in San Francisco that actually had a dress code, so I wore a dark blue, full-length dress with thin straps and a somewhat risky low neckline. This dress was one of the few that gave me a bit of confidence in my figure, mostly because it completely covered my leg but also because it hugged my figure, pushing my breasts up and out. The maître d' at La Table seemed to approve, judging by the lusty look he gave me.

"Good evening madam," he said, reluctantly tearing his eyes away from my chest. "Do you have a reservation?"

"Yes, table for two under the name Emily Saunders."

"Ah yes, your other guest is already at the table."

He walked me over to a little two-seater table at the back of the room. It was in the middle of an aisle and near the restroom, so we would have people squeezing past us all night. I'd been lucky to get a table at all and couldn't afford to be picky about its location.

"Happy birthday Mom," I said, wrapping my arms around her thin frame. She lost a little weight over the last few months and looked damn good. If I looked like her at fifty, I would be very happy.

"Thank you, dear. I cannot believe how fancy this place is. You really didn't need to bring me somewhere like this. Have you seen the prices?"

I smiled. Mom was used to the dirt cheap food they served in Phoenix, so the prices in San Francisco were bound to be a bit of a shock to her.

"Don't worry about that, Mom. It's my treat for your birthday. Just order whatever you want."

"I'm glad you said that, because I have taken the liberty of ordering us a couple of cocktails. Ah, here they are."

Over the next hour we sampled a bit from the cocktail menu, usually ones with rude names that seemed to titillate my mother, and got through our appetizer and main course. The courses had been quite modest in size, so I contemplated squeezing in dessert.

"Mom, you getting anything?" I asked.

No reply. My mom stared into space, deep in thought. "Mom?"

"Huh? Oh, sorry, dear. Did you say something?"

"I was asking if you wanted anything for dessert?"

"What I want for dessert has just walked in through the door. Goddamn, what I wouldn't give to devour that fine specimen."

"Mom!" I exclaimed. "I don't want to hear things like that."

"Look behind you at your five o'clock and tell me you wouldn't do wicked things to that man."

I sighed, but swiveled slightly in my chair to get a better look at the object of my mom's desire. I couldn't see anyone at first, but then noticed the man with his back to me. He was pulling out the chair for his date, a stunning leggy blonde who must have come straight off the catwalk. This man certainly had a nice ass, I agreed with my mom on that point. Rich as well, judging by the location of the table which had a view out over the bay and by the fact that staff were hovering around to see to the couple's every whim and desire.

Finally the lady took her seat and the man turned round to take his own. He was stunning, all right. Stunning and familiar.

It was Carter.

Chapter Six

Suddenly I felt lightheaded and my eyes slipped in and out of focus. I turned back and reached for the glass of water on the table. I gulped that back and then took a few deep breaths.

"Emily? Are you okay? You look like you've seen a ghost." My mom frowned, and I realized that I must have looked a little rough. I felt cold and sweaty at the same time and my dress clung to my skin.

"Fine, Mom," I said. "Just came over a bit funny."

I took another glance toward the table. Carter was already charming the young blonde, who either found him hysterical or was a great actress. That could have been me. He had asked me out on a date. I could have been sitting there right now, gazing into his eyes and having him spoil me rotten. But I'd said no.

Looking at him with yet another attractive woman made me both jealous and relieved. Deep down, I knew I'd made the right decision. Carter was not a one-woman man. It was better to realize that now than three months down the line.

"Oh my God, do you know that man?" Mom asked.

"What man?" I responded, trying to look clueless.

"You know what man I mean. The one that every woman in the restaurant is trying not to look at right now. The one with—"

"All right, Mother, all right. Yes, I know that man. Well, I know his name, anyway. That's about it. He's called Carter and he's from England. He's just in town for a few months."

"He's English, too? Wow. Just wow. I will remember this birthday for many years, my darling. So how do you know him?"

"We bumped into each other in a coffee shop the other day."

"I wouldn't mind bumping into him. In fact, I might just accidentally bump into him on the way out of here."

"Mom! He's half your age."

"I can dream. Anyway, that makes him the ideal age for you, doesn't it? Why don't you...Oh my God, he's coming over here."

Shit! "He's just going to the restroom, Mom. Please don't say anything." I lowered my gaze and stared intently at the dessert menu. I couldn't handle seeing him up close right now.

To Mom's credit, she did actually remain silent, although I could see her tracking him with her eyes as he walked toward us. He came within inches of the table. At one point he was so close I could have reached out and grabbed a cheek on his perfect ass. Then he stopped.

"Emily. Hi."

I took a deep breath in through my nose and looked up straight into his eyes. I melted. He wore a dark suit with a white shirt and black tie. I spotted cufflinks that were probably the logo of a soccer team, but I had no idea which one. His entire outfit was immaculate.

"Carter. Hi. Um, how are you?"

"A lot better now I have seen you, Emily." He turned to look at my mom and I resumed breathing. "You must be Mrs. Saunders?" He held out his hand. Mom placed her hand in his and he planted a gentle kiss on her fingers. Carter probably didn't find it hard to impress in-laws—or at least, he wouldn't if he ever decided to actually stick to one woman long enough to meet her parents.

"Hello, Carter," Mom said. "How do you know my daughter?"

"Truth be told, ma'am, I actually don't know her all that well. Not as well as I would like to, anyway. Unfortunately, Emily will not agree to have dinner with me. I fear she has misjudged me and decided that we are not a good match."

Mom looked like she had been slapped. I was going to catch hell for this as soon as he left.

"My daughter is just shy, Carter. Please don't give up that easily. Emily, darling, I'm sure you could have one meal with Carter just to see how you get along?"

"It looks like Carter is already on a date, Mom," I said. I had no intention of being the second—no, the third—woman that he strung along while on his little business trip.

"That's strictly business," Carter said. "Lydia is a potential new client and my company wants me to network while I am here."

"There you go, dear," Mom said. "You need to get out more, and Carter seems like a very respectable young man."

"I agree with your delightful mother," Carter said, smiling at me. He had one of those smiles that could illuminate a room with no effort on his part. "How about I take you out tomorrow night?"

"I'm sorry, but my mom is in town this weekend and we have plans."

"No, we don't," Mom snapped. "Don't use me as an excuse. In fact, I have plans of my own tomorrow evening. I have booked a massage and spa treatment in my hotel, so there's no need for you to worry about me."

She was lying, of course, but I could hardly call her out on it.

"Okay, but just dinner," I said. "Me and my mom really do have a busy day on Sunday, so I can't have a late night." I caught Mom rolling her eyes, but she didn't call me out on my lie this time.

"Excellent," Carter said. "What's your address?" I pulled a pen out of my bag and scribbled down and address and phone number on the napkin. "I'll pick you up at seven. Mrs. Saunders, if I don't see you again, then I hope you enjoy your trip."

"Oh, I will have some very pleasant memories of this vacation," Mom replied. I blushed enough for the two of us at that comment.

Carter walked straight back to his table, which meant he had come over especially and not just on the way to the restroom. Could he really want to date me? It made no sense. He had gorgeous women hanging on his every word, and even if his current date was just a business acquaintance, that didn't change the rather obvious fact that she clearly wanted to sleep with him.

"I cannot believe you turned him down," Mom said. "Are you insane?"

"Mom, look at him. He's obviously a player. No doubt he is with a different woman every night."

"So? That doesn't mean you can't have a bit of fun with him as well. And you never know, something more serious might develop."

"I very much doubt that," I replied.

"Well, either way, we are going shopping tomorrow. You need a new dress, a haircut, and hopefully a big box of condoms."

The couple at the table next to us looked over at the mention of condoms, and once again I found myself wanting to crawl under the table and hide.

We ordered dessert, but I couldn't finish it. My nerves tied my stomach in knots, but Mom was only too happy to finish off the dessert.

"Can we get the check, please?" I asked our waiter when he came by our table.

"Your check has been taken care of, madam," the waiter replied. "Another guest settled it for you."

"No need to guess who that was," Mom said.

I should have insisted on paying or made a fuss, but I just wanted to get home. I pulled some cash out of my purse and placed a decent tip on table.

"Ma'am, I really cannot accept that," the waiter said, handing the cash back. "Your friend has already been most generous. Please do keep it."

I shoved the money back into my purse and stared at Carter on the way out. He never even acknowledged us; just kept chatting with his business associate.

Mom and I agreed to meet early in the morning to go shopping. I walked back to my place and zoned out in front of the TV for a bit. The whole evening had been surreal and started to feel like a dream until a text came through on my phone.

"You looked great tonight. Can't wait to see you tomorrow. Carter."

Chapter Seven

"You've scrubbed up pretty well," John said, admiring me in my new dress. My hair was almost unrecognizable from before, now bunched up at the top and making me look pretty damn sophisticated. It was all an illusion, of course—I didn't feel sophisticated or any more confident, but the image I projected was more outgoing than usual, at least.

"Thanks, John," I said. "You still want to hang around here for a bit until Carter arrives?"

"Yes, please. Tom says the internet is still down at ours and I don't fancy being offline all Saturday evening."

"You could always try having a romantic night in," I suggested.

"We don't really do the whole romance thing, to be honest. Not at the moment, anyway."

"Things still a bit tense between you two?"

"Yeah. Unfortunately, the whole 'start-up' lifestyle is a little hard to understand for those who are not part of it. All he knows is that I spend nearly every waking hour on my computer. He probably thinks I'm having online affairs or something."

"I'm taking the evening off," I said. "There's no reason you can't too."

"I would take the evening off if someone like Carter was taking me out on date."

"It's not a date," I said. "Not really. I'm just having dinner with him to please my mom."

"Oh, don't give me that. Look at you. You shaved your legs?"

I nodded.

"Thought so. Got some condoms?"

"John!" I cried, slapping him on the arm.

"I'm going to take that as a yes."

He happened to be right, but I felt like such a slut admitting to it. I was not going to have sex with Carter tonight. No matter what happened, I would not be putting out after one dinner. But I took some condoms with me anyway.

There was a loud knock at the door. He was early. I opened the door to see Carter standing there in a dark suit holding a bunch of roses in one hand.

"Oh," I said, taking the flowers, "you didn't need to do that. Let me just go put them in water. Please come in."

Carter walked in while I hunted around in my cupboards for something I could use as a vase.

"Hi, John. How's things?"

"Hi, Carter. I'm good. I'm just round here to steal Emily's internet connection so that I can finish up some code."

"Oh, okay."

"I'm sure Carter doesn't want to hear all about your coding issues," I called out from the kitchen. I didn't want Carter to get scared off by the technical stuff which he did not look the least bit interested in.

"It's okay, Emily," Carter said. "I'd like to know a little more about what you do. I checked out the website, but it was a little light on details."

"Yeah, that's just a placeholder," John said. "We don't have much of a presence with the general public yet. Really our entire business is collecting data and developing an algorithm to analyze it. We're relying on this 'big data' yielding some promising results that hospitals can use to treat those with artificial limbs."

"What's 'big data?' " Carter asked. "Sorry, I'm not really technically-minded. I'm a numbers guy. Computers just get in my way."

I could have pointed out that his job would no doubt be a lot harder without computers, but I resisted the urge to come across as a know-it-all.

"Big data, in this context, is referring to all the information that doctors collect about how their patients use their body and how their limbs interact as they move. For example, Emily is collecting data with every step she takes on that artificial leg of hers. Her doctor can then adjust it to minimize damage to her body."

"And that's where your code comes in?"

"Precisely."

"Sounds impressive," Carter replied. He was doing a decent job of looking interested, but I could tell he was bored stiff with this line of conversation.

I let John explain the current coding problem he was trying to fix while I sorted out the gorgeous roses that Carter had bought me. When no one was looking, I lowered my face to the flowers and inhaled deeply through my nose, taking in the glorious aroma. Just when Carter looked like he might fall asleep, I stepped in.

"Okay, we can leave now," I said, picking up my clutch.

"Nice to see you again, John."

"Make sure you close the door properly when you leave," I yelled over my shoulder. "Sorry about that," I said to Carter once we were in the hall. "He gets quite enthusiastic about his work."

"No need to apologize," Carter says. "He seems like a great guy. I just don't have a head for computer coding."

I laughed. "Yeah, I could tell. No offense."

"Offense taken," he said, returning my smile. "Anyway, now that we are alone, I can tell you that you look absolutely stunning tonight. You will be the most beautiful woman I have ever taken to dinner."

"Oh, don't give me that," I said. "I've seen two of your dates and I know I don't look anywhere near as good as them."

"Maybe we have different tastes in women," Carter said. "Because I'm telling you that I have never been so in awe of someone in my entire life. I'm using all my willpower right now not to just push you up against wall and devour you."

I wanted him too. I wanted to just forget where I was—who I was—and have him do wicked things to me as if we were characters in a romantic movie.

"You'll just have to settle for dinner," I said.

"I will have you, Emily," Carter said. "I'm putting you on notice right now that one day soon, I will ravish your naked body and have you begging for more. Consider yourself warned."

Chapter Eight

"Where are we going?" I asked when we got outside. "Should I hail a cab?"

"We are going to Veniere," Carter responded. "No need for a cab."

He strolled up to a large black car parked illegally in front of my apartment building and opened the door for me. I stepped inside, just barely managing not to fall over in my tight dress. The dress parted slightly, revealing my leg, but I covered it back up before Carter saw. The car wasn't a limo as such, at least not a stretched one, but Carter did have a driver so we could sit together in the back.

When I saw where we were going, I realized why I had never heard of Veniere. It was situated right at the top of Nob Hill, which meant we would have a great view. It also meant dinner would cost a small fortune. Last night's dinner would be a MacDonald's meal by comparison.

Carter and I were greeted at the door and then escorted to a private booth at the back of the restaurant. The view truly was breathtaking. The sun was setting the other side of Golden Gate Bridge and the fog had mercifully decided not to come into the bay tonight. I wanted to take a picture, but that would hardly be appropriate here.

"So, will this be going down as a business expense as well?" I asked after we had ordered some calamari to share for an appetizer.

"Alas, I think I shall have to pay for this one out of my own pocket."

"I don't even know what you do for a living," I said. "What job is it you have that requires you to take beautiful women out to dinner?"

Carter let out a small laugh. "You wouldn't believe me if I told you."

"Try me."

"I'm a hedge fund manager," Carter said. "We are doing due diligence on a company out here and I'm overseeing the process. Basically, that just entails keeping everyone happy."

"I'm sure you kept those women very happy," I said, a little bitterness creeping into my voice.

"I do my best," Carter said. "But I would rather not talk about what I do and do not do with other women right now. That's not important."

"It is to me," I said reluctantly. "Sorry, but I'm just not the kind of girl who sleeps around. I don't judge those that do, but I don't do it myself."

"It sounds like you judge them. Anyway, just because I sleep with other women doesn't mean I am not serious about you," Carter said.

Did he just admit to sleeping with those other girls? Maybe not, but he as good as admitted that he slept around. That shouldn't exactly be a surprise. Looking like that, he would have to have some serious character flaws not to have fun with other women.

"Why?" I asked.

"Why what?"

"Why are you interested in me?" I asked. "You hardly know me."

Carter gave a slight shrug of his shoulders. "You intrigue me."

"I intrigue you?" That was hardly an answer to fill a girl with confidence.

"Yes. I saw that conference you were a part of the other week. There were only a handful of women there, and the ones that I met seemed to just be there for eye candy. I caught some of your presentation."

"You did?" I first saw Carter just before he left and had no idea he had been watching me speak before that.

Carter nodded. "I didn't understand any of it, of course, but I could tell you had a real passion for it. Also, I will let you in on a little secret—sometimes it is nice to actually have a conversation with a woman. I do enjoy a good time between the sheets, but there needs to be more to it than that."

I had no idea how to respond to that, but fortunately the waiter appeared to take our orders. I ordered a steak for the entrée out of habit and then immediately regretted it. I should have gone for the chicken salad or something a little more subtle.

"I'll have the same," Carter said. "But make mine medium rare." The waiter nodded and left us alone again. "I've been meaning to ask you something, actually," Carter said.

"Shoot."

"Why do you Americans refer to the main course as an 'entrée?' It's been puzzling me ever since I got here."

I thought for a second, but had no real idea. It was an odd question. "I don't know really. I think it's French."

"Well, yes, it is French," Carter said. "But it is French for 'starter.' That's why outside of the US, we call appetizers 'entrees.' "

"You're kidding?" I asked. "So if a French person came to this expensive, fancy restaurant, they would no doubt think the waiter was talking gibberish? That's kind of amusing."

Whether he meant it or not, that served as the perfect icebreaker and helped me relax. It also gave me the perfect opportunity to ask Carter to say lots of different words in his English accent. Some things sounded disappointingly similar, but some were so different I had trouble understanding what he said. Even the waiter looked temporarily confused when he asked for a glass of water, which sounded more like 'glarse of warter.' I never did figure out what "bob's your uncle" meant.

"Tell me more about your job," Carter said once I had run out of words for him to say. "In a language I can actually understand."

"Well, as you may have noticed, I have an artificial leg and—"

"How did that happen?"

"Car accident," I said. "Five years ago."

"Oh. Sorry. What happened?"

"I don't really want to talk about it," I said, but then changed my mind. He would find out sooner or later. "We got hit by a drunk driver. Went straight into the side of the car."

"We?"

"Me and my little brother, William."

"Oh I didn't know you had a brother."

"I don't," I said, taking a sip of my drink. "Not anymore. He died in the crash."

"Oh, my God. I'm so sorry," Carter said. I could tell he felt terrible. That hadn't been my intention, but talking about my dead brother did tend to make people feel a little awkward. But Carter looked even worse than most. He went white as a sheet and looked like he was about to throw up. I knew what that look meant—Carter had lost someone close as well.

"Let's not talk about it," I said. "The driver is behind bars and will be for a long time. There is nothing I can do to bring William back, so I try not to dwell on it. What were we discussing? Oh, yes— the business."

I transitioned abruptly back to talking about work and Carter was visibly relieved at the change in topic.

"I studied human biology at college and was planning on becoming a scientist. As you can imagine, Stanford is full of computer geeks, and one day John had an idea to combine my medical knowledge with his coding skills."

"And the idea is to help people like you who need artificial limbs?"

"Yes," I said. "The better medical science can understand the limbs, the quicker they can improve them. Legs aren't such a big deal, but think of someone who has lost their arm. If we succeed, people will have actual working fingers instead of just plastic ones."

"Impressive. And at the conference, you were looking for more investors, I assume?"

I nodded. "Not just investors, though. We were looking for the right investor."

"Is there such a thing as a 'wrong' investor?" Carter asked. "I've worked with a few start-ups in my time, and they are usually desperate for any money."

"We had one company that wanted to use the technology on people who didn't need it. They said it could be used to make bodies stronger, but it sounded more like cosmetic surgery to us. That's not what we got in this for."

"Fair enough," Carter said.

"Tell me more about your job," I requested of him.

"Trust me, you really don't want to hear about my job. Even I don't find it interesting." He was almost certainly right and I decided not to push it for fear of revealing my ignorance.

Carter turned the conversation back to my business, and I was impressed with how quickly he picked up a lot of the concepts.

"I think it's about time I took you home," Carter said.

I looked around and saw that we were the last ones left in the restaurant. Where had the time gone?

"I can get a cab," I said. "No need for you to escort me to the door."

"Nonsense," Carter replied. "The car is outside and I have no intention of letting you go just yet."

I didn't admit it, but that was music to my ears.

Chapter Nine

"Well, here we are," I said as the car pulled up outside my building. Carter got out and went round to open my door. I quickly fumbled for the handle to show him that I was capable of opening a door myself, but I couldn't find it.

"I'll see you up to your room," Carter said, placing a strong hand on the small of my back.

I noticed a few odd stares from others on the street; I was likely not the type of girl they were used to seeing step out of an expensive car with a heavenly man escorting me inside. I tried to ignore them, I really did, but deep down I knew this looked ridiculous.

We stepped into the elevator and a few drunk girls followed us in. One of them smiled at Carter.

"Hi, handsome," she said, thrusting her chest in his direction. Carter was stood right next to me, and yet she acted as if I wasn't there. He ignored her and took my hand in his. It was the first time our flesh had ever touched for any length of time, and I felt the sparks travel up my arm and set my heart racing.

The girl—who could barely stand up—gave me a quick once-over and then turned away to face her friends. She was nowhere near as subtle as she thought she was, and I saw her mouth the words, "oh my God." To their credit, her friends had the decency to look a little ashamed.

The elevator stopped two floors below mine and the girls stepped out. The drunk girl seemed to think that the open doors had the power to block sound, because as soon as she stepped out she said, "How the hell are they a couple?" loudly to her friends.

I tried to pull my hand out of Carter's grasp, but he held on tight.

"Ignore them," he said. "They're just silly kids."

"That's what everyone thinks, Carter," I said as we stepped out of the lift. "We look ridiculous together. People probably assume I have rented you for the evening."

"Are you calling me a whore, Emily?"

I laughed. His English accent softened the word 'whore' in a way that it almost sounded respectable.

"You know what I mean. Anyway, here we are. You have escorted me to my door. Thank you for a lovely evening, Carter. I still don't understand why you did it, but I am very grateful."

"It's me who should be grateful," Carter replied, making no effort to leave. "I take it you won't be inviting me in for coffee?"

"Carter, I can't. I'm just—"

"Not that sort of girl. Yes, I know. I'm still going to kiss you, though."

"No, Carter. Not tonight." But I wanted him. I wanted his lips on me. I kept my hands locked by my side, but they shook, desperate to grab his head and pull him in to me.

Carter's hands grabbed my wrists. I made a feeble effort at resisting, but my heart wasn't in it. He threw my hands up alongside my head and pushed me back against the door. Slowly his lips moved toward mine until they connected, sending a rush of blood to my head. I let him kiss me, his soft lips pressing firmly against mine as his tongue forced my lips open.

I gave in. I couldn't resist any more. My tongue shot forward to meet his as our mouths merged together. My tongue battled against his, but he was too strong and I soon succumbed. When he bit my lip I went weak at the knees, and my fake leg nearly slipped out from under me. Carter's right hand went down and grabbed my thigh, holding it up to support me, now that all the strength in my body had left me. My artificial leg grazed against his calf, but if he noticed, he didn't react or say anything.

He tore his lips from mine and started to nibble my earlobe while he pressed his hard member against my sex. Even through our layers of clothing, I could feel my heat burning against his eager shaft.

"I know you're wet right now," Carter whispered in my ear. "If I put my hand between your legs, I would find you wet and ready for me, wouldn't I?"

No words came forth, but my moan gave him all the answer he needed. Then suddenly he released me and stepped away. My left hand reached down to the doorknob to stop myself from collapsing.

"Goodnight, Emily," Carter said. "I will see you again soon."

I watched him walk away before stumbling inside and out of my dress. My fingers brought release a few minutes later, but it wasn't enough. Next time he walked me home, I would not be able to stop him at the door.

Chapter Ten

When I woke up the next morning, I found my phone stuffed full of messages from my mom and John. I ignored Mom's for the time being and didn't even read John's, but I did ask him to come over as soon as possible. I didn't want to be alone in the apartment today. I didn't trust myself not to phone Carter and invite him over.

There was a trace of a minor hangover plaguing my head, so I made a fresh pot of coffee and sat down in front of my laptop. With the best of intentions I opened up the last thing I had been working on, but my fingers refused to do their dance across the keyboard. Fortunately, John showed up pretty quickly.

"Morning, Emily," he greeted me with a knowing smile. "How are you today?" John looked straight into my bedroom and then the bathroom.

"He's not here, John, so you can quit snooping around."

He ignored me and continued looking, but it didn't take long in my small apartment to establish that we were the only ones there.

"Do you really need to look in the trash can, too?" I asked. "You won't find any used condoms in there, if that's what you are after. Carter never set foot in the apartment last night. We had a lovely dinner and then he went home."

John looked disappointed, but poured himself some fresh orange juice and sat down next to me. "You know I'm going to need more details than that. Tell me everything, and don't leave anything out. I'll know if you're lying."

I told him the whole story, everything except how horny I had been when he had me up against the door and what I did as soon as he left. John probably managed to guess those details anyway.

"So, let me just get this straight," John said. "This guy—who you may have noticed is somewhat handsome—took you out for a meal and wants to get into a relationship with you, but you said no."

"He doesn't want to get into a relationship with me. He wants to fuck me, that's all, and I'm not going to do that just because he buys me dinner."

"Straight people are so weird sometimes. Okay, so I get that you don't want to put out on the first date, but he wants to see you again, right? So he doesn't just want sex. It sounds to me like he wants a relationship with you."

"Don't be silly," I said. "For one thing, he's just visiting here for a few months, so a relationship is somewhat impractical. Second, this whole thing is too weird anyway. Why is a guy like him sniffing around someone like me?"

"Not this again, Emily. You are hot. You have a great body and most men are not going to give a shit about your leg."

"What should I do?" I asked.

"Personally, I would tell him to come over and ravage me on the bed like there was no tomorrow. But I guess you won't do that. Look, you might be right about this being a short-term thing, but that doesn't mean it can't be fun. Have a good time and stop worrying about what people think."

I agreed with John just to keep him quiet, but I didn't think I was capable of letting my hair down like that. My only sexual experience had been rudimentary at best. To be fair, I probably hadn't set Neil's world on fire, either.

We were only eighteen, but I just laid back and let him do most of the work. Was that my fault or his? I liked to think I could be more passionate than that and perhaps I just needed the right man to bring that passion out. If Carter couldn't do it, then I might as well just buy some toys and accept a life of celibacy.

The ringing of my phone snapped me out of my thoughts. Carter?

"Shit, it's the lawyer," I said, answering the phone and putting it on speaker. We usually only heard from the lawyer if something bad was going down. "Hi, Scott. How are you?"

"Hello, Emily," Scott said. "Is John there, as well?"

"Hi, Scott," John called out.

"Oh, good. So, how did the conference go last week?"

I could tell this was just Scott's attempt at small talk. He wasn't very good at it.

"The conference went well," I said. "We got the attention of a few investors and have meetings lined up over the next couple of weeks."

"Good, good," Scott said, and then went silent on the other end. I looked over at John, but he just shrugged. "Listen, this is a little awkward, but as you know there are a couple of unpaid bills now. The company owes my firm about $5,000 and I'm getting questions from the managing partner."

"Oh, yes," I said, cringing as I remembered the crumbled bills littering my bedroom floor. "I have those bills on the top of my list. As soon as we get this funding in I will make sure you are paid in full."

"Great, great," Scott said. "At the moment, we have to put a hold on any further legal services, but once the financing is in place we can do more work for you."

"Thanks, Scott. We do appreciate your help with this. I'm sorry for getting you in trouble with your boss."

"Don't worry about it," Scott said. "I'll leave you to it. Keep me updated."

"Five grand!" John exclaimed once Scott had hung up. "How did we rack up all those bills?"

"He charges $350 an hour, John. It's not hard to rack up a few grand. That was the cost of incorporating and getting some of our intellectual property filings done."

"Christ."

"Yeah. But we'll be fine as long as we get this investment sorted out in the next few weeks."

"I certainly hope so," John said. "We didn't put blood, sweat, and tears into this just so—"

The phone rang again.

"Ignore it," John said.

"It's not Scott," I said. "It's Carter."

Chapter Eleven

"Hello, Emily," came the smooth voice on the other end of the phone. I quickly sat down before my legs gave out. The soft tones of his voice triggered some sort of automatic reflex in my body, making my heart rate increase and my stomach contract, not to mention what happened between my legs whenever I spoke to him.

"Hi," I replied. *Great response, Emily.* God, I sounded like a fourteen year-old with a crush on a boy at school. Why couldn't I act normally around him?

"I'm coming over Tuesday night with Chinese food," Carter said.

"What? You're coming here?" Apparently Carter wasn't going to wait for an invitation.

"Yes. I will be round at about eight. I'll bring food and wine. You just make sure you have the place to yourself."

"But, um, Tuesday isn't good," I said, hoping my lie sounded a little more convincing over the phone than it would have done in person. "I have plans with John."

"No you don't," Carter said. "I checked with John before calling." I glared over at John and he quickly made himself scarce. "I'm going to have you Tuesday night," Carter finished. "I'm going to pry open those legs and taste what is between them. I just thought you should know that so that we are both on the same page."

I gasped and slapped my hand over my mouth. I couldn't believe he had the nerve to say that. But then Carter had never exactly hid his intentions from me.

"I don't know, Carter. This all just feels like it is moving a little too fast."

"No, it's moving too slow. If you don't want this to happen, then just say so and you will never see me again. So what is it? Shall I come over Tuesday night?"

I nodded, then remembered I was on the phone. "Yes," I whimpered.

"Looking forward to it." He hung up.

I closed my eyes and took some deep breaths. Was this really happening? Was I actually going to have sex? With Carter? Everything seemed too good to be true. Then John came into the kitchen with news that hit me like a cold shower.

PharmaTech called, but they didn't call with an offer; they called with a threat. "Meet with us or we'll just copy your code and subject your company to death by legal fees." Those were probably not the exact words used, but it was the summary John gave me.

We agreed to meet with PharmaTech's lawyers at their offices on the thirtieth floor of a high-rise in the city. John and I elected to go to the meeting dressed in the most casual and inappropriate clothing we could find. We wouldn't be able to out-dress a couple of hotshot lawyers anyway, so there was no point trying. This way we could show we were not intimidated by them.

We were shown into a room with walls made entirely of glass, although the pattern on the glass gave us a degree of privacy. Three lawyers entered the room. One was about my age and he looked like a newbie; probably just there to take notes.

Doug, the older lawyer, was about forty and had a harsh look to him. Lisa was probably in her early thirties and would have been attractive without the stick up her ass. I didn't catch the young one's name and didn't really care.

"Thank you for coming down," Doug said. "I understand that our client may have scared you over the phone and I apologize for that."

"Let's just get straight down to business, shall we?" John said. "Your client wants to buy our business, but we don't intend to sell. Not to them, anyway. So what leverage do they have?"

"Our client feels that they can help you a lot with your business," Lisa said.

"We don't need any help," I said. "We are doing quite well by ourselves."

"Sure, sure," Lisa said. "But our client feels that there are weaknesses in your algorithms—something to do with security of the data—and they can help you with that."

How the hell did PharmaTech know about that? We only found out ourselves about a couple of weeks ago and John had been working to fix it ever since.

"Our algorithms are fine," John lied. "If that is all, I think we should leave. This meeting is a waste of our time."

"Our client is prepared to buy you out for ten million dollars," Doug said as we stood up to leave. "That's a lot of money. You should give it some thought."

"We have other investors," I said.

"And do you think they will want to invest after doing due diligence?" Lisa asked. "They will find out about this problem you are having and call the whole thing off. Look, I respect your morals and your desire to do good for the world and all that, but I'm telling you that this business is going nowhere. PharmaTech is offering you a way out. Think about it."

John and I left the building and headed straight to the park where we could talk in private.

"How the hell does PharmaTech know about that problem with security?" I asked.

"I have no idea," John said. "The only people who have access to the code are the few beta users we enrolled."

"Did you mention anything to the potential investors at the conference?"

"No, of course not. What do you think I'm going to say? 'Please give us lots of money, but by the way there is a big problem with our product.' "

"Then how—"

"Oh shit," John said, sinking his head into his hands. "What if they hacked into the program? They must have a dedicated security team—it wouldn't be a big leap to imagine them devoting some resources to hacking our system."

Regardless of how they found out, the business was screwed unless we could fix this problem. I massaged my temples and tried to relax. Suddenly Tuesday night could not come soon enough.

Chapter Twelve

When I heard the knock at the door, I quickly opened up my laptop to make it look like I had been working instead of just sitting around waiting for Carter to appear. After a bit of debate with John, I settled on wearing a formal black skirt with a more casual low-cut top. It felt just right for an evening in, but revealed enough cleavage to keep Carter's attention. The skirt was not long enough to cover my leg; now we would see just how normal he could act around me with a plastic leg on display.

I opened the door to see Carter standing there in jeans and a tight t-shirt, holding a bag of food in one hand and a bottle of wine in the other. He had gone a little more casual than me, but that just meant I would have a great view of his arms all night.

"You look gorgeous," Carter said as he placed the food on the table. He kissed me on the cheek and left me blushing. Carter had never been in my kitchen before, but he immediately took control, finding the glasses and corkscrew to pour us some wine. We elected to eat directly out of the containers and Carter handed me some chopsticks.

It had been a while since I had even attempted to use chopsticks and I had forgotten how bad I was with them. I ended up piercing the food with the end of the stick, but eating the rice was nearly impossible.

"You can use a fork if you like," Carter said.

"Then I'll never learn, will I?" I forced a smile, and it actually helped me feel a little less embarrassed.

"Here," Carter said, "let me help. You are holding them all wrong. Copy me."

I tried to mimic where his fingers were placed, but the chopsticks just fell out of my hands whenever I moved them. Carter got up and stood behind me. He took hold of my hand and gently moved my fingers into the correct position. It felt a little like a scene in a cheesy movie, but I didn't care. If this were a movie, then his help would have worked, but instead I dropped rice everywhere at my first attempt at picking anything up.

Carter made no attempt to hide his amusement, but his eyes contained genuine affection. He wasn't laughing at me, he was laughing with me.

"How about we both eat with forks?" he said, going back to the counter and grabbing some utensils from the drawer.

"Thank God for that," I said. "This food will be cold by the time I get to it otherwise. How did you get so adept at using those things?"

"Lived in China for a bit," Carter replied, as if he had just mentioned something completely ordinary.

"Oh, that's interesting."

"Not really. It was for work."

"I didn't realize that investing could take you all over the world. It almost sounds like a dream job."

"Hardly," Carter said with a smile. "But it did bring me here to meet you, and for that I am very grateful."

"So what you're saying is that you move around a lot?" I asked.

"Less now than I used to," he replied. "But yes, I still move a bit. Now I just travel internationally when there's a big sale to manage like this one."

"A sale?" I asked. "I thought you said you were doing due diligence?"

"Same thing, really. Listen, do we have to talk about work?"

"What else do you want to talk about?" I asked.

"Who says I want to talk?" Carter held out his hand and I placed my fingers on his palm. He lightly pulled me up and led me into the living room. Flashbacks of my first boyfriend ran through my mind, not because he been anything like Carter, but because the nervous feeling he'd given me in the pit of my stomach was almost identical to the one I was feeling now.

Something caught Carter's eye and he wondered over to the bookcase. He picked up a photo; my favorite one of my brother William.

"Is this your brother?" he asked.

"Yes," I said. "Just a few weeks before the accident. He was always that happy; real bubbly kid, you know? I'm pretty sure he would have ended up in show business if he'd managed to avoid getting dragged into the real world."

Carter's hand shook slightly as he placed the photo back down on the bookcase, and once again I recognized the emptiness that comes with losing someone so close. Who had Carter lost?

He turned back and pulled me down onto the sofa. He placed a hand on my thigh, just inches from the stub on my leg just below the knee, but acted like there was nothing out of the ordinary. Like there was nothing wrong with me.

Now he would take what he wanted, just like he had told me he would.

The fingers on his other hand wove their way into my hair and he pulled me firmly toward him. When our lips touched I felt the same thrill I had just a few days ago. Would it always be like this? I couldn't imagine ever losing the spark when he touched me, no matter how long we kept it up.

Except we would not keep this up for long. There could be no relationship with Carter.

He drew me in close, but I pulled my lips from his, placed a hand on his chest and tried to push him away. I might as well have been pushing a brick wall, but Carter had the decency to back off anyway.

"I'm sorry," I said. "I can't do this. I don't want to be just a one-night stand. I'm not just trying to be prudish or frigid. I'd love to fuck you. I want to pounce on you right now and feel you enter me."

"Then let it happen," Carter insisted, moving his hand up my leg.

"But as much as I want it now," I continued, "just think how bad it will be when you go back to England."

Carter backed away and took a few slow breaths. "Emily, I can't promise you that we will last more than a month, but why kill this before it has even started? Look, I'll make you a deal. If we are still going strong when I have to leave, we will keep it going. I don't know how yet, but we will."

"Really?" I asked. "But why? Why are you doing this for someone like me?"

"Because you are quite possibly the most amazing person I have ever met. Because when I look into your eyes, I see someone who is scared and vulnerable and just needs help to let out her true self. And one other thing."

He had me already, but it couldn't hurt to hear more. "What's that?"

"I have a thing for pert little tits," he said, grinning.

I gave him a playful slap on the arm and let him push me onto my back as he slipped between my legs.

Chapter Thirteen

I surrendered to him on the sofa. My good leg wrapped around him, pulling him toward me as I pressed his body up against mine, his eagerness burning against my sex. Our lips crashed together as his tongue explored my mouth.

He pulled his shirt over his head and for the first time I could see the sculpted body underneath. His pecs held firm under my touch and his abs glistened with a hint of sweat as our bodies writhed against each other.

"I need you so much," I moaned. "Please, take me."

Carter responded by moving his lips down to my neck, then my chest, ripping my top down to free my bosoms. He sucked hard on my right nipple before taking it between his teeth and pulling hard. I gasped and bit my lip as I absorbed the pain and transformed it into pleasure.

Carter's head continued down my body until he was between my legs. I cringed as my plastic leg swung against his body. Carter grabbed my right leg and planted kisses on the knee, right next to the stump. He didn't seem disturbed by it at all as his lips worked up my thigh toward my sex. He stopped when his lips were whiskers away from my dripping wet panties.

I felt his breath on my sex until he moved his lips away and started kissing my left thigh, once again working his way up. The wait was torture and I thrust my opening toward his mouth as it approached. Carter's strong, muscular arms kept me under control, but I writhed under his grip, desperate to get his lips on mine.

"Maybe I'll just stop now," Carter said.

"No," I moaned. "Don't stop."

"What do you want me to do?" Carter asked.

"Eat me," I yelled. I'd never said that before. It sounded so naughty, so unromantic. But I needed his lips between my legs.

"You'll have to beg me for it," Carter said. "You made me wait for you, so now you're going to have to beg. Really convince me that you want it."

I writhed under his grip. His arms still had me locked down tight so I couldn't move.

"I need your tongue on me. Please, I need you to lick my pussy."

"Not enough," Carter said. "I don't believe you.

"Aahh!" I screamed. "Stick your tongue inside my cunt and eat me, you son of a bitch!"

Carter grinned. "That's better."

He placed his fingers under my soaked panties and ripped them off, tearing the cheap cotton as if it were paper. He shoved his head down between my thighs and I felt his strong tongue move up and down my lips.

Carter moved his tongue slowly into my hole and then worked up to my bud in one long, slow movement. I rocked my body into his face, moving in time with his strokes, eager to feel every part of his mouth on me.

He placed a finger at my opening. Then a second. As his lips pursed around my clit, his fingers slid inside me, stretching my tight pussy with his thick fingers.

His fingertips aggressively rubbed up against the rough skin on the top of my tunnel while his mouth sucked my clit gently. I could feel it throb between his lips as blood rushed through my body.

"I'm coming," I moaned as I used my hands to force his head harder against my slit. My legs locked tight around his body and my back arched into the air as I came hard in his mouth.

Carter kept kissing my lower lips while my body convulsed and shook against him. I'd never come with a man before, and a feeling of shame and embarrassment threatened to engulf me until Carter lifted his head up and looked at me with hunger in his eyes.

He moved back up to my face; so close I could smell my sex on him.

"You taste so fucking amazing," he said as he planted kisses on my neck. I grabbed hold of his head and brought him toward me, pressing my lips against his. I tasted my juices as we locked in a passionate kiss.

"Thank you," I said as Carter pulled away. "That was amazing."

He collapsed on top of me as I panted, desperate for air and clammy in my clothes. I needed to get naked, but first I wanted to return the favor. I wanted to taste Carter.

"Get on your back," I said, trying to push him off me. "It's my turn to show you a good time."

"No," he said. "Not tonight."

All the self-doubt came flooding back. I'd never known a man to turn down a blowjob before. What the hell did that say about me? I tried to close my legs and cover up my bad one, but his tight body was still firmly between them.

"Tonight I just want to savor the taste of you in my mouth," he said. "And I don't want to give you all the goods tonight."

"You want me to beg you again?" I asked a little irritably.

"You made me wait. Now it's my turn to do the same." With that he sat up and picked the remote control up off the table. "Want to watch some TV?"

Chapter Fourteen

"He slept on the sofa," I told John the next day.

"Are you shitting me? And you slept in your bed?"

"Yep. Best night's sleep I've had in a while."

"I bet," John said. "I mean, I'm a bit disappointed you didn't get laid, but I guess him eating you out is a pretty good second place. And you've been grinning like a Cheshire cat all bloody morning, so I'm guessing he knew what he was doing?"

"He taught me a thing or two about my body," I said. "So yeah, you could say he was good." I knew why he was good at oral, of course—practice. No doubt he had gone down on countless women before me, but I was trying really hard not to let that bother me. After all, I was no virgin either—just—and his past experiences should not be held against him.

"Are you sure he slept on the sofa?" John asked. "Because you don't need to keep up that frigid persona with me."

"Look," I said, grabbing John's hand and dragging him into the living room. "You can still see the mark made by his body where he lay."

John lay down on the sofa and pressed his body into the spot where Carter had been just an hour earlier. "Sorry, Emily, but this is the closest I am ever going to get to laying with him, so please let me enjoy this moment."

I rolled my eyes and walked away, still smiling.

"Wait, what's this?" John said. I turned round to see him digging something out from the back of the sofa.

"That's his phone," I said, stating the obvious. "Shit, he's bound to need that during the day. What should we do?"

"Call him?" John suggested.

"Very funny," I said. I wasn't about to fall for that one.

"No, seriously. Call him at work. You know his firm and it won't be hard to find the number for their San Francisco office."

"Oh, yeah. I suppose I could do that. You don't think it would be a little too creepy, do you? I don't want to be one of those clingy women."

"No, not if you have his phone. Just give them a call. You remember the name of the firm?"

"Yeah, it was Chadwick Ellis," I said. "I remember because a friend of mine interviewed with them a few years back."

"Okay, I have the number." John read out the number for the local office and I dialed.

"Hello, Chadwick Ellis," came the chirpy, but clearly bored voice on the other end of the line. "How may I help you?"

"Oh, hello, I was hoping you could put me through to Carter Murphy."

"We don't have anyone here by that name, ma'am."

"Ah, well, he is actually from your London office, but he is working from San Francisco at the moment for a big deal."

"Just give me a minute," the secretary said before putting me on hold. You'd think she would keep vaguely clued up on which partners were working out of the office, but clearly that was too much to expect.

"Hello, ma'am. Sorry to put you on hold."

"That's okay."

"I'm afraid we don't actually have anyone by the name of Carter Murphy working for the firm. He does not work for any of our offices. I checked the international directory."

"Oh."

"Is it possible you got the wrong name?"

"No, that's the right name. Never mind, perhaps I misheard the name of the firm. Thank you." I quickly hung up and told John the other end of the conversation.

"That's a bit weird," he said. "Why would he lie about the name of the firm he works for?"

"I don't know." The two of us sat there in silence for a few minutes until we were interrupted by the vibration of Carter's phone on the table.

John quickly picked it up and read the screen.

"What does it say?" I asked, conveniently forgetting that reading someone else's messages was a big no-no in my book.

"It just says 'we still on for tonight?' from someone called Joanne."

My heart sank heard in my chest. Once a player always a player, or so the saying went. I had hoped I would never find out, but it looked like I was about to get firsthand experience.

"Could be nothing, Emily. Another business meeting, perhaps?"

"Could be," I said, but didn't believe it. Business meetings were arranged via email, not text messages.

"You're jumping to conclusions, aren't you? Come on, there could be a million and one different explanations for this."

"Like?"

"Well say this is a date—maybe he arranged it weeks ago and never got round to cancelling it. The two of you only really became official last night, and he hasn't had a chance to tell her yet. Or maybe he doesn't think the two of you are exclusive yet. You haven't exactly dated a lot in the last few years, but it's quite common now to play the field a bit until you come to an agreement otherwise."

John was trying, bless him, but he wasn't helping. Even if I had no legitimate reason to be mad at Carter, that didn't mean I wasn't pissed at him anyway, regardless of what the dating rules were these days. He went down on me last night, but tonight he might have his tongue in someone else's pussy—some skinny bitch probably, and definitely one with two legs. Logical or not, I couldn't help but feel like utter crap.

There was a knock at the door. "Emily, it's Carter. I think I left my phone there. Can you let me in?"

"Shit. John, I can't face him right now. You give him the phone back. Ask him what he's doing tonight."

"Emily, I don't think—"

"Please John, just do it."

I ran into the bathroom and quietly shut the door. I heard John open the front door and greet Carter.

"Emily just popped to the bathroom," John said. "Here's your phone."

"Thanks, John. Don't know what I'd do without this thing. Say hi to Emily for me. Tell her I'm looking forward to seeing her again."

"Sure, will do. Oh, speaking of which, Emily and I were going to grab a few drinks tonight at a cool little bar near here. You want to join us?"

"No, can't tonight, I'm afraid. I'm going to be holed up in my apartment going over some papers. Tell Emily I'll be in touch soon."

"He's gone, Emily," John yelled a few moments later.

I didn't reply. I just locked the bathroom door and collapsed onto the floor in a sobbing, sniffling mess.

Chapter Fifteen

"I'm here to see Mr. Murphy in the penthouse suite," I told the receptionist at Carter's apartment block. I still had no idea why I'd agreed to his invitation. I blamed John for talking me into it.

I'd cried for a solid thirty minutes after Carter left on Tuesday, and after plucking up the courage to leave the bathroom, I promptly resumed crying on John's shoulder. He took the tough love approach and told me to stop being pathetic. Apparently, Carter was a single man and therefore entitled to see women in his free time. That was not exactly what I wanted hear, but it was what I *needed* to hear.

When Carter invited me over to his place for dinner on Friday night, I replied with a quick "okay" before my brain had time to take over and remind me that I hated him right now. I made a plan in my head for how to approach the evening—I would be pleasant, eat dinner with him, and then politely decline to let him kiss me again. Simple as that.

Formulating my plan helped clear my mind and for the rest of the week I focused on work, emailing investors back and forth. By the time Friday night rolled around, my entire calendar was full of appointments for next week—that would make it even easier to resist any more invitations from Carter.

Now I found myself in the lobby of an apartment block I clearly did not belong in. The receptionist had made no attempt to hide her glare as her eyes moved up and down my body, presumably wondering what I was doing visiting such exquisite apartments.

"Your name?" she asked.

"Emily. Emily Saunders."

"Ah, yes. Mr. Murphy informed us of your planned visit. Please follow me."

The receptionist led me over to the elevator and waved a keycard over the panel. A light came on for the penthouse suite, which she pressed.

"You're all set."

"Thanks."

The doors closed and I quickly turned round to fix my appearance in the mirrored wall of the elevator. During the short walk from my building to the car, the bay area wind had swept up my hair and dumped it back down in a heap. I frantically pulled my fingers through it, but my hair had always been stubborn and it just fell down in the same position each time.

I heard the doors open behind me and made one quick adjustment to my chest—might as well put my best assets on show, after all.

"Well, this is going to be an entertaining evening," Carter said behind me.

I spun round and saw that the elevator had opened directly into his penthouse. He stood there, sipping from a glass of wine as he checked me out. Like the receptionist downstairs, he made no effort to be subtle about it, but this time I didn't mind. While he undressed me with his eyes I did the same to him, eager to rip off that tight t-shirt and run my hands over his firm chest.

"We're going to have dinner, and that's it," I said, walking out of the elevator and throwing my coat down on a sofa.

"That will not be it," Carter said. "Not by a long shot. Wine?"

I took the glass of white wine and admired the room—or rather, rooms. The main area in front of the elevator functioned as a living room of sorts, complete with a massive flat screen television mounted to the wall with standing speakers on either side.

"Would you like a tour?" Carter asked. "We have a few minutes before dinner is ready."

"Sure. Lead the way."

"I do like to hear that from a woman," Carter said as he showed me into the kitchen.

It was about twice the size of mine and had brand new appliances. A couple of pots sat on the stove with enticing aromas wafting up my nose. Dinner would be a step up from Chinese take-out tonight, it seemed.

The bathroom had a walk in shower and a Jacuzzi. I should have been surprised to see such luxuries in an apartment, but it seemed completely in fitting with the rest of the penthouse.

"So, what do you think?" Carter asked. "Not bad, is it?"

"What about the bedroom?" I asked, somewhat surprised that he had left that out.

"You'll see that later," Carter said as he walked back into the kitchen. My eyes followed his perfect behind as I imagined sinking my nails into his skin.

"Take a seat at the table and I'll dish up dinner."

Carter had decorated the table with a single rose in the middle next to a solitary candle which smelled faintly of the ocean. At least that was what it said on the label.

Carter served up seafood risotto complete with prawns, calamari, and mussels, which went perfectly with the pinot grigio.

"Did you really cook this?" I asked. "Or did you just order from room service and then stick it in a couple of pots?"

Carter smiled. "You know, Americans always seem surprised that I can cook. That stereotype about British food isn't really true, you know. And yes, I did cook. If you like, you can check the bin and see all the mess I made in the process." I smiled at his reference to "bin" instead of trash can. "Anyway, tell me about your week. How is the business going?"

"Looks like we are getting investment within the next couple of weeks."

"Really? Wow, that's good, right?"

"Yes," I said, weighing my words carefully. "It's just all happening rather fast. We are having to fend off a takeover at the moment, and that sort of forced our hand a bit."

"A takeover? I didn't realize the business was that well developed."

"It isn't," I said. "But that isn't stopping PharmaTech from trying. I probably shouldn't be telling you this, but they offered ten million dollars the other day."

Carter nearly choked on his food. "Ten million! Why on earth haven't you accepted?"

"PharmaTech would destroy everything we've worked for just to make a quick buck," I said. "We aren't going to let that happen."

"Well, you are a better person than I am, because I would take the money. Companies like that have a habit of getting what they want one way or another. At least this way you stand to profit from it."

I wished he hadn't said that. I didn't want to hear him reinforce the same fear I had been dragging around these last few days. PharmaTech was playing nice at the moment, but that could change in a heartbeat, and then what? They already knew about the recent security bug. What else did they know about? Was there really anything to stop them from just copying our code and grinding us into the ground with legal fees?

"Speaking of money," I said, putting down my fork as I savored the last mouthful of Carter's meal. "I always pictured hedge funds as being fairly prudent with expenses."

"They are, for the most part."

"And yet here you are in the penthouse suite of one of the most expensive apartments in San Francisco."

Carter narrowed his eyes and looked at me. I held his gaze and did my best to project confidence while feeling like a nervous wreck inside.

"What are you getting at, Emily?"

"I know you're lying to me," I said. "You're lying about working for Chadwick Ellis and you lied about your plans for the other night." I managed to keep my voice calm as I accused him, but my fingernails were digging into the skin of my palm.

"What the hell, Emily! Why did you even come here tonight if you were just going to accuse me of lying?"

That was a good question. Why had I come here? I shrugged. "I guess I was hoping you would be able to explain it."

"I shouldn't have to." Carter looked pissed. His fingers were pressed hard against the table as if he were trying to push through it. I couldn't help but notice the muscles in his forearms rippling as he tried to control his anger. "I get that you have self-esteem issues because of the leg. It's stupid, because you are beautiful, but I do understand. But that does not give you the right to go around accusing me like this."

He hadn't even attempted to provide an excuse for his lies, but had managed to make me feel like crap in the process.

"I'm sorry Carter, I need to get out of here. Thank you for a lovely meal." I stood up and walked over to the elevator, but then promptly made a fool out of myself by not being able to find the call button.

"I did lie," Carter admitted. "I don't work for Chadwick Ellis."

I turned around to face him, hoping to see a hint of remorse in his eye, but there was none.

"Why?" I asked. "Why did you lie? What's going on?"

Chapter Sixteen

"It wasn't a big lie," Carter said. "Just a little white one. I am here on business, but I don't work for a hedge fund. I work for a bank. A big one. People aren't too keen on big banks these days, so I tend to keep it secret. I am in town to work on a deal, though. That part is true."

Shit, that actually made a lot of sense. It certainly explained the luxury penthouse. Big banks threw money around like it was going out of fashion.

"What about the women?" I asked. "Like your date the other night."

Carter gave a quick shrug of the shoulders. "I like women, Emily. You and I are not a couple—not yet—and you can't make me feel guilty for sleeping with other women. I enjoy sex and, if I may say, I'm quite good at it."

Carter walked toward me. I took a step back and leaned against the cold steel of the elevator doors. He was coming to claim me. I could see the look in his eyes. He wouldn't take no for an answer now, and I didn't want to fight him anyway.

He stopped three feet from me and held out his hand. I placed my hand in his and he led me to the one room that had been out of bounds the entire evening. Until now.

I admired the bedroom as Carter spun me round and lowered the zipper on the back of my dress. The light fabric fluttered to the floor, leaving me standing there in just my underwear, my leg exposed to him for the first time. Carter brushed my neck with light kisses as he undid my bra to release my tender breasts. The room was warm, but my nipples stood erect, waiting to be touched.

I cringed as Carter got down on his knees and planted kisses on my belly. I normally hated to be touched there, but he put me at ease with my own body. I relaxed as his fingers slipped under the waistband of my panties.

Carter pulled my panties down to the floor. He slid them off over each foot, the real one and the fake one, before standing up and backing away. He looked me up and down like an art critic examining a painting.

"Emily, you are quite certainly the most gorgeous woman I have ever had the pleasure to see naked. And I have seen a lot of women naked. I am going to make it my mission to kiss every inch of skin on your body."

I laughed. "And the plastic? Don't worry," I added, seeing Carter upset at my negativity, "I'm only messing around. When do I get to see your body?"

The sudden rush of confidence took me by surprise as much as it did Carter, but I wasn't about to complain.

"I'm right here, Emily. You're going to have to do some of the work by yourself."

I approached him and maintained eye contact as I slipped my fingers under the hem of his shirt and lifted it over his head. My body urged me to look down and admire his chest, but I kept staring straight at him while my fingers opened his belt and the button on his jeans.

Finally I allowed my hands to touch him. I started on his chest, digging my fingers in, searching for any trace of body fat, but there was none. I pushed hard against him, but he didn't budge as I moved my hands up to his shoulders and then down the arms. My hands, while not tiny, were unable to get even halfway round his heaving biceps.

My knees were about to give way under me, so I lowered myself to the floor and pulled down his jeans. He stepped out of them, leaving me on my knees staring at his crotch. His boxers were close-fitting and incapable of hiding the generous length contained within.

I subconsciously licked my lips as I slipped him out of his underwear. My eyes opened wide when I saw what hung between his thighs. His member was not yet hard, but I could tell it would put Neil to shame.

My fingers brushed against it—as if not believing it were real—and I felt it twitch under my touch. Before I could get a grip on it, Carter reached down and pulled me up in one swift movement like I weighed no more than a child.

"I want to return the favor," I said, longing to wrap my lips around his shaft. I'd never done that to a man before. I'd never wanted to until now.

"No," Carter replied. "Not tonight. Tonight is all about you."

He ran his fingertips down my chest, lightly brushing my nipples before moving on down to my belly. He planted his palms against me and gave me a soft shove, sending me down onto the bed. I lay back with my legs spread open wide. As Carter climbed on top I realized I'd never let a man look at me in that way before. All my previous sexual encounters involved getting naked under the sheets and often with the lights off. Now I was truly giving myself to Carter in every way.

Carter positioned himself between my legs and knelt there staring at me, his cock now rock hard and ready for me.

"I can see how much you want me," Carter said. "You pussy is wet for me."

"Fuck me," I said. "I need you inside me."

"Tut, tut, tut," Carter said, shaking his head. "Always so impatient for sex. First I want to taste you again." He threw his head down between my legs and put his tongue straight to my sex. My hips raised to meet him and I moaned as his tongue flicked in and out of my hole.

I came within minutes, unable to hold back as his tongue explored every nook of my folds. When his lips pursed around my clit my body shook, and the orgasm hit hard, traveling up from my pussy to my brain. A feeling of euphoria washed over me as I crashed back down onto the bed.

Carter took a few more eager licks of my lips and then pulled his head away and got off the bed.

"No," I whimpered. "Please don't leave me like this. I need you. I need you to fuck me. I need your cock inside me. I need—"

"Emily, calm down," Carter said. "I'm just getting a condom."

"Oh," I replied, smiling. "Well, hurry up, then."

Carter sheathed himself and then lay on top of me, his tip flicking lighting against my wetness.

"You know, for someone who likes to play innocent, you can be very eager for cock between your legs."

"Just yours," I said as he parted my folds with his fingers and slipped inside.

I breathed in hard as inch-after-inch of him filled my aching sex. As wet as I was, there was still some pain as his large member moved deeper and deeper inside me, until I was completely full.

Carter rocked back and forth on top of me. His hands held my wrists down while his mouth explored my body. My nipples stiffened as his tongue moved around my breasts and I ground my hips in time with his.

"I'm coming," I moaned as Carter's thrusts quickened. He stopped kissing me and let his head hover over mine, staring deep into my eyes. I held eye contact as I came hard, my pussy clenching on to his thick cock.

Carter finished soon after and collapsed on top of me, our bodies covered in sweat and my juices forming a sticky mess between our legs. I'd never orgasmed that hard and a wet patch formed on the bed between my legs.

My hands explored Carter's sweaty back and moved down toward his perfect behind. I grabbed hold hard and wished he could just stay here on top of me—inside me—forever.

Finally Carter rolled off, and I placed my head against his chest for the best night's sleep I had ever had.

Chapter Seventeen

I woke to the smell of strong coffee and cooked eggs. Not a bad way to start the day.

"Morning," Carter said, standing over me with a tray of breakfast. There was also orange juice and toast, plus some cooked sausage. I wasn't usually one for big breakfasts, but apparently having two powerful orgasms could give you an appetite.

"In the spirit of complete and utter honesty between us," Carter said, placing the tray on my lap, "I'm going to confess that this is room service."

"I suppose nobody's perfect," I joked, propping myself up on a pillow. Carter stood there in just his underwear; it was an effort to look away and start eating breakfast. He opened the curtains to reveal a view of the city. The Golden Gate Bridge had a layer of fog covering it, but that couldn't be helped. Other than that the view was perfect; both inside and outside the hotel.

Carter sat next to me while I ate, but we didn't talk. The silence wasn't awkward, but I could tell both of us were wondering the same thing, and neither wanted to be the one to bring it up.

"What next?" Carter asked. "What happens now?"

"I was wondering the same thing," I said. "I know what I should do, but it's not the same as what I want to do."

"You think you should end this now because it will only end in heartbreak?"

I nodded.

"But you want to keep going because we have amazing sex?"

I laughed. "I wouldn't have quite put it like that. But you're not far off."

"This doesn't have to end, you know," he said, sneaking a piece of sausage from my plate before I could claim it with my fork.

"If it doesn't end now, then it ends when you go back home."

"No," he said. "It doesn't have to. I didn't sleep last night, Emily. I lay up all night thinking about this. We can work something out. I don't know all the details yet, but I could try and get a transfer, or maybe I just take more holiday leave. And I could fly you out to England as often as you like."

"I don't know," I murmured, trying to think of more excuses. At the moment this sounded too good

101

to be true. There had to be something that would mess this up. "I can't afford to split my focus right now. The business takes up all my time, and I will have to be utterly devoted to it over the next year or so if I want it to succeed."

"I thought the business was going well," Carter said. "Don't you already have investors circling?"

"We do," I admitted. "But it's not quite as simple as that. We are burning through money right now. We already owe our lawyer five grand."

"None of these reasons are insurmountable," Carter said. "We don't have to decide right now. Can we just agree to see how it goes over the next few weeks?"

I nodded. Was I really considering this? My main problem with Carter had been him going home, and now he was saying we could work around that. It was tempting—more than tempting—but it was sensible, and sensible was my middle name.

Decisions like this couldn't be made in bed. "Let's talk about this later," I said.

Carter smiled and pulled me on top of him. As our bodies merged again, I knew that somehow we would find a way to work this out, and my life would never be the same again.

Chapter Eighteen

I came home to find John working at my kitchen table. "Do you spend any time at home these days?" I asked. "Are things really that bad with Tom?"

"Tom and I split up," was John's terse reply.

"Oh, I'm sorry," I said. I didn't think John would be too devastated, but he wouldn't be in the mood to celebrate either.

"Don't worry about it. We just weren't working, so it was better to end it sooner rather than later."

"This might seem a little insensitive, but I have good news about Carter and me." I gave John a summary of the conversation I'd had with Carter earlier. We'd left things with a promise to talk about it later, but I found myself talking to John as if it were a sure thing. Was that a sign I had already made up my mind?

"He'll be meeting the parents next," John said.

I put on a smile, but that was not something I was looking forward to. My relationship with Dad had been strained ever since the accident. Whereas Mom had started attacking life with a "you only live once" attitude, Dad barely spoke to me.

I knew why, although he would never admit it. Whenever he saw me—saw my leg—he thought of William and it ate him up inside. Mom just medicated the pain away. Neither was a healthy solution, but how did you deal with the loss of a son?

"Anyway, to business," John said. "I have good news. In fact, that is an understatement. I have excellent news."

"An investor?" I asked. What else could it be?

"Not just an investor," John said. "A generous investor. I offered her some terms and expected her to come back with a counteroffer. Instead I got sent a load of contracts with our terms in there. This time tomorrow we will have two hundred thousand to play with."

"Sounds too good to be true," I said. "We should send this stuff to Scott. Assuming he will look at it without his fees paid."

"Already have," John said. "In fact, speak of the devil—"

Scott was calling John's phone and he put it on speaker. I'd have to convince him to go easy on the unpaid legal fees.

"Hi Scott," John said. "You're on speaker."

"Hi guys. How're things?"

"Good," I replied. "Scott, before we get into the details, I know there are your legal fees that need—"

"Oh yeah, thanks for the payment," Scott said. "Your account is all clear so we are free to work on this investment."

I looked at John with a furrowed brow, but he looked as confused as me. "You received payment for the fees?"

"Yeah, it went though a few hours ago. "

"Oh, uh, great. I just didn't expect it to go through that quickly. So, what about this investment then?"

Scott gave us the idiot's guide to the investment, but the gist was that we were getting the amount of money we asked for and only had to give up ten percent equity. The contracts included all sorts of restrictive clauses so the investor would not be able to interfere with day-to-day business. The investor was going through a venture capital fund, so details were sparse, but Scott described it as one of the best deals he had ever seen.

That evening, we signed the contract and a "Kerry Woodson" did the same for the investment fund. We had our money. That meant the business would be set for a while and I could keep spending time with Carter. Today had been a good day.

"Hi, Mom."

"Hi, dear. You okay?"

"Yeah, I'm fine. I need to run something by you, though."

"Sounds serious. What is it?"

"You remember that guy who asked me out in the restaurant on your birthday?"

"I'm hardly likely to forget him, now am I?" Mom replied.

"We're kind of seeing each other." Mom was silent on the other end, but I knew I had her attention. "Do you think you and Dad would like to meet him? I was thinking of arranging a dinner with the four of us."

"Oh, things are that serious already?" Mom asked.

"I'm not sure, really," I replied. "It's a bit awkward because he has to go back to England in a few months, which means things have to progress a bit quicker than normal."

"That's understandable. Plus, you really don't want to let this one go. Once you snare someone like that, you need to reel them in and keep them."

"What about Dad, though? Do you think he will agree to meet him?"

"Of course he will, darling. I'll make him."

"And can you tell him to be on his best behavior, please? He's been really rude to some of the friends I've brought home in past."

"He'll be fine," Mom assured me. "Actually, this was supposed to be a surprise, but I'll tell you anyway. Your father finally agreed to go to grievance counseling. He's seeing the same lady you and I saw after William died."

"Oh my God, that's great news." I was under eighteen when William died, so I had been given little say in the decision to go to counseling. I was glad I went, though. I would never get over William and I knew there would never be a day that went by without me thinking of him, but after a few months of talking to a therapist I was able to move on.

Mom recovered too, in her own way, but Dad refused to go to any therapist. Instead he crawled into his shell, and our relationship had been strained ever since. Dad did not even show any sign of relief or pleasure when the driver of the car was given a ten-year prison sentence for manslaughter.

"Don't get too carried away," Mom said. "He's not the life of the party or anything, but he is getting better. I think he'd be only too happy to meet Carter."

Now I just had to get Carter on board. Who knew if he had ever met any girl's parents before? The way he moved from woman to woman, it was quite possible that he had never had the chance. This would be a real test of our relationship and how seriously Carter really felt about me.

Chapter Nineteen

The next time Carter and I met, it was in a cheap diner for some lunch. If we'd met for dinner, then we would only end up going back to mine or his for sex. While that would no doubt be a lot of fun, I didn't want it to distract me from my main goal.

"Can I see you this weekend?" Carter asked while we waited for our food. Judging from the way he scanned the menu, I was fairly sure Carter had never been in a true American diner before. The meals here were cheaper than a bottle of water in the places he liked to take me.

"You can," I said, "but you will have to be prepared to travel."

Carter raised his eyebrows. "Are you suggesting we go away for a dirty weekend, Miss Saunders?"

"Kind of. Except this dirty weekend will have to include a meal with my parents. They want to meet you, so I thought it would be fun to go back to my hometown and spend the weekend in my childhood bedroom."

Carter did not look keen on that idea. In fact, he looked like I had just invited him to spend the weekend at the dentist having his teeth drilled without any painkillers. Suddenly I felt stupid and naïve. He didn't want to meet my parents because he had no intention of staying with me. This was all just a game to him, and I had fallen for it.

"Emily, I'm not sure meeting your parents is a good idea right now," Carter said. "We've only been going out for a few weeks. How about if we're still going strong in a few months, then I meet them?"

"No don't worry, you've made your feelings on this perfectly clear." I considered storming out of the diner, but it was crowded and I didn't want to be one of those people who aired their dirty laundry in public.

"Don't be like that, Emily," Carter said. "It's not even that I don't want to meet them. I just think this could put pressure on our relationship, and we don't need that right now."

"No, we should just keep fucking and not let feelings come into it," I snapped.

"It's not like that. You know this is more than just sex."

"It is for me, but I'm not sure about you. I don't see the big deal anyway. You've already met my mom and charmed the pants off her. And I mean that literally."

"But I haven't met your dad," Carter said. "And from what you've told me, he can be quite a tough character. Not that I blame him—I can't imagine how painful it must be to lose a son—but I think it would be a little awkward."

Not to mention the pain of losing your big brother, I thought. William was the reason I didn't go home as often as I should have and the reason I had been desperate to move away and go to college. My childhood bedroom was right next to William's. Mom and Dad had kept his room exactly the way it was the day he died. Going home meant facing the loss of my brother, and I could only do that so often.

My phone buzzed in my bag just as I was about to continue arguing with Carter. It was Mom. "Dad can't make it to dinner," she'd messaged me. "Can we make it just the three of us?"

"Shit," I said, putting the phone back in my bag. "Looks like you're off the hook. Dad can't make it anyway."

"Oh," Carter said, trying to look disappointed, but failing to hide his pleasure at the news. "Like you said, I've already met your Mom, so why don't we go down to see her? I could do with spending some time out of the city, and I've never been to Arizona."

"Really?" I said. "You mean it? Okay, I'm going to tell Mom and book the flights tonight."

"Leave the flights to me," Carter said. "I'll sort that out."

"Thank you," I said, leaning over and planting a kiss on his lips. He grabbed my blouse and held me close until a cough from the waiter signaled the arrival of lunch.

I dove into my burger and smiled at Carter, wondering what he would make of Mom's cooking.

Chapter Twenty

Carter might have been nervous about meeting my father, but he charmed my mother effortlessly and had her eating out of the palm of his hand. He complimented the house and even helped out with the cooking.

I hadn't realized this until now, but I found men who cooked incredibly sexy. More than once I wanted to drag Carter out of the kitchen and upstairs to my bedroom. Unfortunately, my room was directly above the kitchen, and I didn't want to subject Mom to the sounds of her little girl having wild sex in the room above.

"Can I take Carter away and give him a quick tour now?" I asked her as she placed the enchiladas in the oven.

"Sure, honey. He's all yours for the next thirty minutes."

"We can do a lot in thirty minutes," Carter whispered in my ear.

"Not now," I said, giving him a playful slap on the arm and then squeezing his firm bicep for good measure. "You'll have to wait until tonight for that.

Let's start in the living room." I took his hand and pulled him toward the lounge.

Carter gravitated straight to the childhood photos and took great pleasure in seeing me at various stages of my growing up. There was my milky white phase where I could have won a prize for the palest person in Arizona, and then the chubby phase where my legs resembled tree trunks. He was kind enough to laugh and say I looked cute, but I was not gullible enough to think he would have fallen for me if I were still fat. Although I only had one leg now and that hadn't put him off too much.

"Your brother looks like you," he said, holding up a photo of William and me in the paddling pool. I must have been about five, which would have made William eight or maybe nine. He would have been twenty-seven now, maybe even married or engaged. A tear formed in my eye, so I pulled Carter along the wall to the photos of my parents when they were younger.

"Who's this next to your dad?" Carter asked, pointing at a photo of my father next to his brother. My dad had less gray hair in that photo, so it was probably about six years old, although I couldn't remember the occasion.

"That's my uncle," I said. "That might have been at his fiftieth birthday, but I'm not sure. That's funny though, because most people who look at this photo think my uncle is my dad. Apparently he looks more like me. How did you know which one my dad was?"

"Oh, I don't know," Carter said, quickly putting the photo down and moving on to look at some of my mom on her wedding day. "There is some resemblance there. Maybe you have the same chin or something."

My chin was nothing like Dad's—at least, I didn't think so—but it didn't seem worth arguing about. Not when things were going so well.

As we moved from the living room to the study, I heard a car pull up in the driveway. I looked through the window and saw the familiar sight of Dad's red truck pulling up to the house.

"Mom," I yelled, running into the kitchen. "Dad's home!"

Mom smiled. "He did say he might get home early, but I didn't want to get your hopes up."

"What's going on?" Carter asked, walking into the kitchen with a concerned look on his face. "Do we have another guest for dinner?"

"Dad's here," I said, unable to contain my excitement.

"Your dad? No, Emily. I can't meet your dad."

"Why? I know you think it might be weird, but he's here now and—"

"No, Emily, you don't understand. I really cannot be here. I have to go. I'll—"

The door opened and Dad walked straight into the kitchen as he always did when he could smell dinner cooking. Mom was right; he looked more relaxed and even had a smile on his face.

"Hi, sweetie," he said, as he wrapped his arms round me for a hug.

"Hi, Daddy."

"And this must be—" Dad let go of me and swung round to face Carter, who had shrunk back into the corner.

Carter looked white as a ghost as he made eye contact with my dad.

"I can explain," Carter said, holding up both hands in defense.

"What the hell are you doing here?" my dad yelled, clutching onto the work surface to steady himself. "I'm calling the police."

"Daddy," I pleaded, snatching the phone from his hand. "What are you doing? What's going on?"

"What's going on?" Dad screamed. "I could ask you the same question. I can't believe you have invited this scum into our home!"

"Oh my God," I yelled at my Dad, barely holding back the tears. How would I ever keep hold of Carter now? After this embarrassment he would never speak to me again.

"Emily, don't you know who he is?"

"He's my boyfriend," I replied feebly.

"No, Emily. This is the man that killed William. This man killed your brother."

Part Two

Chapter One

"Are you sure you're okay, Emily?" John asked over a video call. "It's not like you to spend a whole week with your parents, so I know something is wrong."

"I'm fine, John." I wiped my sleeve across my eyes to clear away any traces of the tears that had been there a few minutes ago. "I just wanted to spend some time with my parents. My dad has been going through a rough patch and I'm helping him through it."

That was half true. Dad was having a rough time, but that was only to be expected after I invited my brother's killer to dinner. I wasn't helping him deal with it, because I was taking it just as badly as he was. For the last week I had locked myself in my room and only came out for food and drink.

"And you're not going to tell me what happened with Carter?" John asked for the hundredth time.

"I don't want to talk about it John."

"Okay, but the guy has been hounding me with phone calls and text messages asking to speak to you. Did he do something bad? I want to know whether I should be polite or tell him to fuck off."

"Be polite," I said. "Things just weren't meant to be this time." *Because he killed my brother*, I thought. As excuses went, that was a good reason not to continue dating a guy.

"He keeps apologizing," John said. "I'm supposed to tell you how sorry he is and that things are not what they seem. It all sounds a little mysterious. I'm assuming he slept with someone else?"

"Drop it, John," I replied. How were things not as they seemed? Dad hadn't said much that night before Carter jumped on a plane back to San Francisco, but he made it quite clear that Carter had been the one jailed for killing my brother. He had been drink-driving and the judge classed it as manslaughter. That couldn't be much clearer, could it?

Mom and I had stayed away from the trial. We didn't want to know the gory details of William's death; nothing would bring him back to us. I remember being surprised by the lengthy sentence the judge handed down, but I would be lying if I said there was any pity in my heart for the killer.

Once he'd been locked up, I put it all to one side and tried to just remember my brother with a positive attitude in my heart and not a desire for revenge or vengeance. I'd always imagined the driver as a reckless bum, someone so stupid they drove drunk, someone so reckless they didn't care about other people's lives. But that didn't fit with Carter. He wasn't like that. At least, he hadn't appeared that way to me.

"What was the problem with the business you wanted to discuss?" I asked John.

"Not a problem as such," John said. "I'm just having trouble keeping track of all the money."

I laughed. "That's not a bad problem to have."

"I know. We still have a lot to play with, but we don't have a constant revenue stream yet. I think we could do with getting an accountant or bookkeeper on board to help. Especially with these reports that the investor is demanding."

"What reports?" I asked. That was news to me.

"I sent her the information she requested after the initial investment. She was happy enough initially, but she made it clear that she wanted official reports on a regular basis. I don't think my hack-job spreadsheets are going to cut it with this woman."

"Fair enough, I suppose, given the amount Marissa invested. Okay, let's get an accountant in."

"Got anyone in mind?"

"No. Perhaps we could ask Marissa for a recommendation. She's bound to have a load of contacts in the industry."

121

"Sounds good," John said. "Feel free to call me anytime, Emily, if you want to talk."

"I will," I lied. "There really isn't anything to talk about. Relationships end all the time. Don't worry about me."

I could see from his face on the screen that he was worried and would likely continue to be until he found out the truth. I would probably have to tell him one day, but not for a while.

I simply couldn't bring myself to admit I had fucked my brother's killer. What kind of person did that make me? One that John wouldn't be able to look at in the eye again, probably.

"Mom, can we talk?" I asked, walking downstairs once I knew my dad had left for work. I couldn't handle seeing him right now.

"Sure, honey. What about?"

"You know what about." The color washed from her cheeks as we sat down on the sofa.

"I don't know what you want me to say, dear," she said. "This whole thing has been an awful shock, of course, but we will get past it."

"I thought I knew him, Mom," I said, already fighting back the tears. "I mean, I knew he was a bit of a wild card and it was obvious he had secrets, but I didn't think he was capable of something like that."

Tears welled up in my mom's eyes. I put my arm around her and we just sat there together for a few minutes while she regained her composure.

"It was an accident, honey," Mom said. "I don't know all the details—I didn't go to the trial and didn't want to hear about it—but from what I understand, it was just a kid who had a few too many drinks and then hit a car. William's car."

"Why did he get sent to jail for so long?" I asked. "I've always wondered why he got such a long sentence. Not that I was going to complain, of course, but it did seem odd."

"Yes, I was surprised too," Mom admitted. "I think the judge may have lost a family member to something similar, so he came down extra hard. I don't know. Your father knows more about it than I do."

"I'm so sorry for bringing him here, Mom. I had no idea."

Mom took my hand in hers. "It's not your fault, honey. You couldn't have known. And anyway, when I try and see this in the cold light of day, I know that he may not be a bad person. He was young when it happened, and I'm sure he's changed since."

"But he has obviously been lying to me from the start," I said. "He knew who I was, and then we… well, you know…"

"Are you going to keep seeing him?" Mom asked.

I let out a snotty laugh through my tears. "I don't think that would go down too well with Dad, do you?"

Mom smiled. "No, probably not. But don't worry about pleasing your dad. You just do what feels right."

"Thanks, Mom," I said. She had told me just what I needed to hear and I knew what I had to do. I would see Carter one last time—let him explain why he put me through all this—and then I would say goodbye.

No matter what happened that night five years ago, I would never be able to have a relationship with Carter. I already thought of William every time I looked at my leg; I didn't need that to happen every time I saw Carter as well.

I booked a plane ticket and flew home. I was going to put this behind me and do something with my life. I would make my big brother proud.

Chapter Two

Carter was already at the coffee shop when I showed up. It was a good place for a personal conversation; there was just enough noise to cover up what we said from the ears of nosey neighbors and it was public. I usually managed to keep my emotions in check when in public, but I wasn't entirely sure if that would hold true today.

"Hi, Emily," Carter said, standing up to pull out my chair. He had the decency to not make any effort over his usually pristine appearance, but that didn't make much difference. His hair was a mess and stubble covered his face, but that made him look even sexier. Traces of darkness under his eyes suggested he hadn't been sleeping all that well, but that was the only flaw I could find.

"Hi," I said, sitting down to find a cup of coffee ready for me. Soy milk latte; my favorite.

"Thank you for agreeing to meet me," Carter said. "I know this must have been a tough decision for you."

"Just say what you have to say, Carter. I want to get on with my life, and I can't very well do that when you are constantly trying to get hold of me and John. What did you want?"

Carter sighed and leaned back in his chair. "I deserved that. But I want you to know that this is not what it seems."

"So you said in your messages. What do you mean by that? This looks pretty clear to me. You were driving drunk. You crashed into the car me and my brother were in. You were locked up for ten years, but obviously let out a lot earlier than that. Then for some sick reason, you decided to track down the sister of the man you killed and…"

I took a deep breath and tried to calm down. Without realizing, my voice had gradually been increasing in volume and a few others in the coffee shop were now staring.

"You tracked me down and then fucked me. Do I have a good understanding of all this? Is there something I am missing?"

"It's not as simple as that," Carter said.

Was that all he could say? What could make this any better? No doubt he would say it was all just a horrendous accident and that he shouldn't be blamed for it. But that wouldn't bring William back, and it wouldn't mean I could ever look at Carter without remembering the accident.

"How much of it do you remember?" Carter asked, as if he were reading my mind. "About the accident. Do you remember much of it?"

I nodded. "I can remember a fair bit of it. I wish I couldn't."

"Tell me," Carter said. "I want to know what you went through. I want to understand."

I shook my head. "You'll never understand. How can you possibly know what this feels like?"

Carter didn't reply. He just stared at me with those deep eyes looking right through me. He leaned towards me on his elbows, showing me his perfectly sculpted arms. I hated myself right then. I hated myself for admiring him and for finding him so attractive.

"Fine, I'll tell you," I said at length, just to give myself a reason to look away from Carter's eyes. "We were coming back from the movie theater."

"What had you watched?"

"One of the Harry Potter films. I loved them. William hadn't even wanted to watch it, but I didn't want to go by myself. It was dark when we left, but William had driven in the dark loads of times, so we had no reason to think it wasn't safe. We had been driving for about ten minutes when it happened. We were just five minutes from home. Beyoncé was playing on the radio and I was singing along."

"You can sing?" Carter asked with a slight smile.

"No," I admitted. "Not at all. William was the only person who had ever heard me sing. I would never sing in front of anyone else and never will.

"William turned a corner and there was a car—your car—coming at us on the wrong side of the road. William swerved to avoid it, but it was too late. The doctors told me he died from the impact."

"Do you remember anything after that?" Carter asked.

"Why? Why do you need all the goddamn details? You were there as well, or had you forgotten about killing my fucking brother?" My voice had gotten louder again, but the tables next to us were now vacant, possibly because no one wanted to be near us right now.

"Please, Emily," Carter said, his voice calm and sincere. "Just humor me. Please."

"Fine. I have flashes of memory, but nothing too substantial. I do remember screaming a lot and looking over at my brother. I can still picture him if I close my eyes. He looked good, actually. I mean, you would assume someone who dies in a car crash would look a bloody mess, but he looked peaceful. That's how I like to remember him, anyway."

"Were you in a lot of pain?" Carter asked. "With the leg?"

I shook my head. "I don't even remember feeling it, but I lost consciousness quite quickly. After those flashes the next thing I remember is waking up in hospital. The doctors didn't even tell me about my leg for three days."

Carter looked disappointed, as if my recollection of events was not what he had wanted to hear from me.

"Happy now?" I asked in a somewhat petulant and childish tone which I immediately regretted.

"No, Emily, of course not. Listen, I really need to tell you something about that night, but I don't want to do it here. Will you come to my place for dinner?" I opened my mouth to answer, but he held up a hand to stop me before I could say anything. "I know it's a lot to ask, but I must tell you my side of the events from that night. Please, Emily."

As I looked into his eyes, I knew that if I answered right now I would say "yes." I couldn't say "no" to him.

"I'll think about it," I said, standing up and walking away. I needed time to think, and I couldn't do that while he was sat opposite me. I didn't want to spend any more time talking about the night my brother died, but I felt like he had earned the chance to tell his side of the story.

The story that ended with my brother's death.

Chapter Three

"Boy, am I glad to see you," John said as I walked through the door to my apartment. He almost lived with me these days, although he was actively looking for a new place to stay. He'd lived the life of a bachelor before he had settled down with Tom and I knew I was cramping his style a bit right now.

"Oh, that can't be good," I said. "These days you are only pleased to see me when you need my help with something."

"Am I that predictable?"

"Yes."

"Okay. Well, I do need your help with something. Our illustrious investor would like to talk to you about the new accountant we are going to hire."

"Why does she want to speak to me?" I asked. "I know less than you do about that kind of thing."

"That's what I thought, but because you are technically the 'manager' of the LLC, you need to make these decisions. I guess we may have forgotten about a few of the legal formalities, but she is quite hot on them."

I'd completely forgotten all about my status as manager. I vaguely remembered Scott explaining what it meant, but John and I hadn't put a lot of thought into the details. This new investor was a bit more on-the-ball, but that was probably a good thing. As the saying goes—"short term pain for long term gain."

I pulled up the number for Marissa and gave her a call. It was already past business hours, so I expected to get her voicemail, but she picked up on the second ring.

"Hi, Emily," Marissa said. "How are you?"

"I'm fine, thanks," I replied. John was doing some weird mime with a tissue in front of me. "Sorry I didn't get in touch sooner. I had an awful cold and couldn't focus on work." John gave me the thumbs up.

"Yes, John told me you weren't well. Glad you're better now. I just wanted to chat about this new accountant. As the manager, you have to be the one to make decisions like this, although it is of course preferable if we are all in agreement."

"Sure," I replied. "Do you have someone in mind? I wouldn't know where to start looking."

"My client has recommended a good candidate," Marissa said.

Her client. I kept having to remind myself that Marissa was not the investor; she was merely the lawyer for the investment company.

"What's he like?" I asked.

"*She's* called Jane and has worked with me on other clients before. She doesn't have any particular experience with medical technology companies like yours, but she does specialize in start-up companies. As such, she is clued in to all the issues you will likely face. Plus she is quite cheap."

"In that case, she sounds perfect," I said. "Tell her to send me an email and I'll get her set up with our accounts. Is she okay with working remotely? We don't exactly have any offices yet, unless you count SF Station."

Marissa gave a polite laugh. "Don't worry, she's used to that. Anyway, let me know if I can help with anything else."

"Thanks."

"Well, that was easy," John said once Marissa was off the phone. "This investor has been incredibly useful."

"I know. That *was* rather easy." *Was it a little too easy?* I knew a few other people with start-up companies and they made everything sound like such a chore. All I had to do was phone our investor—or rather, our investor's lawyer—and everything would get sorted out.

"What are you thinking?" John asked.

"Huh? Oh, nothing. Just thinking about what I'm going to work on today."

"I could do with you looking at the data from our beta user with the artificial foot. I've collated the information as best I can, but I need your scientific expertise to tell me what the data is saying."

"Good. I need a task like that to get my mind into action. I'll make us some coffee and then we can get on with it."

"Emily, what are you doing tonight?" John called from the living room. I was working in my bedroom and had been going for about four hours now with barely a break. This was just what I needed, a chance to get my head back in the game and spend a few hours not thinking about Carter.

Except now I was thinking about him again. Crap.

"Working," I replied. "Although I could take the night off, I guess, if you want to catch a movie."

John strolled into my room and sat on the bed. "I had something much more fun in mind, actually."

Oh, no. That didn't sound promising. When it came to nights out, John and I usually had a very different idea of what constituted fun.

"There's a new bar opening up on Mission Street. Mate of mine can't go and has two tickets up for grabs."

"I'd rather not," I said. "I don't fancy going to a loud bar full of drunks."

"It's described as gay-friendly, so you won't be harassed. Straight guys don't tend to go near those sorts of places. Why do you think I'm so keen to go?"

"I don't know…"

"The tickets were going for $30 each and we have them for free. Come on, Emily. You need to let your hair down. How about we just go there, have two or three drinks, dance with a couple of queens and then leave?"

That was how John always dragged me out to bars—with a promise that it would just be for a few drinks. It never was. But I could use a night out and gay bars did tend to be a lot of fun. More fun than going to bars where guys felt you up while you ordered a drink and took dancing as an invitation to grind their cocks up against you, anyway.

I didn't make it onto the dance floor that often—my fake leg was not conducive to sexy maneuvers—

but when I did, some idiot would always thrust an erection against my ass or pussy as if that were a turn-on somehow.

"Fine," I relented. "We go for two drinks and then leave, okay?"

"Yes!" John cheered with a clenched fist. "I was so sure you'd say no. No offense, but you've been a real bore lately."

"I have just split up with someone," I replied. "Doesn't that give me a bit of leeway to be miserable?"

"No," John replied. "Well, yes, I guess it does, but I don't want you to revert back to old Emily. When you were with Carter, you were so much more enthusiastic. You should try and stick with that attitude."

"I hadn't even noticed a difference," I admitted. All I could remember about my time with Carter was that I was jealous a lot. Although the sex had been nice, I had to admit.

"You were glowing, Emily. I don't know if it was specifically Carter or just the fact that you were getting laid, but you were looking truly fantastic. And you'd forgotten about the leg."

"No, I hadn't. I never forget about it."

"You did. I saw you go out during the day with it on display. You never do that."

I tried to think back to what I had been wearing recently. The weather had been warm enough for short skirts, but I usually wore leggings underneath to hide my prosthetic. If Carter had made me forget about my appearance, then I must have fallen for him more than I realized.

"Okay, okay, stop hassling me," I said at last. "I'm going out tonight and I will even try to have fun."

"Excellent, because I have bought you some new clothes to wear."

Chapter Four

I couldn't be entirely sure whether John had bought the new clothes from a store or just mugged a prostitute, but suffice it to say I did not feel comfortable in them. I had a strappy top with a plunging neckline that revealed most of my breasts, which in turn were being shoved up and out by a push-up bra.

The skirt was short and tight and left little to anyone's imagination. I'd never gone out at night feeling so exposed. The cool San Francisco breeze blew under my skirt and left goosebumps between my thighs.

John hadn't bought any shoes for me, at least—I had to get mine specially made—so I slipped into some modest heels. Nothing covered my legs. John had forbid me wearing tights or any leggings which meant both my legs were out in the open.

Most people didn't notice the prosthetic with just a quick glance, especially at night, but as I walked around I heard people behind me start gossiping about it. The prosthetic was thinner than my other leg and the plastic-looking material tended to reflect light in a way that caught people's eye.

The new bar stood out a mile away. In addition to some flashy signage, there was a line that snaked around the block and didn't seem to be moving. For a gay bar, there were more women waiting in line than I'd expected and a lot of the men looked more reserved than was typical in the gay scene on Mission Street.

"I wish you'd let me wear a cardigan or a jacket," I said to John, shivering in the breeze. "We'll be waiting outside for an hour, judging by the size of this line.

"We don't have to queue," John said. "These tickets get us straight past all the riff-raff."

We walked straight up to the door and were let in without needing to show any ID. I suspected a few people in line thought we were getting special treatment because of my leg, but at that point I didn't really care. The bar was lively and loud, but not so busy that we couldn't go straight to the bar to get a drink. No doubt the line outside was just to help the bar get a reputation as being exclusive and hard to get into.

The intention had been to leave after two drinks, but I necked back that many in the space of just thirty minutes and agreed to stay on. Besides, we had a nice table in the corner and the bar was starting to fill out. I always appreciated having a seat more when people around us didn't.

"Just admit it, you are having fun," John said. "This is a cool little place."

"I am, but it's not what I expected. For one thing, I thought you said this was a gay bar? Everyone in here looks straight to me."

"You can't tell if someone is straight just by looking at them," John replied.

"No, but I can tell that the men here are not gay by the way they're checking out other women. It's not exactly subtle."

"Okay, okay," John said, holding up his hands. "I never actually told you this was a gay bar. I said it was gay-friendly. Which it is. I know the owner, and he is friendly to me."

"So, this isn't a gay bar?"

"No. I just said that to get you out for the night."

"You're an ass sometimes, you know."

"I regret nothing," John said. "You're having fun. I can see it in your eyes. Now, I'm going to leave for a bit and let that guy over there come and say hello."

John pointed to a decent looking guy by the bar. He had a tall, slender frame, and while he didn't work out much, he probably did a fair bit of yoga or something to give him muscle definition.

"He's been eyeing you up all night, but he isn't likely to come over while I'm sat here."

"No, don't you dare go anywhere!"

"You'll thank me in the morning," John said with a wink as he left me by myself at the table.

I cast a few nervous glances in the direction of my supposed admirer. Could he really have been looking at me? There were some stunning women in here, so that didn't seem likely.

I took another sip of my drink, carefully glancing in his direction as I did so. The man looked straight at me and smiled. I tried to return it, but still had a mouthful of drink and managed to dribble some of it down my chin. This was like meeting Carter all over again.

My smile vanished as I pictured Carter again. This stranger was handsome, but he was no Carter. In my head, I pictured him looking at me over a glass of whiskey.

What I wouldn't do to have him sweep me off my feet now...

The stranger wasn't short on confidence and he approached my table as soon as he saw me smile at him. This is the bit I was just no good at. I had no idea how to be nice and polite to men in bars while not sending out mixed messages about wanting him to take me home.

Maybe I should fuck this guy? Would that help get Carter out of my system? John clearly seemed to think so, and it had worked for him.

"Hi, do you mind if I sit here?" the man asked.

Last time I'd heard those words had been when Carter sat opposite me in the coffee shop. That seemed like a lifetime ago then. I hadn't known about Carter's involvement in the accident. Everything was different now.

"Be my guest," I replied. "I'm Emily."

"Mason," he said, holding out his hand. "Can I buy you a drink?"

"Oh, no need," I said. "I'm still working on this one, and you've only just sat down."

Mason smiled and got the attention of a bartender. I didn't hear what he said, but just a minute later the bartender came back with two Manhattans.

"Do you work here?" I asked. The bar didn't have table service, at least not for anyone else, and Mason hadn't paid for the drink.

"Sort of," Mason replied. "I own the place."

I rolled my eyes as everything fell into place. Mason must be a friend of John's. This whole thing was one big setup.

"You're John's friend?" I asked. Mason nodded. "Look, I don't know what John has told you about me, but I'm not looking to meet anyone right now. I hope he hasn't given you the wrong impression."

"I'm not exactly looking for anyone myself either," Mason said. "I'm just here to keep my customers entertained. No pressure."

Thankfully, Mason kept to his word and we just talked casually while I sipped my drink. I caught a few glimpses of John with a guy on the dance floor. There was a good chance I would be bumping into that guy over breakfast tomorrow morning.

Mason had crept closer and closer as we talked and I didn't stop him. I even flirted a little bit; playing with my hair and attempting to flutter my eyelashes. Was I betraying Carter? Technically we weren't a couple—probably never had been—but I still wanted to be with him. I would have swapped Mason for Carter in a heartbeat if I could.

"So, how about we go dance?" Mason asked. "I have no ill intentions, I promise. Let's just let our hair down on the dance floor."

No one was more surprised than me when I stood up and walked over to dance. Mason didn't bat an eye at my leg, so John must have already told him. If he didn't care, then I had no reason to be embarrassed about it.

I took a deep breath and tried to relax. Maybe Mason would be the perfect cure to Carter's hold over me.

Chapter Five

The music was loud and quick, but Mason matched his pace to mine. I felt the stares from the other dancers, some smirking, some seemingly in awe at my dancing as if a girl with an artificial leg shouldn't be able to move at all.

When Mason put the moves on I only made a weak effort to resist. I pushed him away, but only feebly. He placed his hands on my ass and pulled our middles together. We ground our hips in time to the music and I could feel his erection building, twitching against my sex.

My heart raced, but I didn't feel that horny. My pussy wasn't wet like when Carter touched me. He only needed to look at me and I would be dripping. Mason wasn't doing it for me.

That's when Mason went in for the kiss. His lips took me by surprise as they pressed mine apart. His tongue forced its way inside me as our teeth clashed in a clumsy embrace.

Mason was nothing like Carter. Carter was forceful, but gentle at the same time. Mason was like a horny schoolboy.

So why was I letting him kiss me? My brain was telling me this was a bad idea, but I couldn't muster the enthusiasm to resist him. Sure, the sex would be a little dull, but at least I would have some cock inside me again. I couldn't stay celibate for the rest of my life just because it hadn't worked out with Carter.

Mason's fingers started wandering up inside my skirt and I felt them brush against my panties. The skirt was too tight for him to move freely, so he pulled out his hand and roughly manhandled my breasts instead. The left nipple popped out of my bra. There was no stopping Mason now.

"Let's go to my office," he said, leading me by the hand. I went with him willingly, just hoping that a quick fumble would cure me of my lust for Carter. Not likely, but a girl could hope.

I looked around me as we went to an employee-only room. Eyes followed us, the women judging me and the men likely jealous.

As soon as we were inside, Mason pushed me onto his desk and spread my legs. He unbuckled his belt and slipped down his trousers. He didn't even bother to take off my knickers; he just pushed them to one side.

"Wait," I said, as I squirmed away from him just before he entered me. "We need a condom."

"Don't worry about that. I'm clean and I know you are too since you're a little on the innocent side, according to John."

"No," I said, trying to shut my legs and push him away. Mason wasn't listening and I wouldn't be able to hold him off much longer. "Please don't," I moaned. How had this happened? It seemed like only minutes ago we had been chatting over a drink, and now Mason was trying to force his way inside me.

I flung out a leg to kick Mason, but he caught it in one hand and spread my legs open wide. "Feisty little bitch, aren't you?" he said. "Why don't you just relax? You'll enjoy a good fucking."

I closed my eyes and gave up, bracing myself for his member to slam inside me. Instead Mason let go of my legs. I opened my eyes just in time to see Carter throwing Mason up against the wall off his office. His thick hand wrapped around Mason's neck as he lifted him off the floor.

"Carter," I muttered as I tried to sit up and rearrange my clothing. "Don't hurt him."

"Why?" Carter yelled through gritted teeth as he tightened his grip on Mason's throat. Mason spluttered and gasped for air as his face turned bright red. "Why should I let this sniveling mess get away with it?"

"He's not worth it," I said. "Please. Can we just get out of here?"

Carter held on to Mason's neck for a few more seconds and then let go. Mason fell to the floor, breathing hard and loosening his shirt. Carter walked over to me and helped me up off the desk. I wrapped my arm around his shoulders for support and could feel the veins pulsing through his body. His muscles were tense and the anger flowed through him. As we walked past Mason, Carter turned to look at him and swung his leg right between Mason's. Mason's now limp dick took the brunt of the impact, causing him to curl up in a ball on the floor.

"Let's go," Carter said, practically dragging me out of the bar and into his car. He handled me roughly, unable to control his anger, and ordered the driver to take us back to his place.

"Carter?" I murmured to break the silence. "Thank you."

He didn't respond and we sat in silence the entire ride home. That changed as soon as we stepped into his penthouse.

"What the fuck were you playing at, Emily?" Carter yelled at me. "You cannot fucking do that. Do you have any idea how stupid that was?"

His words, his anger, hit my like a punch to the gut and hurt almost as much as Mason's actions earlier. Why was he mad at me? This was hardly my fault. I just wanted to go to sleep, not listen to his bullshit.

148

"I can do what the fuck I like, Carter," I yelled. "I don't belong to you. If I want to screw some guy I just met, then I am perfectly entitled to do that. You've probably already screwed a couple of cheap tarts since we split up."

"What has gotten into you?" Carter asked. "This is not you talking."

"You killed my brother—that's what gotten into me." I wanted to take the words back as soon as I said them. It felt good to get them out, but Carter didn't deserve that.

"Shit," Carter muttered. "I'm sorry, Emily, I'm not mad at you. I'm mad at myself for not stepping in sooner."

"I'm tired," I said, my eyes suddenly feeling heavy. "Really tired." Carter just about managed to get me back onto the sofa before I fell into a deep sleep.

Chapter Six

The sun streamed into the room and I squinted to read the time on my phone. Eleven o'clock. God, I hadn't slept in that late since I was in college. The smell of coffee wafted in from the kitchen and immediately gave me a bit of a kick.

"Morning," Carter said, handing me a fresh cup of coffee. "How are you feeling?"

"Like crap," I said. "And not just from the hangover. I don't know how I let that happen, I should never have put myself—"

"Stop, Emily. Stop right there. Do not for one second blame yourself for what happened last night."

"But you were so mad—"

"I wasn't mad with you, for Christ's sake, I was mad at myself. I should have got there sooner. How are you feeling? You went through something traumatic last night. Do you want to talk about it?"

"No, no, it's okay. I can't remember any of it at the moment and I don't want to. Why were you there, anyway? How did you know where I was?"

"John told me. He set you up with Mason to make me jealous. The idea was that I would come along and see you two together and realize that I want you."

"I can't believe he did that. I'm so sorry. I'm going to kill him."

"Don't worry," Carter said. "I've already had a little chat with him. Warned him against setting you up with sick rapists."

I cringed and crossed my legs, still feeling ashamed about last night. Mason had crossed the line, but I had willingly gone to his office and I felt like crap for it.

"And I told John that he does not need to make me jealous. I didn't go into detail, but I told him that you ditched me and not the other way around. He seemed quite surprised, actually."

"Thanks. But now he's going to give me loads of grief for ditching a 'sex god'—his words, not mine."

"You don't think I'm a sex god?" Carter said with a smile. "Now I'm offended."

I rolled my eyes and refused to dignify that with a response. "Should I tell anyone about Mason? Like the police?"

"No," Carter said immediately. "They won't do anything, anyway."

That was fine with me. I had a lucky escape and didn't want to deal with the police. It would have just been my word against his anyway and hundreds of people had seen us getting it on the dance floor.

"I was trying to get over you," I said. "With Mason. I was dancing with him to forget about you."

"You don't need to forget about me," Carter said.

"I do. I know it was an accident and it was a long time ago, but I can't see you without remembering William."

"We need to talk about that," Carter said. "Do you have plans for today?"

"I have work to do. But I'm not really feeling up to it."

"You should spend the day with John. Trust me, he feels so bad right now that he will treat you like a princess. Let's do dinner though, okay?"

"Sure. Um, can you take me home? I don't want to do the walk of shame this morning."

"I told you, you have nothing to be ashamed of about last—"

"Carter, I'm not talking about that. I was referring to the fact that I'm dressed like a whore."

"Oh. That. I'll have my driver take you back."

Carter had been right about John. He apologized for a solid hour after I got home and spent the day spoiling me rotten. Apparently he had been introduced to Mason through a friend, and on paper he had seemed like a good fit for me. Successful, charismatic, and handsome—like a miniature version of Carter, I guessed.

Carter hadn't told John all the gory details, which was just as well, but John knew enough to know not to set me up with anyone again in the near future. That was good enough for me.

"Is there any chance something good will come out of all this?" John asked.

"Out of me being groped against my will by a sleazy bar owner?"

"You know what I mean," John said. "With you and Carter. I mean, he clearly still wants you, right? So that means the ball is in your court, doesn't it?"

"Congratulations on using a sports metaphor correctly," I joked. Much to John's displeasure, he did tend to fit a lot of the gay stereotypes, and not liking sports was certainly one of them.

"Don't change the subject."

I let out a quiet sigh and considered telling John the whole story. My reluctance wasn't because I didn't trust him or that I didn't want to talk to him about it. The problem was I didn't know if I could physically get the words out. How could I tell him that Carter killed my brother?

"You're right," I admitted. "Sort of. But it's not that simple. And I don't just mean like ordinary relationship drama kind of thing. It's messed up in a big soap opera kind of way."

"All right, I'll leave it. For now. But you need to tell me about this at some point, Emily. I'm your friend, but also your business partner. If we start keeping secrets it's going to affect the business, and neither of us wants that."

"I will tell you when I'm ready. How's that?"

John nodded. "Fine by me. So, what do you want to do this afternoon?"

"I can't bring myself to go outside into daylight. Can we just watch a movie and eat crappy food?"

"Perfect."

John streamed a film while I prepared some nachos with melted cheese, a recipe that had helped with hangovers in the past.

Every flash of violence during the movie gave me flashbacks of last night. My memory was still fuzzy on the details, but I remember the explosion of energy as Carter ripped Mason away from me and slammed him up against the wall.

Whatever his mistakes in the past, he had saved me last night. For the first time since I found out about his role in William's death, I actually looked forward to seeing him.

I stopped snacking on nachos to save my appetite. Dinner could not come soon enough.

Chapter Seven

Carter could work wonders in a kitchen. When the elevator doors to his penthouse opened, I was greeted by an aroma of seafood, spicy sauce and something sweet for dinner that was still baking in the oven.

To my slight disappointment, Carter had not dialed up the romance at all. There were no candles burning or flowers on the table.

"The entrée will just be a minute," Carter yelled over the noise of fans and boiling pots. I frowned and was about to ask for an appetizer when I remembered Carter's previous criticism of American vocabulary. An entrée was a starter, not a main course. If I ever went to Europe, I would end up completely embarrassing myself in so many ways.

I sat down at the table and made sure my clothes looked presentable. Everything hung in the right place and my light summer dress covered up most of my leg. When Carter brought out the first course of fried calamari, I couldn't help but burst out laughing.

"Where the hell did you get that apron from?"

Carter had dressed in a shirt and khakis with the sleeves mercifully rolled up to reveal his toned forearms, which hinted at the majesty of what lay higher up. But over all that he had on a garish apron with frilly pink bits around the edges.

"It was all I could find at short notice," Carter said. "I don't bring one with me when I travel and had to pop out and get this an hour ago."

"Well, you look beautiful," I said, standing up and admiring him. "Like a princess."

Carter raised his eyebrows and stared at me. I tried to hide my grin, but ended up snickering like a schoolgirl.

We made small talk during dinner, but I could tell Carter had something on his mind. He'd promised to tell me more about the night William died, but I wasn't sure I wanted to hear it. What could he say that would possibly make it better?

"You want a hand with the washing up?" I asked as I finished off my slice of apple pie. I secretly hoped he would say no, because I felt barely able stand after all that food. It had cured my hangover, though.

"Oh, don't worry about that," Carter said with a wave of his hand. "I have someone who comes and does that."

"Well, lucky you. I have to do my own washing up."

"Does it take a lot of effort to clean up after microwaving pizza?" Carter asked.

I pursed my lips and slapped him on his toned arms. "In the words of your people, you are a 'right cheeky sod' today, aren't you?"

"Did you just do an English accent?" Carter asked.

"What did you think?"

"I think you need to spend a lot more time with English people. Well, one English person in particular. Let's go sit down."

Carter pulled me over to the sofa and sat down next to me, although not quite so close that we were touching.

"I need to tell you about the accident," Carter said.

"Carter, I—"

"Please. Let me tell you. I need to tell you as much as you need to hear it. I'm not sure if it will change things between us, but I will always regret it if I don't try."

Carter wasn't going to let this go. His eyes held the same look of steely determination he had when he told me he was going to have me. And he had most certainly got his way that time.

"Okay, you can tell me," I said. "But if I ask you to stop, you must promise you will. I'm not sure how easy this is going to be to hear."

"Thank you," Carter said. "And yes, I will stop talking whenever you tell me to. In many ways, there isn't that much to tell. Your brother was killed by a drunk driver who stupidly got behind the wheel after too many drinks. Our car was on the wrong side of the road and we slammed straight into your car. You know the rest."

"You weren't alone in the car?" I asked.

"No, Emily, I wasn't. I was with my girlfriend. That's what I want to tell you."

I shook my head. "That doesn't make any difference. Why would I care that your girlfriend was in the car as well?"

"Because she was the one driving. I wasn't the one who killed your brother, Emily—it was my ex-girlfriend."

Chapter Eight

"No," I said. "That doesn't make any sense. My dad was at your trial. He saw you admit to driving the car. He saw you get sent to prison, not some girl. Why are you saying this?"

"Because it's true," Carter replied. "But you're right. I did go to jail and I did admit to being the driver." His thick fingers rubbed the bridge of his nose as he searched for the next words. "I took the blame for her."

"Why?" I asked. "I get that you'd want to protect your girlfriend, but to lie at a trial and go to jail? That's crazy!"

"I know. It all happened so fast. We had been out for a meal to celebrate a friend's birthday and I had necked back two or three beers. I would have been over the limit, but it was Bella's turn to drive. I didn't realize at the time but she had an alcohol problem. She'd been sneaking vodka into her orange juice all night and was wasted by the time we got in the car."

None of this seemed to make sense. I should have been pleased at this news. But he was still intrinsically linked with William. Would I ever be able to look at Carter without seeing William? Even if I could, I doubted my parents would ever accept him as a son-in-law.

"Didn't you notice that she was drunk?"

Carter shook his head. "She was good at hiding it. Even most of her driving had been good up until we approached a sharp corner. The car swung out wide and we went straight into the side of yours."

"Were you hurt?"

Carter smiled and shook his head. "It's sweet of you to ask, but no, I was not hurt. Couple of bruises, that's all."

"How did you end up taking the blame? That's quite a request for her to make."

"She didn't ask. Not directly. As soon as we hit your car she blurted out that she was drunk and way over the limit. In those seconds she told me that she was an alcoholic and would go to jail. I just panicked. I didn't know what to do. So I got out of the car and pulled her into the passenger seat."

"I don't know what to say. I can't believe you did that. And that you kept up the lie all through the trial."

"Once we had started, we had to stick to it. You have to remember that I did not know your brother was dead when we did this. We assumed you would be okay because we were. If I had any idea what had happened then, I would never have gone through with it."

The whole time Carter had been telling his story, something had been at the back of mind, some reason not to be happy with the news, and then it hit me.

"My brother's killer was never punished," I said. "She is still out there going about her life. This Bella girl got away with it."

"I wouldn't say that," Carter said solemnly. "After the accident, she went downhill fast. Kept pouring booze into her, and then moved on to drugs. Not that this makes much of a difference, but the whole thing did mess her up a lot."

"Where is she now?" I asked. I knew the answer before Carter replied. Ever since I had first told Carter about William, I had known Carter had lost someone too. He had shared a look with me and I had seen pain in his eyes, the kind of pain that you only had when someone you loved had died. "She's dead isn't she?"

Carter swallowed and nodded. "Overdosed. A few years ago. While I was in prison."

"I'm sorry," I said. "Not for her—for you. I can tell she meant a lot to you." My heart sank as it dawned on me that Carter had fallen in love. Before he became the ladies' man he was now, Carter had been in love. That hurt me more than anything else he'd told me that day.

"She did," he admitted. "But that was a long time ago." He paused, but I didn't know what to say. Did he want me to throw my arms around him and tell him everything was going to be all right? "Is there any chance you will be able to see past this one day?" he pleaded, placing a hand on my leg.

Sparks flew up my thigh when he touched me. I wanted him to push me onto my back and take me.

"We shouldn't," I said meekly.

"God, Emily. I want you so much, you have no idea." He leaned into me and started kissing my neck while his hand dug into my thigh. "I need you. I need to be inside you."

Carter's words whispered in my ear drove me wild with desire. My pussy was wet and his fingers were just inches away from my opening. If he touched that, he would know just how much I wanted him and I wouldn't be able to resist.

He pushed his way between my legs and pressed up against me. I felt how hard he was. If he just unzipped his fly and slipped my knickers to one side, he would be inside me. I grabbed his ass and pushed his hardness against my clit.

For the first time, Carter placed a hand on my prosthetic leg and moved it to one side, opening my legs wide. He acted as if the leg were completely normal and didn't react to touching it at all. But I did.

The leg was my constant reminder that I was flawed and it was linked to the accident, the accident where my brother had died and Carter sacrificed himself for someone he loved.

"I can't," I said, pressing my hands against Carter's firm chest. Carter didn't move. I dug my nails into him, but he barely noticed. "Carter, please, no. I can't do this. Not now."

Carter let out an animalistic noise, half yell, half moan, and rolled off me onto the floor.

"You should leave," he said coldly.

I grabbed my purse and waited for thirty long seconds for the elevator to arrive. I needed time to process what I had heard. Carter had been in love before. The girl who killed my brother was dead. In pleading guilty to something he never did, Carter had done something incredible for the girl he loved. I should have respected that, but as I stepped into the elevator I realized there was a good chance I would never see him again, and maybe that was for the best.

Chapter Nine

Living with John had some advantages, like easily being able to talk about work and show each other what we had on our screens, but it also had its downsides. Mainly, we talked too much.

After dinner with Carter, all I could think about was the story he told me about the night of the accident. I needed to talk it through with John, just to know if what I was crazy or not. Even though Carter hadn't been the one driving, he was still there when it happened.

But I wanted him in ways I had never wanted anyone else. I craved his body in a way I didn't know was possible. I looked at him how sleazy men look at women in bars. I'd never done that with anyone else.

And we had a connection beyond sex. I could be myself around him and never felt like he was judging me for my leg.

I told John everything from the incident at my parents' house to Carter's full explanation.

"So, am I crazy for wanting him?" I asked after I had finished the whole story. John had listened in a kind of stunned silence the entire time, so I had no way to judge what his reaction would be.

"Shit, Emily. That is pretty fucked up."

"Thank you, John. Yes, I am aware that this is perhaps not the typical boy-meets-girl situation. But that doesn't answer the question."

"Maybe you're crazy. But love and lust can do crazy things to people. I don't think you're crazy for wanting him. Christ, the guy is impossible not to want. I still find myself fantasizing about having him do wicked things to me and—"

"John, I don't want to hear that."

"Sorry. Look, this all comes down to trust. Carter did something stupid by taking the blame, but he did not kill your brother. This Bella girl did, and she's dead now. Good riddance. The question is whether you can trust him."

I didn't trust any man when it came down to it. I never had. Carter hardly seemed like a good place to start, what with his womanizing and lying to a court.

"Maybe," I replied. "But it's not just the accident. He hasn't admitted as much, but him meeting me was obviously not a coincidence. He must have tracked me down and seduced me, even knowing what he knew about my brother. That's fucked up. Maybe he isn't even here on business at all."

John nodded. "I was hoping you hadn't noticed that. You need to figure out the trust issue, but don't rush into it. Trust takes time in any relationship. It'll take even longer in this one, but Carter wants to make this work. Just look at all the effort he's put in to win you over."

"So it's not insane that I still want him?"

"No," John replied. "I don't think so. That doesn't mean it will work out, though. If you can't think of him without remembering your brother, then this will all collapse."

John was right. My therapist had worked me through a similar problem with my leg. In the first few months after the accident, I hadn't been able to go a minute without thinking of William. Dr. Michaels traced that to my leg—every step I took on it was a constant reminder of what I had lost. The leg still triggered memories of William—as it had done back at Carter's—but it was less frequent and manageable.

Would I ever be able to achieve the same thing with Carter? William would want me to. He wouldn't want me to turn my back on the perfect man because of some messed up coincidence. That thought gave me the courage to give it one last shot.

"Hi, Mom," I said cheerily the next morning. The hangover had completely vanished and I actually felt good. A lot had changed in the last twenty-four

167

hours and I tried to remain positive for the time being. "Can I speak to Dad?"

"Don't want to talk to your mom today, then?"

"I need to ask Dad some questions about the trial."

"Ah. Honey, I don't think he's going to want to talk about that."

"Please, Mom. It's really important."

Mom relented and Dad picked up the phone a few minutes later. He wasn't going to like talking about this, but I had to get some answers.

"Dad, I'm sorry to do this, but I want to ask you some questions about the trial."

"Yeah, your mom said. What do you want to know? Has Carter given you a different version of events?"

"Sort of," I confessed. "I just want to know whether anything at the trial seemed unusual? Did the version of events make sense? That sort of thing."

"It made enough sense for a jury to convict him," Dad said. "I don't know what you want me to say. The trial did get a bit messy at times and Carter got caught changing his story more than once. That's why the sentence was so heavy—there were perjury charges tacked on."

"He changed his story?" I asked.

"There were inconsistencies about how events unfolded and he had a crappy lawyer."

"Really?" That did surprise me. I imagined Carter's parents hiring some hot-shot defense attorney for him.

"Yeah, just a public defender who wasn't really up to it. Are you going to tell me what this is all about? Whatever he told you, it doesn't change anything. That man killed your brother. He may have served his time, but he still did it and I don't ever want to see him again."

"I know. Thanks, Dad."

I hung up without waiting for a goodbye. There was no point telling Dad the whole story right then— I would have to work up to it.

What I found interesting was that Carter had a public defender for the case. He was only twenty-nine now and had spent five years in prison, but he had access to a lot of money, that much was obvious. I'd assumed the money had come from his parents, but perhaps not.

The truth was that I knew very little about him. Did he even have a job at a big bank? That seemed unlikely for someone with a serious criminal record. So where was the money coming from?

John had told me how important trust would be in our relationship, and at the moment, I couldn't trust Carter. He had some more explaining to do.

Chapter Ten

"I have more questions," I said to Carter as we met for lunch in a restaurant on Sunday. I'd let Carter chose the place, so it was horrendously expensive and a little snobby.

"I figured you might," Carter said. "I will answer if I can."

"Tell me more about Bella," I said. I didn't want to know about her, but I had to get all the information if I was to ever move on. If she remained a mystery, then that would always come between us. "How close were the two of you?"

"We were close," Carter said. "She's still the only person I have been in a serious relationship with. We got together when we were seventeen and she was on holiday in England. We were both trying to get into a bar, but were underage. We bonded over our distaste for bouncers, I guess. We wrote to each other after that and called when possible. Her parents were loaded, so she came to England a few more times, and when it came time to apply to university, I chose to go to the States."

"That's quite a commitment for someone so young," I said. I couldn't imagine anyone moving to another country for me. Carter tried to keep his voice casual, but his actions for Bella spoke volumes.

"I guess. But I was young and stupid. We stayed together throughout university, but once that was finished, I had to go back home. I managed to get a job that paid enough for regular visits, and she had no problem flying out. I was visiting her on holiday when the accident happened."

"When did she... overdose?" I was going to say "die," but the word stuck in my throat.

"Two years ago while I was in prison. I was allowed out to go to the funeral."

I unconsciously rubbed at my artificial leg under the table as I tried to get my head around her death. All I got was emptiness. It didn't help at all. I was glad she wasn't alive and living a full life, but her death left only a bitter taste in my mouth.

"If your family is poor, why do you now have loads of money? I don't mean to sound rude, but it seems a little unlikely for an ex-con to land a good job with a bank after coming out of prison."

"Her family has connections," Carter said. "They felt like they owed me after what I did."

"Tell me about your parents," I said. "How do they fit into all this?"

"Emily, I can keep answering all your questions, but the fact is you are going to have to decide whether or not you can trust me."

He'd seen right through me like he always did. I sought answers for everything I didn't know, but that wasn't how trust should work in a relationship. We would never know everything there was to know about each other, and sometimes you just had to take a leap of faith.

"You're right. But tell me one last thing. It wasn't a coincidence, was it? Meeting me at the bar the night of the conference?"

Carter shook his head. "No, it wasn't. I sought you out that night, but I had no idea how to approach you. When, well... when everything got a little embarrassing, I just knew I had to see you again."

He placed his hands on mine, and I saw small cuts and bruising on his knuckles. Had he got those the night he saved me from Mason? I didn't remember him throwing any punches, but it all happened so quickly. The cuts only made him look more manly and rugged. I had to have him.

"Take me back to your place, Carter. I want to start making up for lost time."

173

I don't know what got into me—maybe too much coffee that morning—but a passion had taken hold of me and would not let go.

As soon as we got into the back of Carter's car we started wrestling with each other, pulling at clothes and pressing our hands into each other's bodies.

Carter dragged me into the elevator once we arrived back at his building and then threw me down onto his bed. He pulled my jeans off and dove between my legs, greedily lapping at my wet panties. His teeth clasped onto the delicate cotton and he pulled them off me, only needing to use his hands when the cotton got caught on a joint on my artificial limb.

That kind of embarrassment would normally throw me off, but I was gushing between my thighs and nothing could stop me. Carter ate me with a force and passion I had never known, his tongue hammering at my cunt like my fingers had never managed. When he slipped two fingers inside I came hard and writhed on the bed in a sweaty heap.

"Be right back," Carter said, heading to his drawer for a condom.

"No, come here," I replied. I got up onto my knees and pulled him down onto the edge of the bed. I got up and stood there in front of him completely naked. I'd never had the confidence to stand naked in front of anyone, but now I glowed under Carter's lusty gaze.

Looking directly into his eyes, I lowered myself onto my knees and crawled between his thighs. Placing my hands on his legs I looked at his member, seeing it up close for the first time. The shaft pulsed in front of me—not yet hard but stiffening—as I admired its length and girth. No wonder the sex had been a tad painful; Carter's shaft was the size of one of the big black dildos they sold at the sex shop on the corner.

I took hold of him in one hand and slowly stroked up and down. As he grew in my grasp, I lowered my head and slowly licked his tip. Carter gasped and flinched under my touch. The head tasted a little salty, but I had nothing to compare him to. I'd never had a man in my mouth before.

My lips opened slightly and wrapped around Carter's head while my tongue flicked against his slit. I sucked gently and pulled my lips away with a "pop!"

"Baby, you don't have to do this," Carter said. "I know you've never done this before."

"You want me to stop?" I asked, looking up at him with a smile.

"Fuck, no!"

I went back down on his cock and opened my mouth wide. There was no way I would get the whole thing inside me, but I would give it a damn good go.

I sucked hard as I moved down his shaft inch-by-inch until he reached the back of my throat. I held my mouth there for a few seconds before springing back up for air, leaving a trail of drool over his cock.

Carter didn't seem to mind. I kept tossing his shaft—easier now that I had left it wet and slippery—while sucking as much of him as I could fit in my mouth.

"Oh shit, this is so good." Carter squirmed under me, tensing his muscles and revealing his huge quads. He placed a head on my head and let his fingers weave through my hair. "Do you trust me, Emily? I need you to trust me."

I didn't look up at him, but gave a nod with his cock still filling my mouth. Carter pushed his cock further inside me, his hand holding me down. I thought I was going to gag, but I remembered what he said. I trusted him. My fingers dug into his thighs, but I didn't push back. Finally he let me up for air.

"Again," I said, surprising myself. Carter thrust himself back inside my mouth. I sucked hard as he released.

"I'm close, baby." I put my hand back on the shaft and tugged hard at his wet, slippery cock. Just as my lips were about to lock around his head again, a hot burst of thick white goodness sprayed forth into my mouth. I quickly swallowed without thinking, pleasantly surprised by the taste, but didn't get my mouth open in time for the second load. The spray hit my chin and dribbled down my neck onto my breasts.

Carter shook a few more times, then looked down at me in all my messy, sweaty, sticky glory.

"I have never seen you look more beautiful," he said.

Chapter Eleven

After Carter and I showered together, we wrapped ourselves in a couple of thick bathrobes and curled up on the couch. I decided not to question why Carter had more than one bathrobe—I wasn't sure I would like the answer and I knew he would get mad at me for asking.

That was my first ever blowjob and it was not at all like I had imagined. I'd always assumed I would feel dirty and used after doing it, but as I lay under Carter's heavy arm, I had never felt more secure or confident in myself and my sexuality.

The next morning, we went out for a cup of coffee. Carter had expensive taste for the most part, but he rarely had good coffee at home. There was plenty of tea, of course, but that wasn't strong enough for first thing in the morning.

"So, what's the latest with work?" Carter asked. "Tell me in terms I can understand."

"We're moving along okay. I'd like it to go a little faster, of course, but that's the way these things go. We only have a small group of beta users at the moment and need to expand drastically to get more useful information, but that is going to be expensive."

"Is this like clinical trials?"

"Kind of," I said. "We're quite lucky in that none of the technology we use is new, so we don't have to get any special licenses. We are just using the technology in new ways."

"Like what?" Carter asked. "I need a basic description of your business so that I don't sound like a complete prick if people ask me what you do."

"Right, that might not be easy. Well, take my leg as an example." I lifted my leg up under the table and rested it on his lap. "This is a normal prosthetic leg and has been around for quite a few years now. It's not even a particularly good one, actually, because my parents never had good health insurance. What FriendlyLimb does is collect data from that leg through lots of small electrodes that track movement and pressure."

"And you have that in your body?"

"Not really, it's just rubbing against the skin. And again, that is old technology, but we are the first to analyze the data with some damn complicated algorithms."

"Hmm, I think that's about as much as I can store in my head for now," Carter said. "Do you have much of the investment money left? Finances, I can understand."

"Yeah, we do, but if we move forward with this next set of trials, then we will burn through it quick. Essentially, every time we do something big like this we have to keep our fingers crossed it will succeed, because if it doesn't, no new investors will want to come in."

"And I thought banking was a high-pressure job. Speaking of which, I have some work to take care of, so we won't be able to spend the day together."

I shrugged, but was a little disappointed not to be going back to his place to have a bit of fun before getting on with work. My to-do list was huge, so a day without Carter was probably for the best, but that didn't stop my hormones for lusting after him.

"Well, hello," John said when I walked through the door at midday. "Someone didn't come home last night. I take it things are back on with Carter, then?"

Things were as "on" as they were before, but I still had no idea what that really entailed. I had not yet used the term boyfriend and he had never referred to me as his girlfriend. Not with me around, anyway.

"We're on," I said eventually. "Still taking it slow and steady, but we are spending a lot of time together."

"That's great news, Emily. It really is. I know there is a lot of shit to work through, but you look radiant after spending time with him."

"I do feel better," I admitted. "I'm not walking on the air or anything, but I guess I can see the positive side of life at the moment."

"I've got some more good news for you," John said. "I thought about not telling you, but I think you have a right to know. Plus you may find out anyway and I don't want you thinking I kept it from you."

"Uh, this sounds ominous. What is it?"

"You know the bar owned by that Mason guy I set you up with because I am complete moron?"

"I'm not likely to forget that in a hurry," I said.

"You do remember it, then? What happened that night?"

That was an odd question, but he had a point. I was nearly raped, but my recollection of it was hazy to say the least. Not that I was complaining—better than having it burned into your brain—but it was weird to not remember.

"I remember roughly what happened. Why?"

"The police shut the place down and arrested Mason. They found drugs behind the bar."

"What kind of drugs?" I asked.

"Roofies. Seems like Mason was spiking drinks and having his way with women. Emily, that's why you just went along with it. I thought it was a little odd at the time, but that explains it."

"And that's why I can't remember," I added. How could I have been so stupid as to let a stranger get me a drink like that? At least now I could sleep a little easier knowing that I hadn't tried to betray Carter. "So, Mason is now in prison?"

John shook his head. "Hospital. Seems he took a bit of a beating yesterday. We have a mutual friend who says his body now looks like it was used as a punching bag."

I closed my eyes and thought back to the marks on Carter's knuckles. I never did ask him how he got them because I didn't want to bring back memories of Friday night.

"What is it, Emily? Are you okay? Don't spare any sympathy for that man. He deserved everything he got."

"You're right," I said. "I don't care about that prick. I'm going to get some work done today. We should catch up later, though, and talk about the cost of this next trial."

"Will do. And Emily, I don't want to jinx anything, but I'm glad you're happy."

"Me too," I said. I was happy. It was a weird feeling and I wasn't used to it. No doubt something would go wrong soon enough.

The only question was whether it would be the business or Carter—or both.

Chapter Twelve

"Emily, we have a big problem."

That wasn't how I liked to wake up on a Wednesday morning. Carter had insisted on spending time apart during the week because he was busy with work, so that meant John and I were spending more time together than usual. We were still getting along well, but I had gotten used to having my own place and sharing it was a little strange, especially when I wanted to sleep in.

"What is it?" I asked groggily.

"We've been sued."

That woke me up. "What? By whom? What for?"

"No surprises who—PharmaTech. They are suing us for IP infringement."

I quickly threw some clothes on and ran into the living room to see John scanning the papers.

"Oh, this is complete bullshit," John said. "They are alleging that our technology is in violation of one of their existing patents. It's not even close. This is something we already hold a patent on ourselves."

"This is what we feared would happen," I said, taking the pages of the lawsuit from John as he finished reading them. "They are just hoping we can't afford the legal fees and will give up."

"Are they right?" John asked. "We still have some money, but the new trial is going to absorb most of that and Scott's services don't come cheap."

"This could be a problem," I conceded. "They know this is a losing case, but we'll have to pay to get it dismissed. No doubt another lawsuit will follow, and then another and another."

"There must be something we can do," John said. "Surely there are laws against companies filing suits like this."

"Probably. But we'll have to pay a lawyer to find out and then sue PharmaTech ourselves. That'll cost a small fortune."

"Goddammit!" John snarled. "Do you ever wish we had just accepted that ten million dollar offer? I hate them as much as you do, but it would be nice to be a millionaire and not have to worry about this shit."

I thought for a few seconds before answering. Not once since the offer had I regretted our decision to turn down PharmaTech, but I'd never given much thought as to why.

"You know what? I don't regret it," I said. "Because knowing that company, they would have found a way to screw us out of the money somehow. They would have knocked the price down and found ways to make payment contingent on certain milestones. We'd be just as stressed as we are now, but we would have also sold our souls."

"You're probably right," John said. "I'll pass this on to Scott and see what he has to say. You want to be on the call?"

"No, you can handle it. I'll keep on top of this new trial. I want to get that underway before we get distracted."

Carter and I were not ones for sending text messages back and forth, but I decided to send him a quick message with the news that we were being sued.

"You know you've made it when you've been sued. Need any help? I know lawyers," came Carter's reply.

I told him we were dealing with it and didn't hear any more from him. He was busy on some deal this week and couldn't sit there sending me messages each day. Not long ago that would have annoyed the hell out of me, but fortunately I had matured a little in the last few weeks.

John was right—Carter had changed me for the better.

Before getting down to work, I sent a quick email to our new bookkeeper Jane to warn her of the money we would need to spend over the next few weeks and the lawsuit. She expressed some concern over the cash flow situation, but nothing we didn't know already. I managed to get about three hours into work before Marissa called my cell.

"Hi, Marissa," I said. "How are things?"

"Good, thanks Emily. Listen, I just got a report from Jane which had a few disclosures about a lawsuit you just got hit with. I'd like to see a copy, please."

I hesitated. Was it appropriate to send a copy of the lawsuit to an investor? Marissa had been helpful, but she was still an outsider. But she saw our finances, so she may as well see this too.

"Sure, I'll email it over. It's nothing to worry about, though. Complete nonsense about infringing on their IP. I think they are just trying to distract us."

"Probably, but even defending a weak lawsuit costs money. I think you may need further funding."

"Well, we could always do with more money," I said, stating the obvious. A start-up that didn't need money wasn't really a start-up at all.

"Would you be open to selling more equity to my client if I can convince the powers that be to invest more?"

I cringed at the thought of losing more equity. Any sale would probably be at least another 10%, bringing the investor up to 20%. That wouldn't be so bad, except we didn't know anything about who was behind the shell company that Marissa represented.

"It depends on the terms, of course," I said. "But I'm sure we'd be open to it."

"Excellent. I'm going to meet with my client later this week and I'll get back to you, okay?"

"Sounds good."

Most young, cash-strapped companies like ours would have been delighted with such strong financial support, but I couldn't help but worry that we were giving away equity too quickly. One more injection of cash was fine, but after that, John and I needed to focus on retaining control of our company.

To get myself in a better mood, I sent Carter another message telling him that I would be spending Friday night with him. He was likely in a meeting, because he just replied with a smiley face.

I took that as a "yes" and decided to treat myself to a new outfit. For once I couldn't care less about how much of my leg would be on show. If I needed further evidence of how much I had changed, that was it.

Chapter Thirteen

Scott reassured me and John that the lawsuit was not worth worrying about, but he couldn't promise that it wouldn't cost five figures in legal fees to get it to go away. John accepted that further investment was not something we were really in a position to turn down at this point, so we provisionally agreed to go with whatever Marissa proposed.

I spent the week working with Stanford University to get some more clinical trials set up. Stanford had a plentiful supply of cheap, but intelligent students ready and able to work, and was also attached to a top class research hospital, which meant access to patients. Being an alum of the school, I also got a minor discount on the fee they'd usually charge. Every little helped, although even with the discount we were still committing six figures to the project.

With all that going on, I couldn't wait to see Carter. I'd never been one of those girls to throw myself on a guy, but right now I just wanted to jump on and slip him inside me. I had a high sex drive, after all—it had just been hiding behind an inexperienced girl with an artificial leg and lack of confidence.

Carter had told me to come over at six, but I couldn't wait that long. My sex ached for him and I'd already had to change my panties once after the first pair showed traces of my eagerness. I considered taking a self-help approach to relieve some stress, but figured Carter would be worth the wait. He always was.

"Hi, I'm here to see Carter in the penthouse," I said on arriving at Carter's building. At this point, I knew most of the people who worked behind the desk, but there was a new girl in tonight so I had to introduce myself.

"Miss Saunders, I see you are scheduled in for six o'clock, but I'm afraid Mr. Murphy is not available until then."

I looked at my watch. "It's five thirty. Surely you can let me up now?"

"I'm sorry, ma'am, but we are under strict instructions only to let visitors up in accordance with the log book."

I huffed and took a seat in the lobby to wait. I pulled out my phone and tried calling Carter. No response. I sent him a message.

"The bitch in the lobby won't let me up! Can you come get me, please?"

No response.

I resigned myself to spending thirty minutes flicking through my Facebook and Twitter feeds before moving on to browsing a few tech-oriented news sites. Not an ideal way to spend half an hour when you're horny as hell.

My eyes followed those moving in an out of the building, although for the most part it was just people coming back from work looking fed up and miserable.

Then a woman caught my eye as she left the elevator. She was on the phone and in a world of her own; she didn't look twice at me, but I stared at her from the moment she walked out of the elevator until she left the building.

I recognized her. Where did I know her from? She was dressed in a skirt and blouse, very formal, but she had a skinny frame with a generous chest. In a way, nothing about her was familiar, but in other ways I was sure I knew her. Then it hit me.

She had changed her appearance drastically from our last encounter. Her hair was down instead of up and she now wore glasses. Last time I had seen her she had worn a tight-fitting dress that showed off her figure instead of this business suit, but there was no mistaking the face.

This was the woman that had been on a date with Carter the very first night we met. The one he had bought a drink for instead of me. What the hell was she doing here? I knew the answer to that question, of course. It couldn't be a fluke—she was visiting Carter. There was only one reason a woman like her would be visiting Carter on a Friday afternoon and that was for a hook up.

"You can go up to see Mr. Murphy now," the receptionist said with a sweet enthusiasm that I couldn't stomach.

The ride up to the penthouse took forever as I pictured the woman in my mind. Flashbacks to that fateful night at the conference came thick and fast as I relived the shame of tripping over on stage and then making a fool of myself in front of Carter at the bar.

"At last," Carter said with a smile as the doors opened. "Sorry I missed your messages—I've been slammed with work and needed to get something finished. Those dirty messages you sent me today have driven me wild. Come here." He took hold of my hand and pulled me towards him.

"I can't believe the things you wrote," he whispered in my ear. "Are you going to have your way with me?"

My anger didn't fade as I looked into his eyes, but my passion came back with a vengeance and I felt my lips getting wet as his fingers worked their way up my thigh. I was too mad to have him make love to me, but too horny to yell at him.

"Take your clothes off," I said. The words came out of my mouth, but it didn't feel like me saying them.

Carter looked a little surprised, but he was only too willing to undress right in front of me in the lounge. The blinds were still open, so we had a perfect view of San Francisco. And San Francisco had a perfect view of us.

As Carter undressed, I slipped out of my dress and stood naked in front of him. I pulled him over to the rug in front of the television and pulled him down. He tried to open my legs, but I pressed my hand to his chest and pushed him to the floor. He had the strength to resist me, but he didn't bother. He was happy just to go with the flow.

"Tonight, *I* fuck *you*," I said as I lowered myself down onto his perfect body.

Chapter Fourteen

Carter lay sprawled out on the floor. I pinned him down by the wrists and straddled him as my wet sex rubbed against his ripped stomach.

"What's gotten into you?" he asked, grinning up at me. I felt the top of his cock flick against my ass as he hardened beneath me.

"Nothing," I lied. God, I hated him right then. He was so excited and aroused, and yet he had just betrayed me. I couldn't look at his face anymore. I slid my pussy up his body, leaving a trail of my lust behind on his tense, hairless chest until I reached his face.

Carter pulled his hands free and placed them on my ass before burying his face in my cunt. My thighs locked his head in place and I rocked back and forth, pressing my sex hard into his mouth.

Carter's pushed his tongue deep inside me while I used a finger to furiously rub my clit. I kept fucking his tongue until I came hard in his mouth. Carter gasped for air when I finally moved my pussy away from his face.

"Fucking hell," he yelled. "Not that I'm complaining, but fuck, what is going on with you?"

I slid my ass back down his chest until his head pressed against my lips. I didn't have a condom.

"I'm clean," Carter said, as if reading my mind.

"You just fucked that skank from the convention," I said calmly while rubbing my wetness into him. "Why should I believe you?"

"What?" Carter asked. "Christ, Emily, she was here for business. I only want you, I swear. You are the one I want to be with. You are the one I need."

My head told me not to trust him, but my head wasn't in control right now. I moved my pussy back and the wet lips parted to let him inside. It was the first time I had ever felt the flesh of cock in my tunnel and it unleashed the animal within me.

I dug my fingers into his chest and pushed back so that his entire length filled my body. There was still pain as he reached into depths of me that only he had ever been, but it was better this time. Slowly, I sat up straight and felt his whole shaft inside. I was whole.

My hips ground into his as I came hard just seconds before he exploded inside me. I fell forward onto his chest as his cock softened, fluids spilling out of me onto the floor.

"We need to talk," Carter whispered in my ear as I lay on his chest.

"Not now," I said. "Let me just enjoy this for a moment first."

"When are you going to start trusting me?" Carter asked after a respectful ten minutes of silence.

"When you stop lying to me," I replied. His essence dripped down the inside of my thigh as I stood up. "I saw that woman from the conference. She was here to see you. Don't deny it."

"I'm not denying it," Carter said, pushing himself up onto his elbows and looking straight up at my naked body. "We had to discuss business and needed some privacy to do that."

"Why didn't you tell me that she was coming here?"

"Because I know how embarrassed you got that night and I didn't want to remind you of it."

"Well, you should have told me. I don't want to be kept in the dark anymore, Carter."

Carter stood up and ran his fingers through my hair. "I will be completely open with you from now on, I promise. Although—"

"Although what?" I snapped.

"Although if this is the punishment I get for lying, then I must say, it isn't much of a deterrent."

I pursed my lips, trying to fight back a smile. "I was horny," I said. "Next time I catch you in a lie, you won't enjoy it so much."

"Unless you're horny," he added with a grin. I bit my lip and smiled as Carter picked me up by the thighs and carried me into the bedroom. I still didn't know quite what had come over me, but I wrapped my arms around his sweaty, muscular back and let him punish me in much the same way I had punished him.

Chapter Fifteen

"Okay, what have you done to the real Emily?" John asked after I gave him a rough outline of what transpired last night.

"I have no idea what came over me," I admitted. "I was so pissed off with him you wouldn't believe it. But instead of screaming at him, I screwed him."

"It's called 'revenge sex,' sweetheart, and there is nothing better. I've been in relationships where we would get into arguments just so we could have make-up sex after."

"Really? So I'm not being some weird, kinky freak?"

John laughed. "No, it's natural. Enjoying sex doesn't make you a whore, Emily."

"It just feels weird. I can't explain it. I don't even think about my leg while I'm doing it."

"That's because you trust him," John said. "You know he's not judging you or thinking about your leg. He wants you for who you are."

"Thing is, I'm still not sure if I should trust him. He never talks about work and I still don't know anything about his life other than… well, you know…"

"The accident and him being locked up for five years?"

"Yeah."

"I actually think you've made a lot of progress. You may not trust him one hundred percent yet, but it sounds like you're getting there, and that's a start."

"You're right." I did trust Carter more than was logical. I would never have let his flesh inside me if I didn't trust him completely. But he was starting to tell me more about himself, albeit very slowly. "Enough about me and Carter. What places do you have in mind?"

John pointed out the apartments he was scheduled to visit that afternoon and I went to look with him to give my opinion. I told John there was no rush to move out of my place, but he didn't want to impose. I barely noticed he was there most of the time.

Other than that, John and I just worked on our laptops. John tended to be a good influence on me and made me knuckle down to work when my natural inclination was to slack off.

"I liked the place with the big kitchen," I said after we had seen four apartments.

"But I don't cook," John replied. "So I'd be paying for something I don't need."

"You should learn to cook."

"You're one to talk," John said. "I've seen what you eat for dinner. It's hardly healthy."

"It's sexy," I replied, appealing to John's predominant passion. "Men who can cook are sexy. Carter is a good example of that."

"Carter would be sexy scrubbing toilets. But maybe you have a point. I'll sleep on it."

I tried to picture Carter in a situation where he wouldn't look attractive, but found it nearly impossible. Carter was perfect. And mine. Carter was mine.

The next day, Carter told me to meet him for lunch at a small café near my house. He didn't so much ask me as tell me, but apparently he had exciting news, so I went along willingly.

He was sitting at a table when I arrived. He'd ordered me coffee and a chicken pesto sandwich, which was my favorite thing on the menu.

"So, what's this exciting news?" I asked, sitting down at the cramped table. I had to use my hand to shove my leg out of everyone else's way. It was at a rather odd angle, but it was better than someone tripping over it.

"I had a word with the receptionist at my place today, and as of now you can come and go as you please. I can't get you an actual key without you being on the lease, but you will still be able to get into the building even when I'm not there."

It took me a few moments to realize the enormity of what he was saying. Being able to come and go as I pleased would save me having to wait in the lobby, but it was more than just an added convenience. It meant he wasn't hiding anything. Carter couldn't be doing anything in his apartment that I couldn't see. That was huge.

"Aren't you going to say anything?" Carter asked, looking a little concerned. "I thought this would be good news."

"It is," I said. "It's incredible news. It's just taken me a little by surprise. Thank you."

"There's more," Carter said. "I'm going to speak to my employer, and ask for a permanent move out here. Nothing is official yet, but it shouldn't be a problem. They'll need to sort out a visa, but all that stuff can be handled by someone else. The fact is, I am falling for you big time and I don't want us to drift apart in a couple of months time when I go home."

"I... I don't know what to say." If there had been a cold drink in front of me I would have thrown it over my face. I had to be dreaming. This was like a young girl fantasizing about marrying a prince, except I was a woman, and instead of a prince, I was marrying a sex god who made every man jealous and every woman wet.

"Good news though, right?" Carter said, snickering at my indecision.

I nodded. "Good news."

"I can't hang around today. I'm busy. But I want you to come over to my place tonight. I'm going to be gone a few days starting tomorrow, so we have to make the most of this night."

I squinted, blinking a few times to make sure I really was awake. "I need you," I said. "I need you now."

"Sorry," Carter said, standing up. "You're just going to have to wait, you naughty little girl."

Carter leaned over me and placed a kiss on my cheek. As he reached down, his hand slipped between my thighs and went straight to my wet panties. A finger slipped under the cotton and flicked inside my wetness.

"I'm going to smell you on my fingers all day," he whispered.

And then he disappeared. I shuddered in my seat, desperate to bring myself to orgasm in a crowded coffee shop. The sandwich did nothing to crave my lust and I was happy to return to an empty house. There was no way I could wait for Carter this time, so I enjoyed myself between the sheets twice in the space of an hour.

Chapter Sixteen

The next time I entered Carter's building I felt like royalty. As soon as I walked through the door, the receptionist greeted me and had the elevator doors open even before I had reached them. No doubt the staff were wondering how the hell a cripple snared a man like Carter, but at that point I couldn't have cared less.

As soon as the doors opened into Carter's penthouse, my senses were struck with the aroma of another gourmet meal prepared by my favorite chef.

"How did you learn to cook?" I asked, standing behind him and wrapping my arms around his waist. "I can barely make toast."

"I noticed," he replied. "Stir this for me, would you?"

He passed me a wooden spoon and I promptly moved it through a thick red sauce. This was the most I had done in the kitchen in quite some time.

"Believe it or not, I picked up most of this in prison."

"Has television been lying to me about prison?" I asked with a furrowed brow. "Are you telling me that it has Michelin quality food?"

This was the first time I'd asked Carter about his time in prison. The subject had been too painful before, but now that I knew he was not the one who killed my brother, I was able to talk about the subject a little more casually.

"Hardly. But I learned how to cook the staples. Being a cook is considered one of the good jobs in jail—certainly better than cleaning or washing clothes—so I made sure to do a good job. Where possible, I added flavor to boring foods and the inmates liked it."

I kept stirring the pot until my arm began to tire. "Can I leave this for a bit?" I asked.

Carter nodded. "Sure. I turned the heat off ten minutes ago. I just wanted to see how long you would keep stirring it for."

"Bastard," I muttered under my breath. "If this were a cheesy movie, I would flick some of this sauce in your face and we would end up in a food fight."

"I wouldn't mind eating food off your naked body," Carter said. "But right now, I'm too hungry."

"Me too."

Carter served up the food and I did my best to pretend I knew what I was eating. The appetizer was crab, but the main course was not at all familiar. It had some French name that I forgot as soon as Carter told me it.

"What was it like?" I asked. "Being in prison for all that time. For something you didn't do."

Carter sighed and put down his fork. "I said I would be honest with you from here on out, so I will tell you if you want me to. Are you sure you want to hear it?"

I nodded. As long as I kept to generic terms like "prison" and "the accident," I was able to talk about it without welling up. Mentioning William by name was the trigger that led to tears dripping down my cheeks.

"Mixed, I suppose. Obviously no one wants to be in jail, but it wasn't always hell. At first, I actually found it quite easy. I was punishing myself for what happened and prison was the place I deserved to be."

"Except you didn't deserve to be there. Bella did."

"That kept me going too, believe it or not. You have to remember that I was in love with this girl. I knew she had problems, but, well... that's what love is, unfortunately. You accept people despite their flaws."

I nodded and did my best to keep my emotions from appearing on my face. Under the table, my good leg felt weak and my stomach tightened. Did Carter love her all the way up until her death? Did he still love her? I didn't love William any less now that he was no longer with us, so why would it be any different for Carter and his ex-girlfriend?

"The positive outlook lasted for about a year, and then things started going downhill for me. Bella's addiction became impossible to hide, so much so that I even noticed it when she came to visit."

Conjugal visits? I wondered, but didn't ask the question out loud.

"I wanted to get out of jail so that I could help her through it, but I couldn't. Then... then she passed away. You can imagine the rest. Despair. Sadness. Guilt. I went through every emotion at least five times before I just became frustrated. Everything I had done was for nothing. That was when I resolved to make it up to you. Money was not an issue. Bella's family made that clear. I had a friend track you down while I was still in jail and I started counting down the days."

"You had someone spying on me?" I asked. "When? What did they find out?"

Carter's lips crept up into one of his cheeky grins. "Not that you were a closet sex freak. That I had to find out myself."

"Carter, I'm being serious. It's creepy to think that all this time someone was checking up on me."

"It was nothing like that. Just basic details about where you went to school and that you had formed a business venture. Everything came from public records, so it's not like he was sat outside your house or anything."

"Good," I said, shivering slightly. I was still a little freaked out by that revelation, but to be honest, I lived such a boring life before meeting Carter that there wasn't a lot about me to find out. "I've been thinking, though—doesn't your employer mind about your criminal record? I thought banks were quite hot on that kind of thing?"

"They are. Like I said before, Bella's family pulled a lot of strings. Actually, I've been meaning to talk to you about work."

"Oh?" I said, raising my eyebrows. Carter never talked about his work. Maybe I would find it boring, but at least he would be confiding in me.

"I told them I want to stay here."

"In the penthouse?"

"No silly, in America. In California. With you. Permanently. We discussed extending my visa, but I just want to go all out and get a green card."

"You're serious?" Carter's return to England was pretty much the last impediment to the two of us getting more serious. If he was staying, then that meant this might become something real.

"Deadly."

I couldn't take it all in, but I knew I wanted Carter. I had to have him. "What's for dessert?" I asked with a smile as my foot moved slowly up his leg.

"I had something fun in mind," Carter replied seriously. "But I need to know one thing first."

"What's that?"

"Do you trust me?"

I nodded.

"I need to hear you say it, Emily. I need to know that you trust me."

I swallowed a lump in my throat. "I trust you. Completely and absolutely." Whatever doubts I had had completely disappeared. Carter had my trust. He'd earned it.

Carter smiled and my heart raced as he held out his hand. "Come with me to the bedroom. We're going to have some fun."

Chapter Seventeen

Everything started off innocently enough. Carter maneuvered me to the bed and pressed a firm kiss against my lips. The wetness built between my legs as he removed my clothing piece-by-piece until I lay there naked and exposed.

"Close your eyes," he commanded. I did as I was told and felt his body leave the bed. I heard him open a drawer and then close it shortly after. He placed something soft and silky over my face. "Okay, you can open your eyes."

I opened them, but only saw darkness. I blinked a few times, but couldn't see a thing. Carter had blindfolded me.

"You okay sweetheart?" Carter asked. I nodded slowly. "Just say 'orange' if you want me to stop at any point. That's the safe word."

"Is this going to hurt?" I asked. This was all coming a little too quickly. I was scared, but the wetness between my legs gave away my true desires.

"No," Carter assured me. "Not this time."

He gently took hold of my right wrist and wrapped a few straps of silk around it. He then pulled my arm towards the corner of the bed and tied the other end to the bedpost. He repeated the act with my left wrist and then flicked kisses over my stretched chest. My nipples rose to meet his lips as his hot breath left a trail of goosebumps over my breasts.

My pussy ached with anticipation as his mouth moved down my stomach. Just as he reached the tip of my slit, Carter got up off the bed again. This time he wrapped my ankle in silk and tied it to the bottom bedpost. I cringed knowing what was coming next.

The final piece of the puzzle was my prosthetic leg. Carter picked up my plastic foot and wrapped the silk around my ankle. When he tied it to the final bedpost, I was left one hundred percent exposed to him. My legs were spread wide. Carter could do anything he wanted to me and I wouldn't be able to stop him.

"Fuck me," I said. "Please, take me."

Carter didn't say anything. I just heard the bedroom door open and then close.

"Carter?" I kept silent for a few minutes, waiting for him to return.

"Carter?" I yelled more loudly when he still hadn't come back after five minutes. "Carter, what the fuck are you doing?"

I pulled at my restraints, but they just tightened around my wrists and ankles as I struggled. Carter had teased me and left me hanging. My pussy dripped between my legs as I moaned, desperate to be touched.

"Carter, get back here and fuck me you son of a bitch!" I yelled at the top of my lungs.

"Okay, I guess I can do that." Carter's voice came from the corner of the room. He had never left. He'd just been standing there watching me squirm, watching my sex get wetter and wetter as I waited for him.

Carter got back onto the bed and slipped some fingers into my sex. "How much do you want my cock inside you right now?"

"I don't want it," I said between deep breaths. "I need it."

"Talk dirty," Carter said. "I want you to talk like the filthy whore you are deep inside."

I'd never talked dirty. Not on purpose. It had happened when in the moment with Carter, but I'd never really controlled the words that came out.

"Take me," I moaned.

"You're dirtier than that," Carter said. "I only like dirty girls. Boring ones are not worth my massive cock."

"I want you to stick that monster dick inside me and split my tight little hole. I need you to enter me. Fuck my tight little cunt, Carter. Fill my tight pussy with your hot cum."

"That's better," he said. I could tell he was grinning, even with a blindfold on.

Seconds later I felt his thick girth stretching me open as I took him, riding wave after wave of heavy orgasms until Carter spilled his seed inside me.

"I've been meaning to tell you something," Carter said as he removed the straps from my wrists and ankles. "But I don't know if I can handle you looking at me while I say it, so leave the blindfold on."

"Um, okay. Is this going to be bad?" Surely he wasn't going to ditch me after that display?

"Emily, I don't know how this happened and I don't know when it happened, but at some point in the last few weeks, I fell for you. And I fell hard. I think I'm falling in love with you."

It was my eyes that were covered, not my ears, but I was sure I'd misheard him. I nearly blurted out "I love you," but I needed to process what he had just said.

He's falling in love with me. So he's not in love with me? What does that mean?

"Emily? Are you going to say anything?"

"I love you."

Chapter Eighteen

I loved Carter, but after that night I needed a break. Not just physically, although my body was certainly a little sore, but mentally as well.

I had given myself to him in a way I never expected to with a man. Carter's little business trip had therefore come at a good time, and I was able to bury myself in my work. Or at least, I would have been able to if it were not for John's constant interruptions.

"Emily, can I have a word with you?" John asked strolling into my room. "It's a little awkward, but I want you to be completely honest with me."

"John, what the hell is this all about? You have me worried now."

"It's about Carter. Things between you are going well, right?"

"Very, very well," I said, tingling between my legs just thinking of him.

"He doesn't hurt you, does he?"

How the hell does he know about last night? Is that what he means? Or does he think Carter is hitting me?

"You have marks on your wrists, Emily. Like he's been grabbing you."

I looked down and pulled up my sleeves. Damn, John was right. I had light bruising around my wrists from where the material had dug into the skin. This was going to be hard to explain and then look him in the eye after.

"John, Carter only hurts me when I want him to, if you get what I mean."

John didn't say anything, so I looked up at him, blushing bright red.

"Holy shit," he murmured. "You do realize that in a few months, you are going to be able to give me sex tips? How times have changed!"

"I wouldn't quite go that far, John, but we're experimenting, I guess."

"Just when I thought Carter couldn't get any more perfect. You really need to keep hold of this one, Emily."

"I'm aware of that. I don't intend to let him go without a fight." I told John how Carter was now planning to stay in America and that we had agreed to try having a real relationship.

"You should surprise him when he gets home," John said. "Do something cheesy, like throw rose petals over the bed or something. It'll be fun."

"I guess I could. But I'd have to do it tomorrow night, because we are meeting for dinner the day after. What should I do?"

"Leave that to me," John said. "I've got an idea."

John's idea was not as original as I had hoped, but it would make an impression. He had gone all out and bought loads of candles of various shapes, sizes, and aromas. I'd never been much of a candle person, but even I could tell that these smelled sensual and sexy.

We placed a few in the kitchen to enjoy over dinner, a few in the living room, and then filled the bedroom with what was left. As long as the fire alarm didn't go off while I was tied to the bed, then it should have set up a romantic evening.

"So, can I check out some of his collection?" John asked as we put the finishing touches to the bedroom display. He sprinkled rose petals on the bed, which seemed romantic, but I had an awful feeling they were going to end up getting in places they didn't belong.

"No," I scolded. "Don't go poking around his stuff. Besides, I don't know where he keeps it."

"Ah, yes, you were blindfolded when he took out the toys, I suppose. Well, they are bound to be in here somewhere."

"John, come on, we've finished up in here. Let's head out."

"Don't pretend you aren't interested. You do realize he probably has a lot more in here than you have used so far? The other night would have just been a warm up. Don't you want to see the big guns?"

John had a point. Even I wasn't naive enough to think Carter hadn't held back slightly. He was bound to have a few more toys to spring on me, and it would be good to have advance notice. Besides, Carter had given me permission to be here, which must also mean I had permission to look in his drawers, right?

"Okay, but be careful and don't make a mess," I said, opening the top drawer of his dresser. As I worked my way through the drawers, I couldn't help but be impressed at how tidy he was. Or maybe that was just his cleaner?

"Huh," John said, as he routed through the bedside cabinet. "That's weird."

"Oh, God. It's not too kinky, is it?"

"No, it's not that. Didn't you say Carter was applying for a visa or green card or something?"

"A green card, yes. Why?"

"He already has one. A green card, I mean. And it's still valid. Why would he apply again?"

"Immigration is pretty confusing," I said. "Maybe he changed status and needs a new one?"

"I guess," John said.

He sounded uncertain, and to be honest, so was I. At the very least, Carter should have mentioned that he already had a green card. Why would he leave that little detail out? I didn't know a lot about immigration, but I knew that green cards were tough to come by. You needed to be an expert in your field or something like that. How had Carter qualified for that when he had only been working a few years?

John placed the green card back in the drawer, but then pulled something else out.

"Where did you say Carter was today?"

I shrugged. "Some business meeting. What have you found now?" I asked, my heart racing. John's tone made it clear he had found something suspicious. "Has he been lying to me? What have you found?"

"He has I think," John said. "But a white lie. Probably for your own benefit."

"What is it John?"

"I think he's having an operation today. Look at this."

John passed over a medical procedure authorization from an insurance company which gave clearance for a biopsy. "Shit," I exclaimed. "This is worrying."

"Are biopsies bad?" John asked.

"Not always, but this is a series of them and that suggests something a little more serious. Plus the fact that he didn't tell me and has had to stay overnight at the hospital does make me worry."

I sat down on the bed staring at the paper. There was little information on there of any relevance, so it was impossible to tell what was being biopsied. Carter was healthy and didn't smoke. He didn't deserve this to happen to him after everything he had done. But then, no one does.

"I'm going to the hospital," I said, standing up and putting the paper back in the drawer. "I bet you he hasn't told anyone about this and is completely alone. I want to be there for him."

John smiled and gave me a hug. "You two are going to make an amazing couple. Go get him."

Chapter Nineteen

The bus to the hospital took a long, meandering route, so I had an entire hour to sit there feeling sick to my stomach with worry. Every possible negative outcome went through my head. I couldn't shake the "C" word, even though it was unlikely in someone Carter's age.

My brain kept going back to melanoma—that seemed the most likely outcome. Carter couldn't have spent much time in the sun growing up in England, but he had acquired a nice tan at some point, so it was possible.

Stop it, Emily. These thoughts are not helping anyone. You're just making yourself sick.

As I stepped off the bus, I forced myself to start smiling. The last thing I wanted to do was greet Carter with a miserable face. He didn't need that right now.

As was par for the course with hospitals, the entrances were badly labeled and I had no idea where to go. The emergency room was the only thing clearly marked, but I had to walk around the entire building before I found regular admissions and then another ten minutes before I found a receptionist.

"Excuse me," I asked the lady behind the desk. "I'm looking for a Mr. Murphy. He is in here for a biopsy."

"One minute," she replied, typing "Murphy" into her computer. "What's your relationship to the patient?"

I opened my mouth to say "just a friend," but I swallowed the words. Not anymore. I was more than just a friend now and I didn't want to hide it.

"Girlfriend," I answered confidently.

"We have a Murphy in room 203. It's down the hall and to the left. Then take the second right and it's the third door on your right."

I stored the information in my memory and headed to his room. The hospital wasn't warm, but I felt sticky and clammy. I took a quick detour via the restrooms and attempted to make myself look presentable. My blouse still clung to my back, but it would have to do. At least in a hospital no one would look twice at a girl with a prosthetic limb. There were far stranger looking people in these places every day of the week.

Despite the directions the receptionist gave me, the rooms were not numbered and I had already forgotten which one Carter was in. I walked slowly down the hall looking through the window into each room, but I couldn't see Carter in any of the beds. Once I reached the end of the hall I retraced my steps and noticed that there were patient names on a small placard on each door.

Still no Carter Murphy. There was an Isabella Murphy, though. I chanced a peak into her room and saw a young woman hooked up to lots of machines. The poor thing had wires coming out of every orifice and at least three different fluids going into her.

Next to her bed was a man with his back to me. He stared at the woman; not in anticipation or hope, just sadness. The jacket on the back of the chair looked familiar. Carter had one just like it.

Then it hit me: Isabella Murphy. Bella. She was still alive. And she had the surname Murphy. And a wedding ring.

The blood rushed from my head and I felt faint. My prosthetic leg slipped from under me and I fell back, stumbling against the far wall. The collision knocked the wind out of me and I gasped loudly.

The man turned and looked at me. It was Carter. The color drained from his face as he looked at me while I fell to the floor in tears. He was married to my brother's killer and had been lying to me the entire time.

I wanted to run, but my leg was too weak. I just buried my head in my hands and cried while Carter stood beside his wife and stared at me through the glass.

Part Three

Chapter One

The tears came immediately and I fell back against the wall, slipping down onto the floor as my legs gave out on me. This was the second time my world had collapsed in on me while in a hospital. I still had nightmares about the first time. After the accident that took my brother's life, I had spent a few weeks in a hospital while the doctors had examined—and later amputated—the lower half of my leg. After the leg had been cut off, I was monitored for both physical and psychological damage.

The first few days of that had been a blur as I drifted in and out of sleep, and I retained only faint memories of my mom and dad looking down at me with solemn faces. Four days after the accident I was finally well enough to sit up, drink some water, and consume some meager hospital food. That was when Mom and Dad broke the news. My brother was dead. William had died in the crash from serious head wounds. The only consolation was that he had suffered no pain.

That news broke my heart, but while it had never fully healed, I had got on with my life eventually. William was never gone from my memory, and there wasn't a day I didn't think about him, but I managed to put him to one side for twenty-three hours a day. *Most* days, anyway.

As I sat on the hospital floor, tears streaming down my face, I looked back up toward the room in which Isabella Murphy, Carter's wife, was lying with Carter by her side. He was still looking at me, just staring at me with his warm, compassionate eyes. How could someone look so perfect when they had just been caught committing the ultimate act of betrayal?

Married. He was married to another woman, and he had lied about it. Carter had said that "Bella" was dead, and as if that wasn't bad enough, it occurred to me that he must have also been lying about where he was going all the time, as well. How many times had he said he was working or going to a business meeting when he was actually visiting his wife?

I locked eyes with him, daring him to leave the hospital room and give me some excuse, any excuse for this new turn of events. He didn't move. He just stood there and looked at me. I thought I saw tears building in his eyes, but I had far too many of my own to trust what I saw.

My view of Carter was interrupted when a doctor walked in front of me and into Isabella's room. I could see the doctor start talking to Carter, but he didn't look away from me. Finally, he tore his gaze away and gave his attention to the doctor. Whatever the news was, it wasn't good.

I buried my gaze between my knees and resumed my pathetic sobbing. I wanted to move, to walk away and never look back, but my real leg was far too weak to support me. Even sitting on the floor, I knew I had no energy in me to stand up.

After a few moments, I felt a hand on my shoulder and my breath caught in my lungs. I hadn't heard Carter approach and couldn't handle speaking to him right now. Makeup was probably all over my face and I no doubt looked a mess. I knew I shouldn't care about my appearance right now, not for him, but years of trying to look my best and draw attention away from my leg had made me overly paranoid about these things.

"Emily?" a soft voice whispered in my ear.

I knew the voice, and it wasn't Carter's. I wiped my wet eyes and I looked up to see John crouching down next to me.

"John?" I whimpered. "What are you doing here?"

"Sorry, Emily. I'm so sorry. I figured it out, but a bit too late."

"Can we get out of here?" I asked him.

John grabbed hold of my hand and heaved me up. I stumbled a little on my false leg, as if I were getting used to it all over again. It was in a hospital hallway like this that I had first practiced walking on the leg outside the safe confines of my physical therapy room. Now I felt like I needed to learn to walk again for the third time in my life.

"Did you speak to him?" John asked, holding me tight around the waist.

I shook my head, sniffing and unable to speak.

"There might be a good explanation—"

"No," I said, firmly, finally finding my voice. "Don't say that. There's no possible explanation for this. Don't make excuses for him."

"Okay," he replied meekly.

I could tell John wanted there to be an explanation for this. He wouldn't want me to go back to how I was before—not trusting men and throwing myself into work—but that was not his decision to make. To be honest, it wasn't my decision either. Carter had made the decision for me—he had betrayed me, and now I would never let myself fall in love again. Nothing John could say would ever change that.

My ears had been filtering out all the surrounding noise around me, but now the sounds were coming back. Doctors were shouting at each other. Shoes were squeaking on the floor as nurses hurried between rooms, moving from patient to patient at a speed that always amazed me. Among all the noise and clattering of gurneys and carts, I heard a voice call out to me.

"Emily," Carter said weakly.

I was now at the end of the hall and his words should have been lost in the din, but somehow his voice reached my ears. I froze, but John kept walking until my stiff body tugged him back. He looked over my shoulder and figured out why I had stopped.

"What do you want to do?" he asked.

I had no idea. Well, perhaps that wasn't quite true. I knew what I wanted to do. I wanted to pretend that the woman in there was a stranger, or his sister—anyone but his wife. I would run to him, wrap my arms around his firm, wide shoulders and pretend this had never happened. But life didn't work like that. I could never go back to that wide-eyed innocence from just a few days ago.

Deep down, I think I knew that had all been a dream. People like Carter didn't happen to people like me. There would be no happily ever after for a girl with an artificial leg. Save that story for the next Disney princess.

"Let's get out of here," I said, regaining some control over my voice. "Take me home, John."

Chapter Two

"You can't do this every morning," I said, stretching my arms and stifling a yawn. For the fourth consecutive morning since the incident at the hospital, John had woken me up with a fresh cup of coffee and my favorite sugary cereal. People going through traumatic breakups could eat whatever the hell they wanted, so I figured I might was well make the most of it.

"It's not a problem," John replied. "I was making myself some coffee, anyway, so it's easy enough to make a second cup. And this crap you shovel down for breakfast hardly takes a lot of time to prepare. You know these colors are not natural, right?" He picked up a pink shape from my cereal bowl and held it close to his eye. "I think this one glows in the dark."

"Oh, hush," I replied, yanking my breakfast from his hands and managing to spill some milk on the bedroom floor. "Making me coffee is one thing, but you really don't need to stay at my place every night. You just signed a lease on a new apartment—why don't you go enjoy it?"

John shrugged. "It's weird being on my own. I've never actually lived by myself before, and I'm not too sure I like it."

I could actually believe that. John was an incredibly outgoing person—a social butterfly, of sorts—and rarely spent any time in his own company. He was so different from me that I wondered how we remained so close.

"Are you working your way through the internet's collection of gay porn? I'm sure they will keep making more when you run out."

"Very funny," John replied with an exaggerated raising of the eyebrows. "I'll have you know I am spending most of my time working. Two days of non-stop masturbating was more than enough for me," he added under his breath. "That's what I don't like. If I spend too much time by myself, I focus on work to the exclusion of everything else. It's not healthy."

"Why don't you get out once in a while? You're gay and in San Francisco—you're practically living the dream."

"Like I said, I'm busy with work, and—" John paused.

I cringed and looked up at him from my cereal. He'd figured me out.

"How on Earth did you get the topic of conversation onto me?" he asked. "It's you we should be talking about. You're the one who is going to have to get out and about at some point. There is a world outside this apartment."

"That nearly worked," I said. I'd managed to keep all the conversation off me for a couple of minutes—almost a record. "I know you're going to want to give me that speech about how I should try to move on and get my head back in the game, but that's really not necessary. I've had a good cry and felt sorry for myself for long enough. Every woman has her heart broken at some point, but broken hearts do mend. I'm going to be fine, John."

I'd shamelessly copied parts of that speech from a romantic movie I'd been watching the day before. The actress had pulled it off a lot better than I had, of course, but John seemed to believe me.

The part of my brain that processed logic told me that everything I had just said was true. Women—and men—really did get their hearts broken, and those hearts really did mend. I was nothing special. Unfortunately, the logic part of my brain was currently being attacked from all angles by the far stronger forces of jealousy, betrayal, hatred, and love. It was like David versus four Goliaths, except David's slingshot was broken and the Goliaths had tanks.

"I'm not sure I believe you," John said, "but there's not a lot I can do about that. Has he... you know... has he called you, or anything?"

I bit down hard on my lip to stop myself from crying. I would have found it almost impossible to ignore Carter's calls and messages over a prolonged period. At some point in the previous four days I would have caved and responded to him or answered a call. Except he hadn't called. Not once. Nor had he texted me. Not one phone call or message in the four days since I saw him with his wife at the hospital. Did he just not care about me anymore? Perhaps I just wasn't worth all the effort it would take to get me back.

I gave a quick shake of the head and looked back down at my nearly-empty bowl, which now contained just a few soggy bits of color. The comparison to my life was impossible to ignore.

"Good," John said. "It's good that he hasn't tried to get in touch—that way you are not tempted to talk to him. You can get a clean break. What you need is a distraction and I have the ultimate distraction. One that never fails to get your attention."

"Work," I said, knowing the answer immediately. Before Carter, my life had been all about work. Even my best friend was tied to my work. With Carter no longer in the picture, my life would likely go back to just being me in front of a computer.

"We have something new to work on," John said.

"Please don't tell me we are being sued again," I said, exasperated. "It took too much time and money to get the last lawsuit crushed."

"Nope, not that. It's good news. But let's not discuss it here."

"Want to head to SF Station?" I asked. "It should be noisy enough that we can talk with some degree of privacy."

"Sounds good. You should get showered and dressed first, though. You don't want to inflict that—"John waved a finger in my general direction "—on the public right now. We don't want to get banned from our favorite coffee shop."

"Hi, Emily," Jane said as I walked in the door.

There were plenty of customers in the line waiting to be served, but Jane had no qualms about yelling over them. John and I were probably her favorite customers—we caused minimal fuss and always left a good tip. I waved a hello, but waited until Jane was ready to serve us before talking back. I'd not left the house in a couple of days and wasn't ready to have loud, public conversations just yet.

"Morning, Jane. Just the usual today, please." The usual meant a soy milk latte, but after the week I'd had, something stronger might be required. "Actually, make that an Americano with a double shot of espresso."

Jane raised her eyebrows at my out-of-character request. "Tough morning? You're going to be bouncing off the ceilings after this one."

"I expect it will just raise me to a normal operating level, to be honest," I said. Bouncing off the ceiling seemed a long way off for me at the moment. I took my coffee and contemplated adding some milk before settling for strong and black.

"There was a man in here the other day asking after you," Jane said calmly.

My hand shook just as I had started to pick up the coffee. I dropped it back down as if it were hot to touch, with some spilling over the side. I took a deep breath and looked up at her.

It was then that I realized she had been talking to John. He had noticed my mistaken assumption, but Jane was clueless as to the unspoken stupidity on my part. Of course Carter would not have asked after me in the coffee shop. He hadn't even sent me a text message or tried to call, so why on Earth would he be asking the local barista about me? God, I felt like an idiot.

I quickly mopped up my mess and took my coffee over to a corner table, one that somehow remained unused despite it having the best access to plugs and the Wi-Fi router. Sometimes having intimate knowledge of a coffee shop could be useful. Now it was time for business. No more feeling sorry for myself or thinking about Carter—I had a business to run.

Chapter Three

"So, who's this guy asking after you in coffee shops?" I asked John once he had sat down at the table.

"Well, I had been hoping it was Benedict Cumberbatch taking me up on my offer to explore the other side of his sexuality, but alas, from Jane's description, I think it was just Tom making another attempt to get back together with me."

"I thought he was the one who ended it?"

"He was, but I guess he's missing this," John replied, smiling and pointing at his cute, but cheeky face. "We split up because Tom didn't like never getting to see me, so it's not like we fell out or one of us had an affair."

"You're not tempted to get back together with him?" I kept a straight face and hopefully kept my feelings to myself. I had never been a huge fan of Tom and thought John deserved a heck of a lot better. Tom had a good job, a nine-to-five with a solid income. He was a good catch on paper, but he just couldn't understand that some people had less conventional lives, John included.

John paused for a second and then shook his head. "No, not really. The sex was good, but not great, and there are plenty more fish in the sea. I'm not going to settle for mediocrity when I'm living in San Francisco."

"Good point. Anyway, what's this big work-related news you wanted to talk about? I hope it takes a long time to implement, because I could use the distraction."

"It's not a small project," he said. "I only really have the outline at the moment."

"Come on. Spit it out, John."

"What's one of the biggest problems we have when analyzing the data that we get from our beta testers?"

"You're really going to drag this out, aren't you?" I said, rolling my eyes.

"Just play along with me."

"Okay, okay." I paused, thinking back to the last time I really sat down and focused on the data that we had coming in.

LimbAnalytics had a decent amount of information available now. The pool of people with missing limbs was small, but it was also one that was very willing to help out with experiments that may end up improving their quality of life. More data would be better—it always was—but we had plenty to work with.

Our focus at the moment was on the pressure points between the body and the artificial limb, because that was what caused the most problems. Artificial limbs had advanced quite a bit from the days of wooden legs, but they still weren't very good at adapting to the different types of use people put them through.

My leg was the perfect example of this. It was built for walking. If I tried to run in it, then I would quickly fall over. I could change the leg—I did have a spare one that was designed for rapid movement—but that was an additional expense that many couldn't afford. What if one leg could serve both functions? LimbAnalytics' technology could one day help with this. If someone was running, then the software would pick up the additional pressure being applied and adjust the limb accordingly.

When John and I first started out, we had stupidly thought that this would be an easy problem to solve. We were quickly corrected. The problem was people; they don't act in a consistent manner, and that creates a lot of data that our software can't make heads nor tails of.

"Context," I replied, noticing that John was getting impatient. "We get a lot of information that is essentially just white noise and we have to filter it out."

"You're creating some right now," John said.

I frowned and then realized that I was tapping my artificial leg under the table—I liked the noise it made—and that was sending data into the cloud as we talked and drank coffee. Our software couldn't distinguish between me tapping my foot quickly and me running.

"So, what's your big idea, then?" I asked.

"Wearables," John said simply, as if that was supposed to answer my question. "Smartwatches, fitness trackers—things like that."

"You're going to have to help me out," I said. "This coffee hasn't kicked in yet, and I'm in no position to figure out you're cryptic clues."

John sighed. "You're no fun. Look, loads of people are wearing something on their wrists now to track what they do—some people even wear them to bed—and they are all sending data via Bluetooth."

"We can collect that information easily enough, I suppose. But how will it help?"

"You're still tapping your leg," John said. He was right—I'd stopped, but then subconsciously started doing it again straight away. "But you aren't moving your arm."

"Ah, I think I'm catching up. We can use the data from another wearable to eliminate a lot of the white noise from our sensors on the limbs."

"Exactly. So, what do you think?"

I had to take a few moments to consider. We'd had potential breakthroughs in the past—usually late at night after a few too many drinks—where we'd been convinced all our problems were over until the next morning when reality hit. There would be some technological or regulatory problem that stood in the way, and it was back to the drawing board.

But John's idea was a good one. A really good one. And it was quite simple. There would be some work involved in interpreting the data from the wearable, and obviously the company would need to spend a few grand on the fitness trackers to give to the beta testers, but that was nothing compared to their other outlays.

"This could work," I said at last. "In fact, I think it's a great idea. How long will the coding take?"

"I've already started on it, but I will need a few more days. I'll need you to choose a fitness device and get them out to the beta testers and show them how to use it."

"I can handle that. This could really set us apart from PharmaTech. I'm willing to bet they won't have anything like this in the works."

John shook his head. "No, they won't be onto this. They aren't quick on the uptake and fitness trackers are still new."

"Let's do it, then," I said as John immediately got to work tapping away at his computer.

The first thing I did was start researching the various equipment. I pinged out a few emails to the companies in the hope of getting a decent bulk discount. The cost of purchasing all those gadgets was going to put a dent in our budget, but we could afford it. The bigger problem was getting them out there and educating people on how to use them. Still, it was a great idea, and could really help distinguish LimbAnalytics from PharmaTech. That had to be worth the expense.

I was absorbed in spreadsheets when my phone buzzed loudly on the table. I allowed my eyes to glance over at the phone—it was a text message. Only a few people sent me messages these days, and one of them was sat opposite me, hunched over his laptop and oblivious to my phone. The other was Carter.

I took a deep breath and picked up the phone.

We need to meet. C

Chapter Four

Somehow I managed to remain calm. I read the message from Carter, and then I went back to work. John never even noticed me get the message, and as far as he knew, I was working furiously on our next project.

I was working—sort of. I did what I could, but finally I ran out of emails to send and spreadsheets to update. My brain tried to find busywork, but without a clear goal to focus on, my thoughts turned to Carter and his message. *We need to meet.* Not we *should* meet or I *want* to meet. No hint at an apology or a possible explanation. No, Carter had just said that we *needed* to meet, as if that would be enough for me to go running after him.

He made me so damn mad sometimes. The surrounding noise in the coffee shop turned grating. Instead of sitting nicely in the background, each sound felt like someone was deliberately trying to make me snap. The woman next to me was slurping loudly. The man behind me kept fidgeting in his seat and was clearly out of shape judging by the noise of his breathing.

Then there was John. His fingers looked like they were floating over the keys, but to my ears, he was bashing them like a kid hammering a toy car on the kitchen floor.

"I have to get out of here," I said, standing up and slamming my laptop shut.

"You okay?" John asked.

"Oh, yeah. I'm fine. I just sent a load of emails, but need to follow up with some phone calls now. I'll do that from home."

"You should call Marissa while you're at it. Make sure she's on board with what we are planning."

"Good point. She doesn't usually object, but I'll let her know." I walked past him, but then stopped and turned back to him. "John?" He had already resumed typing, but he stopped and looked at me. "You don't need to stay at my place tonight. Honestly, I'm fine."

He opened his mouth to speak, but the clamped it shut and just nodded. He could still keep a close eye on me, but I should have the house to myself tonight, even though that could prove dangerous.

The conversation with Marissa went the same way it always did. She was supportive about the new approach and asked if we needed any more money. I replied that we still had enough cash on hand—just barely—but that we would ask if we needed more. It wasn't supposed to be this easy. Start-up companies usually had to beg and plead for investment, and we were regularly turning it down.

Marissa did come up with some more work for me to do, though. I needed to file a patent for the software that John was using to interpret the data from the wearables. He hadn't finished writing that software yet, but we could still get a patent drafted— or more specifically, our lawyer could.

LimbAnalytics already had a couple of patents, and I was getting pretty good at drafting them now. The applications didn't need to contain every little detail, just the idea and how it would work. I dug up the template that Scott had given me last time, filled out the basic information, and fired it off to him. He would probably have follow-up questions, but that was another job off my to-do list for the time being. Just before closing my laptop, I sent a copy of the application to Marissa to keep her in the loop.

I'd accomplished a hell of a lot since getting out of bed, but I still needed another distraction. A few email replies had trickled in from beta testers confirming that they would happily wear something around their wrists. I added their names to a spreadsheet, but there wasn't much else to do with it right now.

I picked up my phone for the first time since receiving Carter's message. A small red icon reminded me—as if I needed the reminder—that I had a message waiting for my attention. My thumb hovered over the application, and I knew that sooner or later I would open it and reply. It was only a matter of time, but before I could give in to the inevitable, a very welcome distraction popped up on my screen.

"You could have told me you were going to be in town," I complained as I sat down opposite Amy at a table in a cramped French restaurant. "Fortunately, I wasn't busy."

"You're never busy, dear," Amy replied, casually signaling for a waiter and ordering something in awful French. "I took a chance that you'd be free. Anyway, this was all a little last-minute. I only flew in this morning. Technically, I'm here for work, but the meeting finished early."

Amy looked frustratingly fantastic for a woman who had flown across the country earlier this morning. She wasn't even dressed in particularly glamorous clothing, but somehow she managed to look sexy even when covered up. She must have had men eating out of the palms of her hands.

"I'll have you know I actually have a life now, thank you very much."

Amy and I had grown up together, but we only saw each other once a year now, and that was usually when we were back at home over Thanksgiving or

Christmas. My mom often remarked on the strange way we talked to each other, but I loved it. A stranger would think we hated one another, but there was always a lot of love behind our words.

"I heard about your little business," she said, taking a sip of her French roast coffee while I still waited for mine to arrive. "When you hit the big time, let me know."

Amy worked for one of the large accounting firms in New York, but she wasn't a lot of use for a small startup company in Silicon Valley. Should LimbAnalytics ever float on a stock exchange, then I would give Amy a call, but otherwise our work was unlikely to collide.

"What I want to know is when you are going to get a man," she continued. "Or a woman, I suppose. Whatever floats your boat."

"*You* don't have a man," I replied, ignoring her not-so-subtle questioning of my sexuality. I had no idea of her relationship status—Amy wasn't one to update the world on every detail of her life, which was one of the reasons I liked her.

"I don't have *a* man, but I have *plenty of men*," Amy replied. "Don't you worry about me. But I'm detecting something in you today, Emily. There's something different about you. You do have a man, don't you?"

My coffee arrived and I took a sip immediately, scalding my mouth in the process.

"Had," I said. "I *had* a man."

"Oh, my sex-sense is tingling. Is there an interesting story here? Come on, you're going to have to give me more information than that."

I loved Amy, but there was no way I was telling her the whole story of Carter and me in the middle of a crowded restaurant. For one thing, I couldn't trust myself not to burst into tears when talking about the more recent events. The version Amy got was that I'd met a rich English guy with whom I had lots of hot, steamy sex, and then I found out he was married.

"When you say 'married,' do you mean happily married with kids?" Amy asked. "Or is he perhaps separated?"

"No kids," I said. "That I know of, anyway. I don't know much more than that—we haven't spoken since. He sent me a message earlier though and he wants to talk."

"Oh, God, Emily. What are you doing sitting here talking to me, then?"

"It's complicated."

"It always is. Look, I've had my share of married men, and I can tell you that there is no single type. Some of them just want a fling away from their wives, but others are in legitimately unhappy relationships and want out. Of course, I run a mile once they talk about divorcing their wives and settling down with me, but I guess that's what you actually want here."

"That would be nice," I said, thinking back to when Carter had talked about getting a visa and living in the US permanently. Had that really only been a week or so ago?

"You at least need to hear the guy out. Text him now and make him buy you an expensive dinner this evening where he can tell you all his excuses over a few glasses of wine. If he was just looking for a bit of fun, then leave him to pay the check and be thankful for the good sex you got out of him. If he wants something more, then go back to his for some more of that steamy sex you told me about. And still make him pay the check."

I don't know whether Amy's argument was actually convincing or whether she was just telling me what I wanted to hear, but either way, I ended up texting Carter.

Dinner tonight. Pick me up at 7.

Chapter Five

Carter replied instantly with a "Thanks," but offered no clue as to where we might be going. Deciding what to wear was a nightmare. I didn't know whether I was trying to impress Carter or not. Did I want to have the leg on display tonight? Dress or skirt? John could have helped me with the decision, but I didn't want him to know anything about the evening. That way, if it was a disaster, I wouldn't have to explain all the gory details in the morning.

I was ready by six o'clock and resisted the temptation to change outfits. I settled on a skirt which sat above the knee and a top with a plunging neckline and back. It was an outfit that would get some second looks, but it wasn't exactly slutty, either.

I spent the next hour sitting in front of the TV. I stared at the screen, but all I could see was Carter standing next to his wife in the hospital. He loved her. I could see that in his eyes, and if he told me otherwise tonight, I would know he was lying. Did that mean I was jealous of a sick woman? A woman who looked like she was in a coma? Was I a horrible person?

Another message from Carter snapped me out of my self-pity. *The car is downstairs.* Apparently, he couldn't even be bothered to come up to my apartment now. Whatever the evening had in store, it obviously wouldn't involve Carter being nice to me. I considered replying with a message telling him to get stuffed, but in the end I picked up my bag and walked downstairs. I would hear him out and then say goodbye. He wasn't worth it.

Not only had Carter not bothered to come up to my apartment, he hadn't even joined me in the car. I stepped into the back and said hello to the thin air on the seat. Carter's driver apologized for him and said that he would be waiting for me at the restaurant. What had happened to the man who swept me off my feet not so long ago? The man that I was physically incapable of resisting, who could make my body shake with orgasm after orgasm?

Most women with any self-respect—someone like Amy—would have got out of the car and not gone anywhere near that man ever again. I considered asking the driver to stop and let me out, but a part of me thought that Carter would take some satisfaction from me getting mad at him. I wasn't going to give him that pleasure. I strolled into the restaurant and sat down opposite him at the table before he had even noticed me arrive.

"Emily," Carter said, looking up from the wine glass he had been staring down. He sounded surprised to see me. "I'm sorry for not meeting you in the car. Work stuff."

I nodded, but didn't ask for any more explanation. The man had lied about being married, so whether or not he was busy working late tonight didn't seem to matter all that much in the grand scheme of things.

The thing that struck me most about Carter was his appearance. I wouldn't go so far as to say he looked bad—that was impossible for someone like Carter—but he did look different. Instead of being alert and clean-cut in a sharp suit, he looked tired—exhausted, even—and his suit was wrinkled like he had slept in it. If he had, it couldn't have been for long, because the heavy bags under his eyes were impossible to ignore. Women around the restaurant were still gawking at him, but I could tell the difference and it made me feel better. I'd been through a living hell these last few days, and I took some pleasure from knowing he had, as well.

"This had better be good," I said, picking up the menu. I had been referring to his forthcoming explanation, but it probably looked like I was talking about the food.

"I took the liberty of ordering for you," Carter said. "I don't want you to have the time to reconsider your being here."

"I've spent enough time considering that," I said. "You might as well get on with it."

"Fair enough," Carter said before taking a sip of his wine. He'd ordered a dry white which seemed an unlikely pairing for French food, but what did I know? "Where would you like me to start?"

That was a good question. Whenever I thought about that day at the hospital, the questions all came to me at once. *Why didn't you tell me you're married? Do you love her? Will you stay with her?*

"You told me she was dead," I said. It wasn't really a question, but it struck me as the first lie from which all the others stemmed.

Carter just sighed, which infuriated me, although I did my best to keep my emotions hidden. Surely he had planned this out in his head? Or was this all just a second thought, something he was just doing to clear his conscience?

"Sometimes I wish she was," Carter said finally. "Life would be so much easier then."

Chapter Six

"You shouldn't say that," I said quietly. In my darkest moments, my brain had come to the same conclusion, but it was wrong and irrational. It wasn't Bella's fault that Carter had lied about his relationship with her.

"I know, I know," Carter said, rubbing the bridge of his nose between his thumb and forefinger. "I'll tell you everything, Emily, but it's not going to be easy. Not for you to hear, or for me to say. Before I start, I want you to know that regardless of all this, I do love you. I mean that, and I think you feel the same."

I sat there silently and continued to stare at him. I did still love him, of course, but I wasn't going to say that to him. He hadn't earned the right to hear that yet.

"Bella didn't die of an overdose," Carter said. "You've figured that much out already. Everything else I told you about the crash is true. She was the one driving, and she had been drinking. I took the blame and went to prison."

"But all this time, Bella has been living her life and not been punished at all for killing my brother? That's... that's not fair."

Not fair. Those words were grossly insufficient, but I couldn't think of any better ones right now. Life was not always fair—if it was, then William would still be with us—but this was more than that. I had no control over what had happened to William, but Bella could have owned up to what she did. She didn't deserve anyone's sympathy.

"I wouldn't say she went unpunished. She punished herself every day. She had a drinking problem before the crash, but that soon spiraled out of control. She moved onto hard drugs—heroin, I think—and she started wasting away before my eyes."

"Did she come and visit you in prison?" I asked. It was a stupid question. She must have, otherwise he wouldn't have seen the signs of her drug use. But I couldn't help but dwell on the two of them having conjugal visits in some seedy trailer.

"At first," Carter said as the waiter brought out our food.

He had skipped the appetizers, which was for the best as I wasn't a fan of French starters. He had ordered two steaks—medium-rare for his, by the looks of it, and medium for me. I couldn't recall ever telling Carter how I liked my steak, but he had ordered perfectly.

257

"Even just seeing her once a fortnight, I could still tell that she was in a bad way. Her eyes, her skin—she had all the signs of a junkie. It was painful to watch, and I felt completely helpless."

"Sounds like she didn't deserve you," I said, unable to understand how Carter had ended up with a druggie. Carter was smooth and sophisticated and didn't look at all like the type to get mixed up in all that.

Carter shook his head slowly. "It wasn't like that. *She* wasn't like that. When we first met, she was wonderful. You know those people who have energy all the time? She was one of them, and she used all that energy to make people's lives better. When we first met, she was volunteering in an old folk's home and a homeless shelter. Admittedly, she was from money, so she didn't need to work, but still…"

"People with money don't always use it so selflessly," I said, finishing Carter's thoughts when he trailed off. His words didn't sting as much as the look in his eyes did. When he thought back to Bella there was a glow behind his eyes like he was remembering better times.

"But all that money meant a continuous stream of temptations were thrown her way. We would go to expensive bars and get treated like royalty, but with regular offers of drink and drugs. Eventually that took its toll."

"You stayed with her, though," I said, sounding a little more accusatory than I had intended.

Carter nodded. "Yes, but we were drifting apart. If it hadn't been for the accident, then we would have probably split up within the next few weeks, anyway."

I probably shouldn't have been so quick to trust Carter after recent events, but the pain in his face didn't look fake to me. Just having this conversation was taking a lot of the energy out of him, almost as much as it was me.

"So why did you take the blame for her? Why not just be honest with the police? She should have gone to jail, Carter, not you. Now everything is messed up." Deep down, I knew I shouldn't be mad at Carter—in some ways, he had done an honorable thing—but the rational part of my brain was losing out to raw emotion again, and I couldn't control it.

"It all happened so quickly. It's not like I knew your brother was going to die. I got out of the car, and she moved into the passenger seat. The police and ambulances showed up within minutes, and before I knew it, the lies were pouring from my mouth."

"You should have told the truth," I said again, sounding less angry and more defeated now.

"I don't regret going to prison," Carter said. "Bella had to be punished for what happened and watching me go to prison was more painful to her than if she had gone herself."

I could feel tears building up inside. I took a quick sip of water and then some wine. Neither worked. My mouth opened to say something, but my lips were quivering and I knew any words would set me off crying.

"Emily, there is a lot more I need to tell you, and I will, but I can't keep going like this. Can we finish this off another day? How about I cook for you Friday night?"

I nodded. Carter still had many more questions to answer, but I wasn't ready and neither was he.

After a few minutes of silence, he asked me about work and I told him about our new project. He even managed to feign a basic understanding. By the end of the dinner the mood had lightened considerably, and I was even able to laugh a few times. I still welled up whenever I pictured Carter with his wife, but somewhere inside I let myself believe there might be a light at the end of this wretched tunnel.

Chapter Seven

Before Carter, my life had revolved around either studying or business. I had friends too, but they were distractions from achieving other goals in my life— or at least, that was how I treated them. Even when my career was going well, there was still a touch of emptiness inside me and I tried to fill the void with more work.

With a man now in the picture I knew I could be truly happy, however when things were going well with Carter the business would be struggling and vice versa. If I ever got both parts of my life in sync and going in the right direction then I would be walking in the clouds.

Things with Carter had hit rock bottom. In fact, they had crashed through rock bottom and had melted in the molten core of the Earth. But even though he hadn't explained everything, I had a strange feeling of confidence in our future. Something deep inside me felt that we wouldn't end things as they stood, and that perhaps maybe we could somehow make it work.

Unfortunately, while one part of my life may have been on the up, the other part was a disaster. Any hope or expectation of pulling away from

PharmaTech disappeared with a phone call from our lawyer. Once John and I were on the line, he broke the bad news.

"There's been a problem with your new patent application," Scott said. "The one you emailed over the other day."

"You need more information?" John asked. "I've taken a closer look at the technology now, so perhaps I can do a better job with the description."

"No, it's not that," Scott said. "I had all the information I needed and I submitted the application to the Patent and Trademark Office. You're in patent pending status."

"That's good, isn't it?" I asked, waiting for the bad news that Scott was supposed to deliver.

"The problem isn't with your patent as such it's with someone else's. Before I go on, I just want you to know that my firm filed your application incredibly quickly. I prepared an initial draft the same day I received your email and sent it to a partner for review. We then filed it electronically the next day."

"That's fine, Scott," I said. "A couple of days to turn around a patent application is quick, in my book." I didn't add that it often took me a few days just to reply to an email from my mother, let alone respond to every client at the drop of a hat.

"Well, someone else filed a patent the day before we did. It must have been the same day you sent me the email. Anyway, this other patent is for a similar technology to yours."

"How similar?" John asked, unable to keep the panic out of his voice. "Could our patent be declared invalid because this other one was filed first?"

"Probably not," Scott said. "I'm going to email you the details after this for you to have a look at it. You have a more technical mind than me, so you are in a better position to judge. I think there are a few differences in yours, so you should be okay,"

"Phew," John exclaimed. "I suppose that's not so bad. We may have to incur legal fees once again to defend our patent, but it's better than the alternative."

"John, I think we're missing the bigger picture here," I said, putting a dampener on John's blossoming enthusiasm. "Someone else has had a similar idea to us. That means they may develop a competing product. I have a bad feeling I know who filed that patent."

"Oh, shit," John muttered.

"Emily's right," Scott said. "I did some digging, and the company that filed the patent is a new subsidiary of PharmaTech. They won't let this one go without a fight."

"Oh, this is bad," John said, as he poured over PharmaTech's patent application. "This is really bad."

"Please don't tell me that we are infringing on their patent, which they filed one day before us?"

"No," John said, with a slow shake of the head. "No, I don't think we are. PharmaTech is approaching this in a slightly different way. In essence, they are combining the wearable data and the data from the limbs and crunching it in the cloud before sending the analysis back to the limb. It's not a bad approach, but it won't work as consistently as our method of having the wearable and the limb talk to each other directly."

"But they are definitely doing the same thing as us?"

John nodded, and I saw the disappointment in his eyes. LimbAnalytics was far from dead, but the idea around wearables could have sent us into the stratosphere. I knew that if PharmaTech cracked this problem first, then it would completely twist the information to suit its own ends. Our technology would be more likely to end up enhancing athletes than it would helping those who had lost limbs.

John went into the kitchen to make some lunch while I just sat at my desk, lost in thought. When it came to passion and technical prowess, John and I had all the bases covered. We had built this company from the ground up with our own hard work. We'd had some funding along the way, but that was more in recognition of our success than it was any kind of handout or charity.

What we needed was some help dealing with the big boys. Companies like PharmaTech didn't work like startups. Perhaps once it'd had noble aims, but those ethics had disappeared long ago.

"John," I yelled into the kitchen, "I'm going to speak to Carter. He might be able to help." John still had no idea I'd met him for dinner the other night. If the next dinner went well, then I would tell him, but otherwise I didn't see the need to go through all that right now. He would just ask questions that I wasn't ready to answer.

"Are you sure?" he asked, walking back into my room. "You don't have to do that."

"I know. I know. And to be honest, I'm not sure what he will be able to do, but he is much more accustomed to dealing with big companies like this. We may need to get dirty at some point, so it's best to be prepared."

"Well, I'm certainly glad you suggested it. I had the thought myself, but it was your decision to come to."

"You think he can help, then?" I asked. I had no idea what Carter might be able to do, and the suggestion was just partly an excuse to speak to him again before Friday.

"Maybe. Investment bankers have access to a metric shit-ton of information on companies like PharmaTech. Most of it's public, anyway, but I wouldn't have a clue what to do with it. He may know their intent behind all this, or what they will do now that we have a conflicting technology out there."

I nodded, grateful for the opportunity to hear Carter's voice again without the conversation being about his wife. More than his looks, his eyes, and even his ability in bed, the voice could captivate me like a drug, a drug I was well and truly hooked on.

Chapter Eight

"I know I have no right to ask this of you, but do you think you can help?"

I had called Carter completely out-of-the-blue, and he had answered the phone with more than a hint of trepidation in his voice. He probably thought I was calling to cancel our dinner plans on Friday night. Instead I spewed out everything about the new wearables idea, how we had filed a patent, and how PharmaTech seemed to have beaten us to it.

"You have every right to ask, Emily, but to be honest, I'm not sure what I can do for you. You're right about this being a potential problem, but I wouldn't let it affect what you are doing now. Just keep going, and if a lawsuit comes, then deal with it. If not, well... if not, then there is no problem."

"You don't think we should just abandon the idea? I mean, we can't compete directly with PharmaTech. If they decide they want to go after this, then who are we to stop them?"

"Emily, I mean this in the nicest possible way, but that is one of the stupidest things I have ever heard. You've scared them already. They tried to buy you out, for Christ's sake. Businesses don't do that unless they have to. Think about this: who are your customers?"

I thought for a few moments before answering. At the moment, LimbAnalytics didn't really have any customers. We had those beta testers who had agreed to test the product, and they consisted of a variety of people missing a limb. There were a fair few from the military, of course, some young children, and even a handful of others who had been injured in car accidents like me.

"People," I answered eventually. "Our customers are people. Human beings who need help."

"Exactly," Carter said. "And do you think PharmaTech cares about people? They see those customers as test subjects. You treat those people with respect, and that makes a lot of difference when you are asking someone to be a human guinea pig. It helps that you are one of them, so to speak, but it's more than that."

"You're right," I said. Something clicked in my head. "I don't think PharmaTech has a big pool of people to work with on this. That's why they wanted to buy the business. They need our beta testers."

"And it's safe to assume that they are not doing all this to improve the lives of these poor people. I don't want to stereotype, but people with artificial limbs are often not all that wealthy. PharmaTech might be testing this on that group now, but you can bet they have bigger plans for the product."

John and I had always had the same suspicion. It was that suspicion which kept us from considering PharmaTech's offer to buy us out. It came down to trust, and we didn't trust that company one little bit.

"Thank you, Carter. I needed to hear that."

"Happy to have helped, I guess, although all I did was speak the truth. You are an amazing person, Emily, and you are working hard to improve people's lives. That sort of attitude and commitment always gets rewarded in the end."

I let out a short laugh. "You can be awfully sentimental for a banker, you know. If people always get their just desserts, then you lot will go out of business."

"We aren't all bad, you know. Okay, most of us are pretty dubious, but there are some good eggs too. Keep doing what you're doing, Emily. It will pay off. I'll see you on Friday, okay?"

"Thanks. See you Friday."

I still didn't feel like giving John too many of the details about my relationship with Carter, so I just said that Carter couldn't help, but recommended we persevere with our plan. John looked a little disappointed, but it wasn't long before Carter was proved right. Being a nice person really could pay off in business.

"It seems too good to be true," I said, reading the email on John's laptop. "How do we know is even real?"

"It comes from legit a military email address," John said. "Those .gov domains are hard to fake. For what it's worth, I traced the IP address back to a military base in San Diego. That's hardly conclusive, but the email seems genuine enough. He's also offering to meet us, so it's not like we have to send them money."

Carter was right. What you put out in the world really could come back to help you. Some of the beta testers for LimbAnalytics' technology were military personnel who had lost limbs in conflicts. In fact, they made up our largest single group of beta testers. In most cases, these people had been given a cheap limb and told to make do.

When LimbAnalytics first started advertising for beta testers, we got a few responses from former military personnel. Both John and I were little nervous about going to meet with them. Being Stanford University students, we were not exactly accustomed to the military way of life. In the end, I just acted normally and the people we spoke to really appreciated it. One guy called Sam remarked on how refreshing it was to have a normal conversation with someone. Apparently, everyone who came to speak to him in the hospital spent the whole time thanking him for his service and getting overly emotional. I spoke to him as I would speak to anyone else, and we got along just fine.

Sam was doing well with the technology we had given him, but I hadn't spoken to him in a couple of weeks. Obviously he was happy with how things were going, because he recommended us to his former boss who was still active in the Army. Next thing I knew, John got an email from someone important in the Army who wanted to discuss a contract with the company.

"This could be huge," I said. "Contracts of the size he is talking about could be what it takes for LimbAnalytics to explode."

"No shit," John said. "This contract is a game-changer. And even better, we don't have to worry about PharmaTech stealing this one from us."

"Why's that?"

"We were chosen for this contract in part because we are a small business. There is an attachment on this email that we have to fill out to give information on our company size, but given that we are a two-man operation, we shouldn't have a problem meeting the definition of 'small business.' The federal government has lots of programs to ensure that small businesses get government money.

I didn't think we would ever benefit from them, but it looks like we will now."

"Are we ready for this?" I asked. "This is huge with a capital 'H.' You have to be extra careful when working with the federal government."

"This is what we set out to achieve," John said. "We want to improve people's lives, and this will help us do exactly that. You're right about being careful, though. We might want to consider bringing the bookkeeper on full-time; will need our financial records to be one hundred percent accurate."

John and I read the email about five times each before it really sunk in. The Army officer wanted to meet us to discuss the details, but it sounded like the contract would include a research element. That meant we would actually be paid for additional research and development and wouldn't have to find the extra money to fund it ourselves.

I forwarded the email to Marissa. No doubt she would pass the message on to our elusive investor, who would now be seeing a return on his investment a lot quicker than he or she had initially anticipated. Best of all, I could now go to dinner with Carter tomorrow night without having to worry about the business. I could focus on worrying about his wife and why he had kept her a secret.

Chapter Nine

The receptionist in Carter's building had my name down as a "permitted visitor," so she didn't need to call Carter and announce my arrival. But it didn't feel right to just walk into Carter's building. I wasn't his girlfriend—not anymore—so I shouldn't act like one. The receptionist looked a little confused, but she called Carter to get his permission before I went up to his apartment.

"You can come straight in, you know," he said as he took my coat. "I don't have anything to hide."

I just shrugged. I wasn't about to apologize for being suspicious of him.

I looked over to the kitchen and was pleased to see that Carter had turned it down a little bit in the romance department. There were no flowers or candles on the table this time, although two glasses of red wine had been poured and a bowl of pasta sat steaming on the table. The smell of fresh pesto drifted over to my nose and my stomach reminded me with a gentle growl that I hadn't eaten in over six hours.

"I've been thinking about how to tell you the whole story," Carter said. "I feel like I should have a speech prepared or something, but the more I try to plan my words, the harder it becomes."

I shoved a few bits of pasta into my mouth to give me some time to consider what to say. I knew how he felt. I had been doing the same thing, trying to think of questions I would ask him and answers I would demand. But it really wasn't that simple, and I knew my emotions would end up dictating the conversation. The same thing seemed to be happening to Carter.

"How did you get married?" I asked. "I get that you were in love with her, and I can believe that she was someone different before the drinking and drug problems, but that doesn't explain how you ended up married to her."

Carter took a sip of wine, probably buying time like I had just done.

"I suppose in some ways that's easy to explain," Carter said, carefully placing his glass down. "We got married about four years into my prison sentence. Needless to say, it was a small ceremony."

"Family and friends?" I asked with a sly smile.

"Something like that. But without the friends. It wasn't my idea—not exactly. Bella had mentioned marriage on a couple of her previous visits. She would always profess her love for me and thank me for what I did. I always just said I would think about it, but I had no real intention of marrying her."

"What changed?"

"Her sister, actually. Bella has a sister, Julia, but she is older and far more sensible, and she came to visit me while I was in prison. Bella hadn't told her family that she was driving that night, but her sister had figured it out. She pleaded with me to marry Bella. She thought marriage would set Bella straight. She even promised me money, lots of it, but of course I didn't want it. As Bella got worse, I finally agreed to marry her. There didn't seem to be any other choice at that point."

"So you were just trying to save her again?" I asked. "All this, everything from the car crash that killed my brother to you marrying her, was just you trying to help Bella and stop her from destroying herself?"

"It didn't work."

"It's not your fault. She had every chance to improve her life, but she chose drinking and drugs. You did everything you could for her, but I think you can let her go now."

"I have," Carter said. "Honestly, I have. She's been in a coma for a while now, and every week they find something else wrong with her. It's only a matter of time, and I have come to terms with that. The woman I first fell in love with died many years ago. I've moved on, Emily."

Another battle raged in my brain, or perhaps it was a battle between my brain and my heart. I knew I couldn't blame Carter for previously having loved someone else. Lots of people fell in love when they were young, but that didn't mean you couldn't fall in love with someone else later. I knew that, but my inexperience made this a lot harder to deal with.

I had accepted one thing, though: I wasn't going to blame Carter for keeping his marriage a secret. He did lie to me, but we had only known each other for a few weeks, and if he had told me the whole story I might have dashed out on him. At least this way there was still hope for us.

"Is that where you got your money from?" I asked.

Carter frowned. "How do you know I wasn't always rich?"

"My dad mentioned that you had a public defender in your trial," I replied. "I'm guessing that after you married Bella, you got access to money and connections."

Carter smiled. "Sometimes I forget how clever you are. Yes, I got some money from her family and this job. As you mentioned once before, it's not easy to get a good job when you have a criminal record. Her family helped me and paid for a very expensive lawyer, who was able to secure my green card. They don't exactly like giving them out to criminals, but he was a hot-shot who used to work for the US immigration department."

"So her family is really rich, then?"

Carson nodded. "I tried to turn it down the first—the money, that is—but they insisted. Julia told her parents about what I did, and they were grateful. They don't blame me for the drinking and the drugs. In fact I think they blame themselves. I don't think they were there for her that much when she was a child."

"What happens now?" I asked. "You're still married to her. Is there any chance you two will get divorced? Or does that mean you will lose your job?"

"I don't have to worry about the job or the money. Julia is very supportive and made sure that the money is mine with no strings attached. I never need to work again, to be honest, although I do anyway. I'd be bored otherwise."

"So why not get divorced?"

"She's in a coma. It doesn't feel right to divorce someone who can't consent to it, and before you came, along it wasn't a big deal whether or not I was married. I never intended to fall in love again."

Carter had told me he loved me before, but the words still carried just as much impact. I hoped they always would.

"I'm not going to make you get a divorce," I said. "It's too early for that. Do I know everything now? About your marriage to Bella? And how you feel about her?"

"Completely. I loved her and I married her because I thought that might save her. I don't love her anymore. I love you. I'm going to speak to my lawyer in the morning about getting a divorce, because I don't want to put you through anything like that again. I know it's too early for us, but I want Bella out of the picture so that we have a chance. Do we have a chance? Can you forgive me?"

I didn't need him to divorce Bella—not right away. Marriage was just a piece of paper, at the end of the day. What I needed to know was how he felt for her right now and I believed him when he said he was no longer in love with her. More importantly, I believed him when he said he was in love with me.

"I'm out of wine," I said.

"I'll go open another bottle," Carter replied, standing up and walking into the kitchen.

"Good," I said. "I'll be waiting for you in the bedroom."

Chapter Ten

I could still count all my sexual experiences on my fingers. But when I entered Carter's bedroom that night, I was not nervous. I was still inexperienced, and no doubt I had a lot to learn, but that didn't seem to bother me anymore—Carter would teach me.

He walked into the bedroom with a fresh bottle of red wine and a large grin on his face.

"You look stunning," he said, setting his glass down by the bed.

"I'm still dressed," I said. "I'm wearing exactly the same thing I've been wearing all night."

"Yes, but now you're lying on my bed. Before you were gorgeous; now you're irresistible." He poured me a fresh glass of wine and laid down next to me on the bed.

I took a sip and then kissed him gently on the mouth, a few drops of wine parsing from my lips to his. Carter put a hand on the side of my face and moved his lips from my mouth to my neck. I let out a soft groan and placed my hand on his firm chest. I squirmed and fidgeted as I felt a pressure build between my thighs. I wanted to spread my legs and pull Carter against me, but he was controlling the pace and seemed to want to take things slowly this time.

I opened the buttons on his shirt—not shaking for once—and felt the firm flesh underneath. Carter hooked his fingers under the straps of my blouse and pulled them down, exposing the tops of my breasts. His lips moved down to my chest as he pulled the top down, freeing my nipples. Tiny goosebumps erupted on my pert breasts as his lips covered them in warmth.

I ran my fingers through Carter's hair, holding him close as I wrapped my legs around his. I pushed my sex against his body, desperate to feel him inside me. He took his mouth away from my now stiff and erect nipples, pulling my top off as I fumbled to remove his shirt.

He pulled off my skirt and panties in one swift movement, throwing them to the side of the bed before unbuckling his jeans, pulling them down to the floor, and standing naked in front of me. Now I was nervous again, but it was a good kind of nervous, a nervous that would help send me to the edge once Carter was inside me.

He picked up his glass of wine and took a long sip before lying next to me on the bed, naked and still holding the wine. He leaned in to kiss me again, but as he did, he drizzled some of the wine over my chest. Dark red droplets weaved their way down the valley between my breasts before trickling down my belly, leaving a crimson trail behind them.

Carter placed the glass back down before letting his tongue chase the wine that he had spilled over my body. He lapped up what had pooled in my navel and then moved down between my legs. The red wine had left a warm sweetness in his mouth that I felt as he began to lick my wetness.

I reached out for my glass and took a long sip of the wine, letting the rush of alcohol go to my head combined with the rush of ecstasy that had taken hold of my pussy. With my newfound confidence, I poured more wine down my chest and watched it trickle down until it reached Carter's mouth as he licked at my swollen bud.

I quickly put the glass back down by the side of the bed, unable to keep it still as my orgasm approached, and then grabbed hold of the posts making up the headboard. As Carter's fingers slipped inside me, I tightened my grip on the wooden posts and shook them as I exploded into his face.

We shared more wine while I took Carter's manhood in my hand and felt him stiffen in response to my gentle strokes. When he moved to climb between my legs, I put a finger on his chest and pushed him onto his back. I straddled him and looked deep into his eyes as my hips moved down and let his shaft plunge deep inside me.

"I want all of you inside me today," I said. "Everything."

Carter gave a gentle nod, but didn't let his eyes leave mine as my hips rocked slowly back and forth until he erupted inside me.

My lack of experience meant that I didn't really know the difference between sex and making love, but I was certain that whatever we did that night was making love. We stayed up talking, drinking, and trading orgasms for hours until I finally fell asleep with my head on his chest, rising and falling with his slow, steady breath.

Despite drinking more than an entire bottle of wine, I still woke up in the morning in relatively good spirits and with little to show in regards to a hangover. Our night of passion, however, had left us with quite an appetite.

Carter took me to a small café near his apartment where I polished off a chocolate croissant in less than two minutes.

"I'm going to have to start leaving clothes at your place," I said. "I'm wearing the same ones from last night, and it's quite clear I will be doing the walk of shame when I go home later."

"I'm sure I can find some space in the closet. Hell, I'll buy some more closets if it means you'll be staying over more often. In fact, I'm going to grab a few essentials, like a toothbrush for you. That way, you have no excuse not to stay over more often."

"Thank God for that. I chewed through an entire packet of mints this morning trying to disguise my breath. Although I must say, I actually quite like feeling a little *dirty* the morning after. I wasn't one of those girls who did that kind of thing in college, so it's nice to make up for lost time."

Carter grinned. "Don't worry. You didn't miss anything. Sex in college is nothing like that; it's nowhere near as special. I guess I'm going to need some new clothes as well, although I can't imagine I will stay at yours as much. Not unless you improve your cooking. I can't quite believe I'm going to say this, but how about we go shopping sometime soon?"

"You really are the perfect man, aren't you?"

Chapter Eleven

Despite wearing crumpled clothes that screamed "walk of shame" from a mile away, I decided to walk home after my breakfast with Carter. I caught a few grins from passersby but did my best to ignore them. I was in far too good a mood to let a few judgmental idiots spoil my day.

By the time I got home, I had resolved to tell John that Carter and I were an item again. He would know something was up just by how good a mood I was in—my body language the morning after three orgasms was hard to miss—and I saw no reason to keep it a secret. In fact, I wanted to tell people about it. What was the point in having a man like Carter if you couldn't shout it from the rooftops?

As I entered my apartment, I almost tripped over a pair of sneakers that had been left in front of the door. John must have been here again and obviously he had no qualms about letting himself in unannounced.

"Good morning," John said, walking into the hall and wearing a grin from ear-to-ear. "Or should I say, good afternoon? I trust you had a nice evening."

"Yes, thank you, it was very pleasant. You should feel free to let yourself into my apartment whenever you want, by the way."

"Don't try to change the subject, missy. I know you didn't spend the night here. That means you either hooked up with some random guy or you and Carter are suddenly back on. Since you seem positively terrified by the concept of one-night stands, I'm going to go ahead and assume Carter had a damn good explanation for the whole being-married thing."

"Can I at least make myself a cup of tea first?" I asked, kicking off my shoes and filling the kettle. "I'm kind of tired."

"Tea?" John said, practically spitting out the word. "Christ, Emily, what happened to coffee? Is Carter turning you British?"

"Oh, calm down, I've had a coffee already today, that's all."

I resisted the urge to add milk to my tea—that really would have John worried—and then sat down to recite Carter's story. I hadn't realized just how much I needed to tell it. A part of me still thought I was being stupid to trust Carter again and that I was being taken in by his lies. John was a good friend, but more importantly, he was brutally honest. If I was being stupid here, he would tell me and wouldn't mince his words in the slightest.

"Wow, that's one messed up series of events," John said once I had finished. "You might be able to make a movie out of this one day."

"It would have to be R-rated if it depicted some of the things we did last night," I said, turning a little red on the cheeks.

"I'm so proud of you," John said. "My boring virgin is become a fun sex freak. I've lived for this moment, I really have."

"So you don't think I'm being stupid, then? Getting back together with him?"

John shook his head. "You can't punish the guy for being in love with someone else before he met you. And the marriage thing explains his money and green card. I don't even disagree with him lying to you about this. Sometimes, white lies are for the best."

"Being married is hardly a white lie," I said.

"In this case, I think it is. He doesn't love her, and she is in a coma. You would have never spoken to him if you'd have known he was married. What's one small lie in the grand scheme of things?"

"All right, you've convinced me," I said, holding up my hands in defeat as a buzz from John's phone distracted him. "I'm in too good a mood to argue."

"Not for much longer you won't be," John said, throwing his phone at me. "What the hell is all that about?"

I scanned the email John had opened on his phone. It was from the Army officer who had emailed us yesterday about potentially entering into a new contract. This time, it was bad news.

"Is he canceling the contract offer?" I asked.

"Certainly looks that way," John said. "He says something about us using overseas labor. Apparently, we don't qualify for the small business program if we use overseas labor instead of American workers."

"But we don't use overseas labor. You and I are the only employees. We have an American accountant, and all of our beta testers are American. This doesn't make any sense."

"We should call Marissa. She got pretty excited when I told her about the contract. What the hell is going on, Emily? Could this be PharmaTech again?"

"I don't know, but I admit to being worried. I'll call Marissa now."

The phone rang and rang with no answer. I was actually hoping she wouldn't pick up; even though this didn't seem to be our fault, I felt like she would be pissed. She had been supportive so far and the investor had never put us under any pressure, but I felt that at some point he or she would want to see us

287

generate some revenue, or at least get some good contracts in place.

Finally, after at least ten rings, Marissa picked up the phone.

"There is one possibility that springs to mind," she said after we told her what happened. "How confident are you in your security? Is there any chance you have been hacked?"

John sighed. "It's always possible. No company can completely protect against that kind of thing, but I like to think we have peace and security in place."

"Take a closer look," Marissa said. "That's the only thing I can think of right now. It's one thing for PharmaTech to one-up you on the wearable tech thing, but this Army contract should have been secure. They sure as hell didn't hack into the Army email server."

"So, you do think it's PharmaTech?" I asked. "It could just be a coincidence."

"I certainly hope it is," Marissa said, remaining completely calm. This was probably a small amount of money for her and her investor, but for us, it was our lives. "But do some checks anyway."

"Do you think she has a point?" I asked after the call ended. "If PharmaTech really wanted to hack in, then I'm sure they could."

"Probably," John said, but he didn't look convinced. "But we aren't soft targets. We don't use any of the traditional email platforms, so that makes hacking our email tougher. And then there is the special authentication stuff we use. I'll look into it—see if we have left any backdoors open—but I'm not convinced that is the problem."

"Thanks. Is there anything I can do to help?"

"No, I'll do it. I set up the system, so it'll be easiest if I look at it. Sorry to bring you down after things had just got sorted with Carter."

"I'm not going to let this bring me down," I said defiantly. "This is just a hiccup. We'll recover."

"Wow, when did you become so positive?" John asked. "I like this new Emily. When are you seeing him next? I'll make sure to stay out of the way."

"He's taking me shopping. We're buying spare clothes to leave at each other's houses. Should I be scared of that?"

"I would be," John said. "But then, I'm scared of commitment. You probably thrive on it. Make sure you buy some sexy undies, though—no Bridget Jones knickers."

I hadn't even thought about that. I'd never bought underwear with a man before. I wasn't scared before, but now I was a touch nervous. Nervous, and excited.

289

Chapter Twelve

"Are you okay?" Carter asked as we walked along a popular shopping mall in downtown San Francisco. "You seem a little nervous."

"This is going to sound a little stupid," I said, "but I usually go shopping for clothes and underwear by myself. John has helped me out a few times, but I've never gone shopping with a boyfriend before."

"And here I was thinking women were always in their element when they were shopping for clothes."

"Most women probably are, but I am definitely not. I get funny looks when trying on clothes because of my leg; the shop assistants seem to think I need all my clothes specially made, or something."

Carter tried to take me to some of his favorite fashion stores, but I insisted on going to my good old favorites. I knew if we went to the expensive stores he would insist on buying me something fancy, and knowing me. I would go and spill tomato sauce over it the next day.

"Can we buy the fun things now?" Carter asked. "We've got all the comfy tops and sweatpants you will ever need, so let's go get you some new underwear."

"Do we have to?" I asked. "I think I would be more comfortable buying that myself." The thought of browsing through bras and panties with Carter was strangely awkward. He had seen me naked plenty of times and had done things to me that would make even John blush, but doing such a normal thing in public made me feel weird.

"Oh, I definitely want to be there for this bit. It's my reward for putting up with all the boring stuff that we just bought. Anyway, I have a few other purchases I would like to make. Come on, let's go."

Carter took me by the hand and led me down some streets I didn't recognize. At first I thought he was going to take me to another expensive store, but the area we found ourselves in certainly wouldn't have any of the top fashion labels for sale.

"You're taking me to a sex shop, aren't you?"

"What gave it away? All the neon lighting? Or was it the mannequin wearing leather in the window? Come on, it's not that bad. I promise."

I had to admit that despite its outward appearance, once inside the store, I could have been in any store in the mall. Well, if the mall sold dildos and whips. I had no idea where to look, so I just went straight for the underwear, although even that freaked me out a little.

"Do you really want me to buy crotchless panties?" I asked him.

"Actually no, you can buy the normal ones. Tell you what, I will go pick out some nice knickers for you while you go and explore that corner over there."

Carter pointed to the corner of the store I had been avoiding—the one with the not-so-subtle vibrators. I wanted to argue with Carter and have him go look at the dildos, but it occurred to me that if we were going to buy one, I would rather have some say in the matter, otherwise we may end up with something far too large and misshapen for me to enjoy. I took a deep breath, lowered my gaze—although I was fairly sure I wouldn't see anyone I knew in here—and walked over to the corner of the room.

Sex toys were one of those things that I knew existed, and I knew lots of women owned them, but I just couldn't bring myself to buy one. The shop had a huge variety, and the vibrators came in all shapes and sizes. Some were small enough to fit in a handbag, while others were too big to fit anywhere—at least, in my opinion. A sleek, silver one looked like something out of a science fiction movie, and I didn't want to imagine being probed by aliens when getting intimate with Carter.

The only one I could bring myself to pick up and hold was a six- or seven-inch piece of pink plastic with a gentle ribbing. As I was holding it, my fingers slipped and pressed a button on the base, causing the toy to twist in a circular motion. I nearly dropped the thing in shock and fumbled at the button to get it to stop. I heard a girl and a guy snicker behind me, but didn't turn around to look.

"Maybe she's shopping for a new leg," the guy whispered to his girlfriend who laughed in response.

I froze. I thought I'd heard all the jokes about my leg before, but apparently I was wrong. This was definitely a new one on me. Thank God Carter hadn't heard him; I still has vivid memories of his reaction to the incident at the nightclub. I loved him, but there was no denying that he had a temper when it came to me.

I didn't want to turn around until the guy and his girlfriend had disappeared, so I waited a few moments, grabbed a box with the pink dildo in it, and walked over to Carter. He had collected a basket full of bras, panties, and some leather items that were hidden underneath.

"Found one you like?" he asked. "I picked up a few things you'll like, but I'm going to keep them as a surprise for later."

I gave a weak smile and nodded as we went to pay for our goodies. As Carter handed over his credit card, I heard a girl screaming at a guy before storming out of the store and slamming the door behind her. I turned around to see the guy who had made the joke about me earlier now standing in the middle of store, looking thoroughly confused.

"What was that about?" I asked, looking back at Carter. He was staring at the guy and grinning with a knowing look on his face. "Did you have something to do with that?"

"I don't know what you're talking about, dear."

"You heard, didn't you? You heard what he said. What did you do?"

"The moron had his Bluetooth open on his phone, so I sent him a few messages. Looks like his girlfriend found them, and now she probably thinks he is having an affair."

I couldn't help but smile. "I think he deserved it. Does that make me a bad person?"

"Not at all. You don't have to take it, you know. You hear someone say something like that, you could always confront them."

"I don't have time to deal with the idiots in the world," I said. "You know what, that sort of thing just doesn't bother me as much as it used to. Come on, let's go take our tawdry purchases back to your place. I want to try on what you bought me."

Chapter Thirteen

No sooner had I slipped into the underwear than I had to slip back out of it again, but not for the reasons I liked. Instead of spending the afternoon being ravished by Carter, I had to head home alone while he went back to work. I began to grumble about being abandoned until her reminded me that it was in fact a Thursday and not everyone could live the startup lifestyle of working whenever they pleased. Fair enough, I supposed.

The new panties and the toys stayed at Carter's to be fully explored at a later date while I brought some of his stuff back with me. Every item, including the perfectly-sculpted boxers, had a designer label inside them. He had socks that cost more than my skirts. Still, he looked damn fine even when dressed, so I couldn't complain too much.

By the time I arrived home my legs and feet were exhausted. For once I hoped that John was already at my place. I could have used a bit of looking after. I dropped the bags inside the door and collapsed onto the sofa before realizing that my laptop was all the way over on the table. I should have taken a nap or just chilled out, but my laptop was chained to me when I was at home and I felt naked without it. Just as I was about to get up, I heard a rustling from the kitchen. Thank God for that.

"Bring me my laptop, will you, John?" I called out. "And put the kettle on. I need a cup of tea."

"I could have been a burglar," John said, passing me my laptop. "How did you know it was me?"

"Most burglars don't stop in the middle of a job to eat chips."

"Fair enough. You look exhausted. No offense."

"I was with Carter all day," I replied.

"Ah, so you're all shagged out, then. Poor thing; my heart bleeds for you."

"We were just shopping," I said with a flick of the hand toward the bags of clothes by the door. "Unfortunately, that was all." I neglected to mention some of the more intimate purchases we made that day; John didn't need to know everything, and he was already of the opinion that Carter was some closet sex freak. "What have you been doing all day?"

"Looking for holes in our security. Didn't find a single one, but I have a plan, and it's quite a good one, if I do say so myself."

"Do tell."

"We come up with another idea for the business, but not a real one. Something that sounds vaguely real, but is beyond our capabilities to actually do. Or maybe just something we don't care about because it's too small a market. The details don't matter. It just needs to be a fake plan."

"You're going to set some bait," I said, sitting up and suddenly feeling a lot more invigorated.

"Yep, that's the plan. Leave an idea out there and see if anyone reacts to it. Got any plans that are borderline believable?"

"We were going to design the hardware ourselves at one point, but we didn't because it would have been horrendously expensive."

"And there were already patents on the tech," John pointed out. "That's perfect, actually. Let's have a fake email exchange where talk about the hardware and pretend to be all excited. I will copy the plans based on an existing patent and leave them on our system. If PharmaTech gets hold of that information, it may make them waste money on developing a product that already exists."

"Not to mention that they might go and file a patent for a product that is already patented. That would get them a slap on the wrists, at least. Let's do it."

John and I sat opposite each other and sent a few carefully constructed emails where we discussed plans to use money raised from a private round of investment to get into hardware. A small business like ours wouldn't usually get into product development, but PharmaTech seemed to be reacting to whatever we put out there without giving it a second thought. I was willing to bet they would act first and think later.

When your business was under threat from a hacker and you were laying traps for them like something from a spy novel, regular work had a tendency to look rather dull and uninspiring in comparison. The next few days floated by in haze of normal emails from our customers and the odd query from the accountant. The business was still ticking along nicely even when operating on autopilot, but I had to admit to being rather bored.

My boredom wasn't helped by the lack of contact with Carter. We had sent each other lots of text messages, plenty of which I would be embarrassed to show my mother, and we had talked over the phone, but I needed to see him in person. In the flesh. I needed him. I refused to let myself become the needy girlfriend, especially since I knew he had a stressful job. If I had been busier it wouldn't have been so difficult, but I had far too much time to myself that moment.

Finally, I got a message from Carter inviting me to dinner. The message was a little cryptic about where we would be going, but apparently I should dress warm. He didn't mention anything about a car to pick me up, so I decided to walk over to his apartment. It wasn't that far away, but San Francisco had lots of hills to climb on the way. I ended up making it there in good time. In fact, I was early and decided to wait outside for him. The weather was pleasant and I didn't see the need for the jacket Carter had insisted I bring.

Even though I was standing outside Carter's building I still heard the ping of the lift doors opening. I recognized the person who walked out, and it wasn't Carter. It was that woman again—the woman I had seen at the conference and who was a business partner of Carter's. This had happened before; I had seen her leaving his building and jumped to the wrong conclusion. That was before Carter and I had really established our relationship, and I now had the perfect chance to show him how much I had grown from the jealous girl he met a few weeks ago.

I held the door open for this woman as she left the building. "Hi, you're a business partner of Carter's, right? I'm a friend of his." I probably could have introduced myself as his girlfriend, but that felt a little unprofessional.

"Hi," the woman said, keeping her gaze on the floor. She seemed determined not to talk to me and just muttered something under her breath as she walked away.

"Well, that was weird," I said to myself. Perhaps she was some high-flying investment banker who looked down on the mere mortals like me. She had seemed a little stuck-up when I saw her at the conference. Frankly, as long as she was just a business colleague, I couldn't have cared less. I only wanted Carter, not his work friends.

Chapter Fourteen

"My God, I'm freezing." I shivered as the breeze from the bay made light work of the flimsy jacket I had brought with me.

"I did tell you to dress warm," Carter said.

"Yes, but you were a little light on the details. Had you told me we were going on a cruise of the San Francisco Bay, I might have known to bring a coat. The only part of me that's not cold right now is my fake leg."

"Well, this is a little too public a place for me to warm your leg or any other intimate parts of you, but my jacket should stop you shivering a bit."

Carter slipped off his dark gray suit jacket and placed it lightly on my shoulders. I felt like such a stereotype, but as the goosebumps faded and I stopped shaking, my body was grateful. Now that I was warm I was able to enjoy the evening as the boat headed toward the Golden Gate Bridge. Carter had booked a romantic meal for two aboard a floating restaurant with an onboard chef who owned two Michelin-star restaurants.

The view in front of me wasn't all that bad, either. At some point amongst the fighting and mistrust, I had somehow forgotten just how dreamy Carter was. He wore a light blue shirt with a pink tie that matched two small jewels on each of his cufflinks. A hefty silver watch protruded from under the cuff of his shirt, and I smiled to myself, thinking that he would not be quick to embrace the newfound obsession with wearable fitness trackers.

"Can you hear that noise?" Carter asked.

"Yes, I can hear something. What is it?"

"Baseball fans. The Giants are playing tonight. If you keep an eye out and get lucky, you may catch a home run."

I laughed. "You really don't know a lot about American sports, do you? We won't be catching a baseball all the way out here. Not unless the players are on some fancy new steroids, which come to think of it, is not all that far-fetched, I suppose."

"Okay, I admit it: I'm not much of a baseball fan. I do know a bit about football—your kind of football—so don't go making too many assumptions about us Brits."

"I only know about baseball because my brother used to watch it. Sometimes it was on TV five or six nights a week. I still watch it, occasionally. It helps me feel close to him, you know?"

"Tell me about him. About William. If that's okay?"

"It's fine. I like talking about him, actually. It's tough to talk about him with my parents, but it's different with you. William was not at all like me, but I think you would have liked him. I suppose everyone says that about people who died, but I really believe it. He was so much more outgoing than me. I like to think he would have become an actor or a presenter, but it's equally likely he would have ended up working as a barista, or something. But you know what? He would've been happy in whatever he did. He was just that kind of guy."

Carter nodded. "I know people like that. I wish I could be like them."

"Oh, come on!" I exclaimed. "You're hardly lacking in confidence, are you?"

Carter laughed. "I'm not sure whether I should take that as a compliment or not. But since I'm confident guy, I will assume it was a compliment."

"I thought you would. You investment bankers are all a bit too cocky for my liking."

"Hey, don't lump us all together. We aren't all that bad, although I admit some of my colleagues do fit the 'one-percenter' stereotype rather well. And don't forget I wasn't always an investment banker. I only got this job because of Bella's sister."

In all the confusion about Carter's past, I'd completely forgotten that he used to be quite poor—or at least, his parents were. The career as an investment banker was new; Carter had another life before that.

"What did you do before?"

"I'm tempted to make you guess, but this cruise only lasts another two hours and I think it would take all night."

"It must have had something to do with numbers," I said. "You can't just have walked into a job as an investment banker without being able to read a spreadsheet. And I think it's safe to assume you went to college before the crash. I'm going to guess that you did a degree in accounting or something similar and maybe worked in that field for a bit."

"I can see from the big grin on your face that you think you have me sussed out."

"And I can tell from the way you are avoiding answering me that I am right."

"Actually, little Miss Smarty-pants, you are completely wrong. I was a writer. Still am, I guess. I have a book out, although it's under pen name; I still get the odd royalty check." I don't know what surprised me more: that Carter was an author, something far more creative than I would have expected, or that he just called me Miss Smarty-pants.

"You don't hear the name 'Miss Smarty-pants' much in America, you know," I said.

"Well, I think it's rather apt here, don't you? I suppose now you're going to ask me what type of book I wrote and want to read it. That's what everyone used to ask when I told them I had written a book."

"You know what? I don't want to know. That's not who you are anymore, and given everything that has happened, I want your past to remain in the past. Like it or not, you are now an investment banker. You're *my* investment banker."

"Thank God for that," Carter said, visibly relieved. "Frankly, the book is dreadful. I used to keep it a secret, but one of my friends found out and I ended up being the laughingstock of the pub. You were right about one thing, though: I do have an accounting degree. I suppose it's actually useful now, but at the time, I just did it so that I would have time to write."

"I *knew* it," I gloated, taking my victories where I found them.

"Smarty-pants," Carter mumbled under his breath. "Enough about me and my crappy book. How's the business going? We haven't spoken about it in ages."

I grimaced, not entirely sure how to answer. On the face of it everything was progressing rather well.

LimbAnalytics wasn't ever going to make money quickly, and we always understood there would be a large costs upfront while we perfected the technology, but I couldn't deny that the recent events had shaken my confidence a little bit.

"Good, I suppose. We're on track and meeting our goals."

"You don't sound entirely convinced. Getting pressure from your investor?"

"No, the investor is great. He or she stays behind the scenes and is really supportive of us. The perfect investor, really."

"He or she? You don't know the investor?"

"We deal with an intermediary. The investor is another LLC, and we deal with the manager, not the owner."

"Is that common? It seems a little sneaky, but lots of investors try to hide their identity, I guess, especially through offshore companies. Maybe the investor is just trying to hide from the IRS. As long as you're comfortable with the situation, that's all that matters."

"It's working so far, that's all I know." Then I looked over Carter's shoulder and saw that the boat was approaching the Golden Gate Bridge. "Come on, let's go enjoy the view."

We stood at the front of the boat and Carter wrapped his arms around me. I couldn't help but think of the cheesy scene in the Titanic movie, but hopefully my story would have a happier ending.

Chapter Fifteen

I was spending more time with Carter than ever, but it felt like an eternity since we had last had sex. Carter's work schedule had become completely erratic over the past few weeks. He had a lot of international clients, and that meant he had to be on conference calls at crazy times. He promised that this was an unusually busy period and it wouldn't last forever. Still, I was getting increasingly frustrated knowing his apartment was full of sexy underwear and even sexier toys. I was still a little nervous about using some of that stuff with him, but it was an excited kind of nervousness.

John was still spending more time at my apartment than his own, but at the moment, I appreciated the company.

"Still no news?" I asked, referring to our attempts to catch whoever was hacking into our security.

"No, nothing. I'm starting to think that no one has hacked into our systems."

"That's good news, right?"

"I suppose," John said, sounding not at all convinced. "I would be happier if I knew what the hell was going on. Someone is getting the information somehow. I guess a part of me was hoping it was just a hack, because that's something I might be able to stop. Now I just feel helpless."

"If it isn't a standard hack, then we have to look into the possibility that we have a more traditional leak."

"God, I hope it isn't that. Where would we even start?"

"We can rule out the beta testers," I said. "They didn't have access to that kind of information. Plus, most of them have been with us for months now. All these leaks started in the last few weeks, so it has to be someone who has recently come into the fold."

"What about that new group at Stanford University?" John asked. "We didn't start using them until we got all the investment money in. Although I guess they don't have the same information, either."

"No, I don't see how they could have deduced our plans from just what we have been doing with them. They are running relatively basic tests and interpreting data; again, nothing that reveals our plans for the future."

"I don't like where this is going," John said.

We had ruled out the majority of the people we worked with, and there were only three left of any significance. If it was one of those three, and at this stage it had to be, then we could be in real trouble.

"Scott knew about the patent applications," I said. "In fact, he has access to a lot of information regarding our business. He has for a while. Maybe he's been leaking information to PharmaTech this whole time. It would explain their early offer to buy our business."

"But he's a lawyer. They have pretty strict confidentiality rules, and you have to assume that if he was screwing us over he would be doing it to others, as well. I can't imagine he would get away with that for long. Plus, to be honest, I trust him. He's a nice guy, and he doesn't ask lots of questions of us. If he was leaking information, he would probably be digging for lots of juicy details."

"I agree," I said. "And he didn't know anything about the military contract. That leaves two people."

"I mentioned the military contract to the accountant," John said. "But she didn't know a thing about the patents."

"So that leaves…"

"Marissa? Why would she do that? What does she have to gain by hurting the business?"

"If it is Marissa," I said, "we have to assume she is doing its on behalf of the investor."

"Okay, so why would the investor do it? I don't want to sound like I'm stating the obvious, but surely the investor wants this company to succeed as much as we do." My head sunk into my hands and I expelled a loud sigh. How could we have been so stupid? So naïve?"

We're screwed. We're completely fucked. PharmaTech has been playing us all along, ever since we turned down the offer, probably."

"I'm not following," John said. "If the company fails, then the investor loses his or her money. Why would they want that?"

"How much will they lose? A few hundred grand. That's nothing compared to the millions PharmaTech can spend. The investor is probably PharmaTech, or at least someone they have control over. Think about it. They invest in us and get to hear all our secrets, everything we are doing before we do it. That's worth losing a few hundred grand over."

"But that's got to be illegal," John said, exasperated. "Surely you can't use information in that way. There has to be security laws or corporate law… things that prevent it!"

"Probably," I said. "But I expect they covered their tracks. The investor is probably not directly connected to them. Maybe it's a friend of a board director, or something like that. Either way, I guess they stayed just within the law or close enough that we won't be able to sue them easily."

"My God. It's genius, when you think about it."

"I'm not going to take this lying down. Let's find out for sure the leak is coming from Marissa. Once we know, we can think about what to do. There's no way we are going to let them win."

"I'll call Marissa later with a fake piece of information. We should know for sure within a day or two, but this won't be easy. I'm with you. I want to take them down, but they are a huge corporation— and not just that; they are a huge corporation that's plays dirty."

"Then we will play dirty, too."

There was one positive aspect to receiving this new information about our supposed investor: it completely eliminated any regrets or doubts I may have had about rejecting the initial ten-million-dollar offer from PharmaTech. In the back of my mind I had wondered whether they were really as bad as John and I made them out to be. Perhaps they really would use the technology to help others in the same way that we were planning to do. All right, they would make a bit more profit along the way, but that didn't make them a bad company. Corporate espionage of the type that seemed to be at play here did make them a bad company, though. If they were prepared to use the investors to obtain information about their competitors, then they were every bit as dirty as I had suspected.

I left John to make the call to Marissa while I sent a message to Carter. *I'm coming round tonight. It's been a tough day and I need to work out the stress. E xx*

Looking forward to it, came the reply.

I put the phone down and took a deep breath. Demanding sex from Carter was surprisingly empowering and went some way to improving my mood. I slipped out of my clothes and into the shower, making sure I was shaved where I needed to be. I planned to spend a lot of time naked tonight and wanted to look my best. At times like this, I needed Carter more than ever.

Chapter Sixteen

I took a taxi to Carter's so that I wouldn't be hot and sweaty by the time I arrived at his apartment. Unfortunately, this being San Francisco, the traffic was horrendous and I ended up in the back of the car for thirty minutes. Once I got to his apartment, I practically ran into the elevator and tapped my foot, eagerly waiting for the lift to arrive on his floor.

The elevator doors opened and Carter reached in, grabbed me, and pulled me into a tight embrace. He pushed me against the wall, lips locking against mine as he started to undress me.

"Slow down," I said, forcing myself to push him away even though I was more than ready for him to take me. "I want to slip into something more comfortable." I had a feeling the underwear would be far from comfortable, but I had heard women say something similar in TV shows.

"Hurry up," he growled. "I can't wait much longer."

I ran into the bedroom and saw some of the underwear we'd bought the other day laid out on the bed. I chose a pair of lacey, light green French panties and the matching bra. John had told me I looked good in green, although I had never been brave enough to wear green underwear. I usually stuck with whites and only occasionally wore black when it would be well hidden anyway.

My clothes hit the floor in a heap, but I left on a pair of high-heeled shoes. Knowing my luck I would end up sticking a heel through Carter's expensive sheets, but being a bit taller made me feel sexier, and right now, that was all that mattered. Once I was "dressed" I looked at myself in a full-length mirror. Usually my eyes were immediately drawn to my prosthetic leg, but now it faded into the background. If Carter didn't care, then why should I?

"I'm ready," I shouted out as I walked over to stand by the bed. My eyes flicked around the room, but I didn't see any of the toys out on display. Sex with Carter was more than enough without any additional contraptions, but I knew he liked to play around in bed, and I wanted him to know he could do that with me.

Carter walked into the bedroom, already unbuttoning his shirt. "I don't know what to say. You look gorgeous, obviously, but that is such a criminal understatement at this point."

"You don't look so bad yourself," I said, admiring his smooth, chiseled stomach. Somewhere in his busy schedule he was obviously finding the time to work out. You didn't get a stomach like that without doing serious time in the gym.

Carter approached and placed his right hand on my left cheek, pulling me in slowly for a kiss while his left hand went to my waist. I was sure I could feel his fingers itching to touch me between my legs, but he managed to resist. I unbuckled his belt and opened his trousers while his tongue moved gracefully inside my mouth. I sat on the bed and pulled him down with me, giving him just enough time to yank off his trousers in the process.

My head hit the pillow as my legs opened, eager for him to take his rightful place between them. Instead he lay next to me on the bed with his lips still pressed against mine, his right hand caressing my stomach, but moving up to my breasts. Suddenly the underwear felt constricting, like it didn't fit and was too tight.

"How long is an appropriate amount of time to wait before I rip this clothing off you?" Carter asked.

"Get it off me," I moaned. "And get the vibrator."

I caught a brief look of surprise on Carter's face, but he quickly went to a drawer and pulled out the combination of pink plastic and rubber that I was surprisingly eager to get inside me.

"You sure?" he asked me. "I don't want you to feel like you're under any pressure."

"You're the one who should feel under pressure. You never know; if I take a liking to this, I may not need you anymore."

Carter flashed a smile that drove me wild. "I think you'll still need me either way. At least, I hope."

After pulling off my panties, he couldn't resist taking a few long, slow licks at my wet slit. He paused to take my firm bud between his lips, sucking gently as his tongue flicked against it. Carter was right; I would always need him, at least until they invented a sex toy that could replicate his strong, knowing tongue. Finally his mouth moved up my body, kissing my stomach and then sucking lightly on my breasts before rejoining my lips. I tasted the hints of my sweet sex on him and closed my eyes as I felt the tip of the toy press against my entrance.

"We can use some lube, if you like?" Carter asked.

"I'm not going to need it."

My eyes rolled to the back of my head as I tore my lips from Carter's, and I let out a loud moan as the toy slipped up inside me and made me whole in a way that only Carter had done before. The vibrator was slightly smaller than Carter's manhood, but it still managed to reach all the places it needed to. He slipped back down between my legs and took control of my pleasure. The toy started to vibrate gently inside me while another part of it buzzed against my button.

I grabbed the headboard as I writhed about on the bed. My back arched off the mattress as I lost control. Carter's firm hands pressed me back down while he turned up the intensity that hummed inside my pussy. The shaft inside me started to spin gently, each turn bringing me new pleasure as it pressed against the rough skin on the top of my tunnel.

Carter's hand still kept my body pressed down against the bed, but my hips were twisting and moving in time with the toy inside my sex. My body strained against him as my orgasm took hold of me.

"I'm coming!" I moaned. "Oh, my God, I'm going to come so hard!"

Carter looked into my eyes as once again he turned up the intensity and strength of the shaft inside me. I forced myself to keep my eyes open and locked on his, staring into his soul until the orgasm hit and my eyes shut and my head snapped back into the pillow. I came so hard that my hips shot into the air despite Carter's hold on me, and the vibrator only just stayed inside me as I covered it with my lust.

When I opened my eyes, Carter was smiling at me and stroking my erect and sensitive nipples. "I take it you enjoyed that?" he said as he slowly removed the toy from my dripping wet pussy.

I was panting hard, barely able to breathe, but I managed a quick nod. "More. I want more."

"I think I can manage that," he said as he pressed the vibrator back against my wet slit.

"No," I groaned. "I want you." I pushed Carter off me and onto his back before climbing onto him. "It's your turn," I said as I sat down on his hard member.

Chapter Seventeen

If there was ever a good time to call my mother, it was the morning after a night with Carter. I loved my parents, obviously, but conversations with them could sometimes get a little tense. Everything would start off pleasant and happy, but after ten minutes or so the conversation would turn to boyfriends and why I don't have one, or work and why I don't have a proper job. Mom tried to be more supportive, and for the most part she was, but she still didn't really get it. She couldn't understand why I didn't just go and work for a big firm and collect a paycheck. But after a night like last night, I was in such a good mood I could handle whatever topic they threw at me.

"Hi, Mom," I said when she finally picked up the phone. "Sorry it took so long for me to return your call. It's been pretty crazy here." Mom had called me two or three times in the past week, but with all the business stuff going on, I didn't really feel in the mood to talk.

"That's all right. I assumed you were busy. How are things going?"

I couldn't tell whether she was referring to work or Carter, so I chose to start with work. "Good. The business is ticking along nicely." There was no point to telling her all the gory details about PharmaTech and their attempts to sabotage us. She would be appalled in that way mothers always were toward someone or something who had hurt their child, but I didn't really need to hear that right now. Mom wouldn't understand that it wasn't as simple as speaking to a lawyer and suing them. Real life wasn't like the trashy TV shows she watched.

"I was actually referring to this man of yours. Carter, isn't it? Is he still yours? I do hope you manage to put the past behind you. From everything you told me, it wasn't his fault, and even Dad is coming around. I think knowing that the driver ended up killing herself has given him some type of resolution. I know that sounds horrible, but it's true. And I think it has tied up a few loose ends, because he always thought Carter's trial was a little odd."

I knew Dad would have been pleased with the news. He reacted badly to Carter being released from prison, and I knew deep down he always wanted the guilty party to pay a bigger price. He would never admit it, but thinking that Bella was dead was the best way for him to move on with his life. I wasn't about to take that away from him by telling Mom the full story.

"We're back together," I said. "Things are going well actually, although there is a minor snag."

"Don't tell me—he's married?" I paused, just long enough to let Mom know she had stumbled on the correct problem. "Oh, Emily, you really shouldn't get involved with a married man. I know he probably tells you he is going to leave her, but—"

"It's okay, Mom. I know everyone probably says this, but it really is okay. The marriage was… odd. It happened while he was still in prison, and they are well and truly separated."

"While he was in prison?" Mom asked. "He's not married to a guy, is he?"

I sighed and rolled my eyes. "No, Mom, he's not married to a guy."

"So they are getting a divorce?"

"Yes," I said, just about managing to hide the uncertainty in my voice. It was a white lie of sorts, but it seemed harmless enough. If Carter and I stayed together, then he would get a divorce. If we didn't, then this minor lie to my mother wouldn't make much difference in the grand scheme of things.

"If it's okay with you, I think I'll leave the being-married thing out of the story when I tell your father. Believe it or not, I think he will be pleased you two are still together. We both like the idea of you having a boyfriend at last, although I can't pretend family meals like Thanksgiving aren't going to be a little awkward."

"That's probably for the best. Dad can be a little old-fashioned with these kinds of things, especially where his daughter is concerned."

"I'm afraid you're still his little girl and always will be."

"I take it Dad isn't there right now?"

"No, he's gone out to buy groceries for dinner. I can't believe I'm going to say this, but tonight he is cooking me dinner. Even more surprisingly, I'm actually looking forward to eating it."

"Does this mean things are a little better between you now?" God, I hoped so. I could really do without my parents fighting right now.

"Yes, I guess you could say that. Like I said, he has improved a bit in these past few weeks and is going to counseling again. I think it's helping this time. We even talk about William now, and we never used to do that. It still hurts, obviously, and the conversations usually end in tears for both of us, but we end up crying on each other instead of alone."

"That's good, Mom. I'm happy to hear that."

With all the important stuff out of the way, Mom and I were able to relax a bit and chat about the usual mother and daughter things, although my mom still had a habit of asking questions about my sex life that I didn't want to answer. I certainly couldn't tell her about last night. I still blushed when I thought about some of the things Carter and I had done in bed. It continued to amaze me that I had the self-confidence to do those things with another man. But Carter was no normal man, and I couldn't believe how lucky I was to have him.

Chapter Eighteen

"I really must stop letting you choose the restaurants," Carter said as he examined the menu at a nice little brunch place I had chosen.

"I thought we had a deal: you choose where we eat for dinner, and I choose where we eat for lunch."

"This is brunch, not lunch."

"And brunch is closer to lunch than dinner, so I get to choose. Stop complaining. This place is great. Just look at the line for a table."

"I don't need to look at the line. We just spent forty minutes waiting in it."

"Oh, hush up, you. I promise you that it's delicious."

"Okay, okay," Carter said, putting down the menu. "I admit, some of the food does sound good."

No sooner had Carter got settled than a waiter came over with water. I cringed, waiting for the inevitable comment.

"Emily, I can't help but notice that our water has been presented to us in glass jars. Not glasses—glass jars. Is this some weird San Francisco hipster thing?"

"It's fun, go with it. Think of it as a type of recycling."

Carter held up his hands in defeat. "As long as our food doesn't get served on cardboard, I suppose I can get on board. You'd think eating prison food for years would make you immune to places like this."

"I like that you don't feel at home in places like this. Now you know how I feel in those expensive restaurants you take me to for dinner. It's kind of funny seeing you look so confused when reading the menu."

"At least it's noisy in here. I actually like that. It may sound a little counterintuitive, but I feel like we actually have some privacy here because no one can hear our conversation."

"Oh yeah, I'd forgotten you actually invited me out for a reason. What did you want to say? Good news, I hope?"

"I certainly hope so, yes. You know how I've been busy a lot lately and we haven't been able to spend much time together?"

"I had noticed, yes." The lack of sex had been driving me crazy. When we did spend the night together, the sex was mind blowing, but then I would have to wait a week for more. I'd spent enough of my life being sexless, and now my body was desperate to make up for lost time.

"The good news is that I should have more free time now. I just had to get something sorted out, and it involved speaking to lots of different people, which made things stressful. But now it's done and I can finally tell you."

Carter had told me he was busy with work on a big deal, but from the way he was talking, it sounded like something else entirely. I certainly hoped he wasn't about to tell me the intimate details of his work; I would struggle to stay awake.

"Go on, then," I said. "The suspense is killing me."

Carter took a deep breath. "I'm getting a divorce. Officially. Everything is in place. I don't know exactly how long it will take—obviously the situation with Bella makes things complicated—but it will happen soon."

I had been staring at Carter, but when he said the word "divorce," my eyes lost focus but had to blink rapidly before I could see again.

"Divorce? Are you sure? I don't want you to do this just because of me."

"I *am* doing it just because of you. You are the reason I do everything now. Can I assume you are pleased with the news?"

I bit my lip and smiled. "You can definitely assume that, yes. Have you mentioned it to her family? How will her sister feel?"

"I have mentioned it to them, yes. They are all fine with it and are still grateful to me for what I did for Bella."

"What happens next? Will this put your green card at risk? I want you to be able to stay in the country, obviously."

"That's what took the most time to figure out. It's all pretty confusing, but the gist of it is that I may lose the green card, but I should be able to transition to a work visa. It's one of the advantages of working for a big international bank. They make it easy to move around."

"Those visas tend to be short-term, though, don't they?"

Carter shrugged. "It isn't a long-term solution, but it will do for now."

I already had a longer-term solution in mind, but I kept it to myself for the time being. If Carter and I could just get through the next couple of years, then with any luck he could get another green card by marrying me. I would even go and live in England with him as long, as I could work remotely on the business. That was the future, though, and right now I just wanted to enjoy the present. John and I had business issues to figure out, but that felt a lot more manageable when my personal life was as strong as this.

Chapter Nineteen

"It's her," John said after I asked him whether Marissa took the bait.

"You're sure? We can't be wrong about this. If we are, we will blow our relationship with our only investor and probably be blacklisted from any further investment opportunities in Silicon Valley."

"I'm sure. I passed on the information to her, and her alone, and now PharmaTech knows." John let out a loud sigh and rubbed the bridge of his nose. I noticed the bags under his eyes and realized he must have been up all night working. "What the hell do we do now?"

"I'm not sure," I admitted. "But we sure as hell aren't going to take it lying down."

"Do we confront her?"

"No, not yet. For one thing, I have no idea how we would do that. She is still an investor—or rather, she is the manager of the LLC that has invested in us—and therefore we will need to tread carefully.

Thank God we didn't give up too much control over the company."

"I have an idea. Or rather, the beginning of an idea. I think we should use this to our advantage."

"How?" I asked.

"Let's give them bad information. I'll need to think on this a bit more, but if we feed her misinformation, we may be able to send PharmaTech off on a wild goose chase."

"Sounds good to me. Let's talk to Scott first, though. I want to get a legal opinion on all this, as well. I'd rather not sue them just yet, but I want to know if we can."

John called Scott's office was able to get us a meeting with him that afternoon. Only an hour, but it was better than nothing.

We walked over to Scott's office, but once again I had dressed inappropriately for the weather. There was a cold wind snapping through the narrow streets and I had nothing covering my arms.

"We're not far from Carter's," I said to John. "He's at work, but I'm just going to nip up to his place and grab a jacket I left there."

We took a short detour and I left John in the main lobby while I popped upstairs. It was nice to be able to enter Carter's apartment without notice, but it felt rude to bring John up there as well. He had already been in Carter's bedroom going through his drawers, and I had felt a little guilty about that ever since.

My jacket was hung on the wall by the entrance, so I barely needed to leave the elevator to get it. But I spotted a pen and paper on the table and couldn't resist leaving a little note for him to find when he got home.

Wish I was here with you right now. E xxx.

I walked into the bedroom and left the note on his pillow. For brief moment I even considered leaving behind the panties I was wearing for him. Unfortunately, my slightly more pragmatic side took over control of my mind and reminded me how cold and windy it was outside. I could do without a cold breeze between my legs if I was going to go commando.

A ping from the elevator told me that Carter was home. Either that, or John had somehow convinced the receptionist to let him upstairs. He was a charming guy and could play the camp gay guy when it suited him, but fortunately, that wasn't very often. I walked to the bedroom door and was about to open it when I heard a woman's voice.

I froze by the door, keeping it slightly ajar but staying out of sight. I hadn't heard what the woman said, but the voice that responded was definitely Carter's.

"We need to be careful or this will fall through," the woman said.

I recognized that voice from somewhere. From the faint footsteps it sounded like the two of them had headed to the kitchen, so I risked a peep through a gap in the door. It was Carter's business colleague, the one he had to spend a lot of time with. At least it wasn't some new woman. I hesitated for just a second, still a little concerned about his relationship with her, but they were standing a few feet apart and didn't look overly touchy-feely. Why did I recognize the voice? I had never spoken to her. In fact, the one time I did try to speak to her, she had practically ignored me and walked away.

"We don't want them to get suspicious," the woman continued.

I froze. I did recognize the voice. It sounded a little different now, because I had only heard her speak over the phone. But there was no doubt about it: I knew that the voice, and my mind went into overdrive trying to figure out what it meant. Carter's colleague, the woman he had been spending so much time with, was Marissa, the woman who was trying to destroy our business on behalf of PharmaTech.

"We're okay for now," Carter said. "They won't suspect their investor."

No. No, it couldn't be. I went weak at the knee in my one good leg. If it weren't for my prosthetic, I would have fallen to the ground.

Carter had been the investor all along. It was Carter who was trying to destroy our business by leaking information to PharmaTech. He headed toward the bedroom, but still hadn't seen me. If this were a movie I would probably have hid in the closet, but I didn't have time. And besides, I had no reason to hide.

"What the hell is going on?" I asked, storming out of the bedroom. "You're the investor," I said, pointing at a bemused-looking Carter. "You've been working with her this whole time to destroy our business. Tell me I'm wrong. Tell me you're not the investor." My voice remained remarkably strong despite both my love life and work life collapsing at the same time.

Carter held his hands up in defense while Marissa walked calmly over from the kitchen and sat down on the sofa.

"You're right, Emily," Carter said softly. "I am the investor. But it's not what it seems—I can explain. Please, sit down. There's so much I need to tell you, and I promise you, you'll want to hear it."

Part Four

Chapter One

"I can explain, I promise," Carter pleaded as he stood just a few feet in front of me.

I glanced down at Marissa, who was sat looking relaxed on the sofa. Even to my jealous eyes, it didn't look like there was anything going on between the two of them, and Marissa certainly didn't look concerned about being caught in the act. That either meant she had covered her tracks well and we wouldn't stand a chance in any lawsuit against her, or there was some other explanation to all this. I desperately wanted to believe it was the latter—both for the sake of my business and my relationship with Carter—but wanting something rarely made it so.

"Sit down, Carter," I said, finding a source of strength inside me I hadn't known existed.

He paused at first and didn't move, but I stared at him until he retreated to take a seat on an armchair. *He didn't sit next to Marissa. That has to be a good sign, right?*

"John is downstairs in the lobby," I continued. "You must have walked right past him. Whatever your supposed explanation is for all this, it is as much John's business as it is mine, so I'm going to get him. I'll be right back."

I forced myself to walk slowly and deliberately to the elevator. I stepped inside and waited for the doors to close before I let the situation overcome me. My legs felt weak, like all the blood had been drained from my muscles. Even the artificial part of me felt drained and I only remained standing by leaning on the handrail. The elevator doors would open in a few seconds, and by that point I had to be composed and ready to talk to John.

This was a business issue that affected both of us. It wasn't the time nor the place to deal with my love life. From a business perspective, nothing much had changed. We knew the investor was screwing us over and that was still the case, even with the knowledge that the investor was Carter. It was a fine distinction, but I tried to keep focused on it.

"John," I said as I approached him. He had taken a seat on one of the sofas and was flicking through a trashy magazine to keep himself up-to-date with celebrity gossip.

"Oh, hey," he replied, standing up and chucking the magazine back on the table. "Are you ready to... Where's your jacket?"

"You need to come back upstairs with me."

"Uh, okay. Why?"

I took a deep breath and blurted out the words. "Because Carter is the investor. Our investor. He's up there now with Marissa. Come on. Apparently, they have an explanation, and I don't know about you, but I'm dying to hear it."

Carter at least had the decency to make some coffee while I was gone. Stimulants might not have been a good idea just then, but I picked up the cup anyway so I would have something to hold in my hands while we talked.

"Emily said that you are the investor?" John asked. Carter nodded. "And you're Marissa? If that is your real name."

"I am, but it's not," 'Marissa' said. "My real name's Kerry, for what it's worth. Kerry Woodson. I signed the investment documents with my real name so you might recognize it."

"I have a few choice names for you, as well," John said.

I'd never known John to be one to keep his emotions hidden—especially anger—but he was doing a decent job of that now. Did that mean he was feeling something else? Fear? Anxiety? I knew I had all those emotions going on, and they were playing havoc with my stomach.

"I'm going to save you the trouble of coming up with any more lies," I said, my eyes fixed on Carter. "Not only do we know you are the investor, but we also know you and her," I shoved a thumb in the direction of Kerry, "were passing our information along to PharmaTech."

"That's correct," Carter said. "But—"

I held up a hand to stop him mid-sentence. "There'll be time for your excuses later. First, I want to know how far back this goes, because there's one thing that has me confused."

"Just the one?" John whispered to me. Now I knew why he was so quiet—he was as confused as I was.

"You never had to have any contact with me," I continued. "You could have invested in our company and taken the information without having a relationship with me. I never gave you any secrets about the business, and you never persuaded me to give them to Marissa. I mean Kerry. Why manipulate me romantically, too?"

I had a double motive for asking that question. I obviously wanted the answer, but it was also my way of letting John know that I hadn't been spilling secrets during pillow talk. A million and one things must have been going through his mind, and I couldn't blame him if he held me partly responsible. This way, I could let him know that we were both in it together and always would be.

"It wasn't like that," Carter said. "Not at all. When I went to that conference I knew you were going to be there, and I knew you were going to be presenting about your company. I went there to see you and find out how you had been doing since the accident."

"And when you saw me, you thought, 'there's a girl I can screw over—literally?'"

"No," Carter said, shaking his head. "I just went to see you. I swear."

"It's my fault," Kerry said, suddenly butting into the conversation. "Carter invited me to the conference, as well. When I saw your presentation, I knew immediately that LimbAnalytics was the perfect company to invest in on behalf of PharmaTech."

Something about Kerry's version of events wasn't ringing true, but I couldn't put a finger on it. "You gave him your business card," I said, thinking back to when I first saw Carter from the stage. He had been talking to a woman and she handed him a business card. "Why would you do that if you already knew him?" That wasn't all that was bugging me, but maybe the answer to that question would lead me down the right path.

"That was a new one," Kerry replied. "Carter didn't believe I worked for PharmaTech until I showed him the card."

She wasn't lying. I wasn't sure how I knew she was telling the truth, but I was confident. Strangely, when she lied, she had more conviction in her voice. Now she just sounded a little fatigued, as if being found out had taken all the fun away and she was just going through the motions.

"Why?" John asked.

"Why what?" Kerry answered.

"Why did Carter invite you to the conference? He said he was there to see Emily, and that kind of makes sense, but what about you? Why were you there?"

That was it. That was the thing that had been bugging me about Kerry's explanation. I could understand why Carter would want to see me; he would have felt guilty about the crash and had probably spent five years in prison thinking about it. But why would he invite Kerry to see me too?

She let out a long, deep sigh. "Carter invited me because he knew I wanted to meet you, as well."

"But why?" I said through gritted teeth.

"Because Bella is my sister."

Chapter Two

I stared into the overly milky coffee that Carter had made, unable to look up and meet Kerry's gaze. "I think I'm going to need something a little stronger."

"Me too," John said, putting his coffee down on the table. "Where do you keep the good stuff?"

"There's whiskey over there on the bookcase," Carter said. "Although even that may not be strong enough for this conversation."

"Sounds like I'll be pouring four glasses, then," John said.

I grabbed some glasses from the kitchen while John brought over the decanter. I didn't consider myself an expert on whiskey, but even I could tell this was a good one just by looking at the smooth texture fill the glass. John and I took the drinks over to Kerry and Carter and sat back down. Judging by the tense look on Carter's face, I felt like the biggest revelations were still to come.

"So, you're the sister?" I asked. Carter had mentioned Bella's sister a few times in passing, but John probably hadn't heard of her. "You were the one who encouraged Carter to marry Bella?"

"Yes," she replied. "At the time, I honestly believed that would make a difference. I was desperate. I would have done anything it took to save my sister, but I regret what I made Carter do. I shouldn't have asked that of him."

"Maybe I'm just being a little slow," John said, "but let me just see if I understand this: even though you two were not the ones responsible for the accident, you both felt some guilt for how things worked out. Once Carter was released from prison, you both decided to go and see Emily to see how she was getting on?"

"That's about the gist of it," Carter said.

"So, where the hell does PharmaTech come in to all of this?" John asked. "And more specifically, why did you bring our company into your weird machinations?"

Kerry and Carter shared a look as if debating just how much they should say.

"I hope you're not considering withholding anything from us right now," I said. "You owe us both the truth after what you did to our business. And you," I looked at Carter. "You owe me for other reasons."

"We decided—" Carter began.

"Let me explain," Kerry said. "It was my idea. The whole thing. I want you to know that, despite how this may look, I *hate* PharmaTech. More than you. Trust me, no one hates that company as much as I do."

Now it was mine and John's turn to share a confused look. "Then why did you give them our secrets? Why go work for them?"

"To take them down." Kerry went silent as if that would be a sufficient explanation for the whole thing. When John and I simply stared back at her, she finally continued. "They killed her. PharmaTech killed my sister. Yes, she made mistakes, but they are responsible for her death."

"This next bit may be a little awkward for you to hear," Carter said.

He was only looking at me, not John, so I knew it must be about his relationship with Bella.

"Bella was on birth control at the time of the accident," Kerry said. "I won't go into all the details, but suffice it to say that she had tried a number of different pills, but they all had side effects. Finally, her doctor prescribed a new one produced by PharmaTech."

At some point, perhaps later today, perhaps next week, the thought of Carter and Bella sleeping together would enter my mind and torture me. I knew they had, of course, but I could have done without such a direct confirmation. For now, my mind was allowing me to focus on what was really important.

"Oh, God. You're not one of those extremist nut jobs, are you?" John asked. "You can't hate every company that produces birth control pills?"

Kerry sighed, frustrated. "No, I'm not. It wasn't that she was on birth control. The problem was that the pill was faulty. It messed her up pretty bad."

Oh, God. Bella was pregnant. Carter had a child.

"Not in that way," Carter quickly said, reading my mind.

"We later found out that the pill had not gone through all the required testing. PharmaTech had bribed and leaned on a few people at the FDA to get approval. Once they had that, they shoved the drug out to market."

"I'm sure I'm going to sound like a jerk now," John said, "but this doesn't explain why you would give them our information. If you hate them, why help them?"

"We didn't help them."

"You gave them information on our patent," I said. "And you messed up a big contract for us. That was plenty of help, by my standards."

"Not really," Kerry said with a shrug. "I altered the patent design enough so that PharmaTech thinks it has something useful, but it doesn't. I admit we blew the contract with the military for you, but trust me, that is going to work in your favor when the time comes."

I looked at John but he just shrugged, none the wiser than I was. Kerry was speaking more cryptically than I liked, so I turned to Carter for better answers. "I assume you were doing it out of some sense of loyalty to Bella, but what was the point of the whole scheme?"

Carter sat forward in his seat and interlaced his fingers. "Yes. I formed the company to be the official investor. Kerry needed to be separate so that there was no doubt she did what she did on behalf of PharmaTech. We're going to take them down, Emily. But we'll need your help."

"Everything I did, legally speaking, I did on behalf of PharmaTech, and that means they are responsible. They stole your patent, interfered with a military contract, and generally screwed you over in other ways you don't even know about yet."

"So, your big plan is for us to sue them and get damages? How is that going to punish them? They can afford it. And by the time we've paid the legal fees, that will hardly benefit us."

"Damages aren't the main goal," Carter said. "We just needed a strong case that can get us into federal court—that's why we made sure there were lots of different issues at play. Patent law, contract law, interference with a military contract. We could take this case into any court in the country because of that."

"But we don't want to end up in court, anyway," Kerry said. "Once the case gets started, we can start asking all sorts of questions about their business affairs. With a bit of luck, we can get information about their bribery in the drug trials and then leak that to the public."

"The only way you can hurt people like this is through their wallets," Carter said. "This will make their stock price crash and burn like you wouldn't believe."

"In other words," John said, "Emily and I are just the unlucky ones stuck in the middle of your little vendetta?"

Carter nodded. "Sorry."

"Well," John said, standing up. "This has been fun and all, but I don't want anything to do with this. What about you, Emily?"

"I agree with John," I said. "I'm still trying to process all this, but what I can comprehend is that you have used our business to suit your own ends." I kept the topic of conversation on business while John was present, but I knew this would affect my relationship with Carter too. It had to. This wasn't a typical romantic betrayal with another woman, but it was still a lie, and our fledgling relationship had seen its fair share of them already.

"We still need you," Kerry said. "Your company has to be the one to sue them."

"Why the hell should we do that?" I asked. "This isn't our fight."

"She's right, Kerry," Carter said, taking a long sip of his drink. "We have to leave it now and let them move on with their business."

Kerry threw a look at Carter that even made me lean back in my seat. "Carter, we have to—"

"Drop it Kerry."

"Uh, hell no," John said. "Whatever it is, you are going to tell us, or we *will* be suing someone and it won't be PharmaTech."

"You want to do this as much as we do," Kerry said. "Well, Emily—you do, at least."

"What do you mean?" I asked.

"The problem with the birth control pill is that it could mess up the body's nervous system," Kerry explained. "You can probably understand it better than me, but basically, certain triggers could react with the drug and you would lose all control of your body."

"What type of triggers?" I asked.

348

"Certain alcoholic drinks. Not mainstream drinks, for the most part—that's how PharmaTech managed to keep this secret. They didn't tell doctors about this, so Bella had no idea that drinking would cause so many problems."

"What does this have to do with me?" I asked, trying to remain calm. I was ready to storm out, and Kerry's sob story was dragging on far too long.

"That's what caused the accident, Emily," she said. "The drugs produced by PharmaTech wreaked havoc on Bella's nerves that night and sent her off the road. She shouldn't have been drinking of course—and the drug doesn't excuse her behavior after the accident—but that doesn't change the fact that it was a reaction to the drug that caused the crash. You need to help us get back at PharmaTech because that company is responsible for your brother's death."

Chapter Three

"Do you have any idea what you want to do?" John asked the next morning.

After the conversation with Carter and Kerry, I had insisted we both go our separate ways to give us some time to think. I knew I needed time alone, and John probably needed it even more. This was his company too, and the problem with PharmaTech was much more my issue than his. I reminded him that we didn't have to make every decision together—we weren't a married couple—and that he needed time to dwell on it as much as I did.

"Not really," I lied. I knew exactly what I wanted to do; the hard part was convincing myself it was the right thing for all parties. I wanted—no, needed—to take down PharmaTech. How could I not, after what they did? But that didn't make it the right decision. I had no idea what I would be getting into. More importantly, I wasn't sure if I could live with myself if it all went tits-up and I took John down with me.

"We don't *need* to do anything," I said. "I shouldn't let personal issues affect the business, especially not when I have a business partner."

"I'm quite capable of making my own decisions," John said tersely. He didn't look like he'd had much sleep and his hair was unusually disheveled. "I agree, though. We don't need to do anything. We were chugging along quite nicely before they got involved, and I'm quite sure we can cope without them if they disappear—uh, business-wise, at least."

"My relationship with Carter cannot come into this," I said, and I meant every word. "We have to make a business decision, first. After that, I will worry about my love life."

"I *would* like to see PharmaTech suffer," John admitted. "None of what Kerry and Carter told us changes the fact that they were using our information for their own ends. And if all that stuff about the drug is true, then that company is every bit as bad as we thought and then some."

I'd tried not to think too much about the faulty birth control pills. Not because it reminded me of how close Carter was to Bella, although that didn't help, but because it made me angry with PharmaTech. I couldn't let anger cloud my judgment right now; this was a life-changing decision for John and me.

"I'm sorry," I said.

"What for?"

"This is all my fault. If it hadn't been for me and my past, none of this would have happened. Kerry and Carter only started playing around with our business because of me. I wish we'd never done that presentation at the conference. I'm sorry I inflicted all this on you."

"There's so much wrong with that, I don't even know where to start. For one thing, if it weren't for you, then there would be no business in the first place. I'm just a tech guy. I wouldn't have known where to start with all this. If I'm honest, without having known you and seen the trouble you went through with your leg, I doubt I would have even been interested in this type of business. But more importantly, I can assure you that PharmaTech would have come after us, anyway. In the end, Kerry was the one to feed them information, but if she hadn't been around, they would have got it some other way."

"You don't know that," I replied, though I was grateful for his confidence in me.

"Oh, come on. This is a company that bribed people to get a drug on the market without proper testing. People have died because of this company, so don't go blaming yourself."

I sighed and slouched down onto the sofa. I didn't think well in silence and I needed some background noise. I grabbed the remote and switched on the TV. I hardly ever watched it and usually just relied on Netflix or some other streaming service for my binge-watching pleasure. Still, at least there was some noise around me other than my gears turning.

"Sounds like we are leaning toward fighting them," John said. He sat down next to me.

"Yes, but are we doing this for the right reasons? You know this could end in a courtroom."

"Well, it's a good job Judge Judy is on TV right now, then. Maybe we can learn something."

I laughed louder than the joke probably warranted, but it was nice to smile again. I had a feeling Judge Judy would be on our side, but I couldn't see PharmaTech agreeing to have such a big dispute decided on national television.

I had just gotten interested in the case at hand— some former couple arguing about whether the woman should give an engagement ring back—when a commercial break interrupted the show.

"If there's one thing worse than daytime television," John said, "it's the adverts on daytime television."

We were watching images of a young family frolicking in the sun and enjoying life thanks to some miracle drug that had cured their daughter's illness. The long list of grim-sounding side effects seems to contradict the happiness of the family, but the whole idea was that you weren't supposed to think about the negatives, I guess.

The writing at the bottom of the screen was hard to read because the text was white on a white background, but at the end of the commercial, I caught a glimpse of the company that developed the drug. It was none other than PharmaTech.

"Did you see that?" John asked.

I nodded, and then realized John wasn't looking at me. "Yes. I saw."

"I know this sounds stupid, but in all this I kind of forgot they were still pushing drugs out there. I've been seeing them as our rivals—and they are—but they are much more than that."

"You're right. They're marketing drugs to be used on children. How do we know those drugs weren't pushed through the approval process the same way the one that killed Bella was?"

"Are you thinking what I am thinking?" John asked.

I turned and looked at him before giving a slow, deliberate nod. "Let's go get them."

Chapter Four

"Are you absolutely sure about this?" Carter asked. "Both of you? Because you shouldn't underestimate what you are getting into. Kerry downplays it sometimes, but this is huge."

I had waited another day before messaging Carter with our decision. We figured that if we still hadn't had any second thoughts after a night's sleep, then it must mean we had come to the right decision. Carter invited us round to his place again to discuss the next steps, and he'd insisted we get there before Kerry so he could talk to us alone.

"I'm with Kerry in all this, obviously," he continued, "but you don't have to be. There's still time to back out."

"We're sure, Carter," I said. "We wouldn't be here otherwise."

"But don't go thinking you've gotten away with the whole lying-to-us thing," John said quickly. "I'm still pissed about that, and you can be damn sure Emily will have some choice words to say to you in private, as well."

I nodded, but after making sure that John couldn't see my face, I smiled at Carter. We'd already had a few conversations over texts where he apologized profusely and swore I knew everything now. Much to my surprise, I hadn't even been that mad at him. Maybe if he'd used me and our relationship to get information on the business it would have been unforgivable, but he'd rarely asked me for any details and had seemed completely disinterested.

During his apology, he told me he had compartmentalized the PharmaTech issue from the relationship with me, and looking back on our time together, I could completely believe that. Plus, there was some comfort in seeing how far Carter would go for someone he cared about. If he would do that for Bella, someone he gave up loving a long time ago, I could only imagine how far he would go for me now.

"First of all," I said once Kerry had arrived, "John and I will be making all the key decisions."

"We will listen to what you want to do, of course," John said. "But if we don't like it, we don't do it. It's our company that will be doing the suing, and once we do this, our company name will be on all the official complaints filed with the court. I'm still not entirely comfortable with that, but at least we are the ones filing the suit and not being sued."

"We completely understand," Carter said. "Don't we, Kerry?"

Kerry nodded. I wished she would be a little less standoffish with us, but she seemed to like staying behind an emotional barrier. The only times her voice betrayed any emotion was when she was talking about PharmaTech.

"So, how does this all play out, then?" I asked. "What's the first step?"

"First, we need to get a lawyer," Kerry said. "I know some good ones who have experience in this kind of complex litigation."

"We already have a lawyer," I said. "Scott's good, and he has looked after us so far."

Despite our speech about how John and I would be making the decisions, Kerry looked to Carter for his opinion on the matter.

Carter shrugged. "This Scott guy, he works for a big firm, right?"

"Pretty big, yes."

"Then I'm sure that's fine. As long as they don't have a conflict of interest by representing PharmaTech in other matters, I am okay with it."

"This way, we keep the number of people involved at a minimum," John said. "Scott already knows some of the details, anyway, because he filed the patent applications."

"All right," Kerry relented. "We'll keep your lawyer. Unless this Scott guy has any better suggestions, we will try to initiate a lawsuit in military court, first. That will never work—they will have the case removed and sent to another court—but it's a good first play to get them worried. Companies like PharmaTech have huge contracts with the U.S. government and won't want their name involved in a dispute with the military."

"That's when the really interesting stuff will start," Carter said. "They have done so many different things to your business that we can get into federal court."

"Why is that so good?" I asked.

"Because the federal courts in this district have a good record of looking after the small guy and awarding large sums in cases of corporate abuse like this."

I had no idea how Carter knew all this stuff, but I suspected the information had come from Kerry. She obviously had substantial resources and had probably done, or paid someone to do, the research before she started down this road.

"Will the case be heard by a jury?" John asked.

"Maybe," Kerry said. "It's possible, and that will be part of the negotiation. But the actual court case and the trial are just side issues. Most cases don't make it to court."

"So, we're just doing all this to settle?" I asked.

"No, not exactly. But the damage will be done before the trial, if there is one. Companies like PharmaTech get hit with lawsuits every day, and most of the cases are easily dismissed or they just settle. With this one, what we want to do is make sure it gets publicity, because that's where we really do the company—and more importantly, the people in charge of the company—the most harm."

"I have some contacts in the press," Carter said. "At the appropriate time, I will leak a few juicy bits of information to them. Enough to get them taking a closer look at the court filings."

"What about the faulty drug?" John asked. "The court case is just going to be about what they did to us, so how we can get information about the drug out there?"

"I must admit, I don't have that entirely worked out yet," Kerry admitted. "Maybe that is where Scott will be able to help us. There will be lots of depositions—which is where we get to ask them questions under oath—and I intend to get them to comment on the drug somehow. Anything they say on the record goes into the court filings, so we just need to get them to trip up once."

"There's something else you need to think about," Carter said. "It's nothing to worry about, but whenever you sue someone, the other party nearly always initiates what's called a counter suit."

"But we haven't done anything wrong," I said.

"That doesn't matter," he told me, shaking his head. "They will find something, or just make something up."

"Why?"

"Just to put you under pressure and scare you. They will take your deposition and ask lots of questions. Obviously, your lawyer will protect you and make sure you don't answer any questions you don't have to. I just wanted to warn you, because they can be quite intimidating."

"Bring it on," John said. "I quite fancy being grilled by expensive lawyers. You never know, I might even get a date out of it."

I knew that wasn't just bravado on John's part. He really wouldn't be concerned or nervous about being questioned by lots of men and women in suits. Unfortunately, the thought of that scared me more than I was willing to admit. Even if I could answer their questions, I would still feel nervous. It would be like going for a job interview where you knew you were qualified for the position, but were still worried you would mess it up.

"So," Kerry said, "are you two definitely okay with this? It's going to be a tough battle, but they deserve what's coming to them."

"I'm down for it," John said. "Let's get to them and see what that we can dig up."

"Emily?" Carter asked. "What about you?"

I took a deep breath in and slowly exhaled out, trying to control the slight shaking I felt in my body. "I'm in. Let's do it."

Chapter Five

Over the past couple of days I had seen plenty of Carter, but only when Kerry and John were around. When we were discussing the business, Carter was professional at all times, as if the whole thing were just another business transaction. I suppose it was, in some ways, but it left me frustrated that I hadn't seen enough of his smile or heard enough of his jokes. I even found myself longing to hear more of his comments—or more accurately, criticisms—on American life.

Thankfully, once we had all agreed on the plan of action and set up a meeting with Scott, Carter invited me out to dinner at another insanely expensive restaurant that was so out of my price range I had never even heard of it.

As I got ready, I started to wish I had let him buy me some high-end designer dresses for the evening. Not that I needed to wear them, or even felt comfortable wearing them, but at least I wouldn't feel quite so out of place in restaurants like the one I was on the way to now.

Carter had picked a great night for a date. I was having a horrendous day and I really needed to see his face and feel the touch of his hand on mine.

When shopping in the morning, I had gone to pay for groceries and noticed that my bank card was missing. I searched everywhere for it at home, assuming I had just left it on my dresser, but after an hour of searching the entire house it was nowhere to be seen. After forking out for groceries, I had $50 in cash on me and my bank promised to get a new one out to me tomorrow. It wasn't a huge deal until I remembered that without a credit card I couldn't use the app on my phone to get a ride to the restaurant. Instead, I ended up in one of the overpriced San Francisco taxis that took half of my measly cash from me.

By the time I got to the restaurant, I was hoping Carter had arrived before me and ordered some drinks because I really needed a glass of wine. Instead I was escorted to an empty table in the back corner of the restaurant. The walls were almost entirely made of glass and I had a great view of the city, although at night it was mainly lights. But still, the frenzied movement of thousands of cars through the streets, like ants bringing food to and from the nest, was kind of fascinating when you sat back and looked at it.

"Will your friend be here soon, ma'am?" the waiter asked, appearing beside me.

I glanced at the time on my phone; Carter was fifteen minutes late, which was not like him at all. I didn't mind too much—my phone and the decent Wi-Fi connection were more than enough to keep me amused—but it wasn't like him to be late.

"I just got a message from him saying he was running late," I lied. "He'll be here any minute, though."

"Would you like to drink while you wait?"

"Oh, God, yes," I said. "Just bring me a dry white wine. A large one."

"Certainly, ma'am."

Once the waiter was out of sight, I sent Carter a message asking him where he was and then went back to answering emails. If I was going to be stuck here by myself, I might as well make the most of the time to be productive.

"Your friend has still not arrived, ma'am," the waiter said as he placed my glass of wine on the table. It wasn't so much a question as an accusation.

"Traffic must be bad, I guess. You know how it gets in San Francisco."

"Quite."

The waiter made no effort to hide his displeasure and I made a mental note to tell Carter not to tip as generously as he usually did—assuming he ever actually arrived. He was now thirty minutes late. I sent another message and this time made it clear that I wanted a reply, at the very least. I didn't mind if we had to cancel or postpone dinner, but I did want him to at least tell me.

As I sat there alone at the table, I noticed why the waiter was concerned about Carter's late arrival. The restaurant might have been expensive, but it was popular, and I could already see some disgruntled guests looking less than pleased that I was taking up the best table in the restaurant by myself and not eating. The restaurant was small and I felt like all sets of eyes were on me. Finally a message came through on my phone.

Sorry, I can't make it tonight. C.

That was it. No explanation or excuse at all. The waiter was already on his way over having no doubt noticed the expression on my face.

"Ma'am, I am very sorry, but it doesn't look like your friend will be coming this evening."

"How much do I owe you for the wine?"

"I will go bring the check."

"Just tell me how much the damn glass of wine cost," I said, raising my voice just loud enough for the entire restaurant to hear.

The waiter pulled out his notepad and pen and wrote the price down, as if speaking it aloud would somehow spoil the illusion. I had just enough cash left to pay for my one measly glass of wine, although probably not enough for the tax and tip. I threw all my cash down on the table, picked up the glass, necked back the remaining wine, and then stormed out of the restaurant.

California was suffering from a drought, so the chances of it raining were slim. But as I said, I was having a really bad day. I ran out of the restaurant and straight into the rain, which was hammering down hard enough that anyone without a strong umbrella was ducking under shelter or running into nearby shops.

I had no credit card, and after paying for the wine, I had no cash. There was no way I could get all the way back to my place in one piece, but Carter's was not that far. Besides, I owed him a piece of my mind. I stayed under cover of the restaurant for a few minutes until I finally decided to make a run for it. Well, "run" might not be quite the right word—I had on high heels and only one real leg, after all—but I moved as fast as I could.

After only a few seconds, I had got as wet as I was going to get, so I slowed down a little bit to avoid slipping and falling on my ass; that would really top off this fantastic day.

The receptionist in Carter's building didn't say anything, but did give me a sympathetic look indicating that she knew she was looking at a woman who had been stood up. If I hadn't been angry before, I soon became mad as hell as I stood in the elevator, shivering and shaking with the cold. With everything that was going on right now, the last thing I needed was a cold or flu to deal with.

As soon as the elevator doors opened, I started pulling off my wet clothes, making my way to the bathroom to get changed. I hadn't expected Carter to be at home. I assumed whatever weak excuse he had for not showing up for our date was related to work. Instead, I opened the bedroom door and found him sat on the end of the bed with his head down.

"What the hell, Carter?!" I yelled, throwing my wet shirt down on the floor. "You've been here all this time?"

Carter looked up at me, and I could see from the redness around his face that he had been crying.

"What's happened?" I asked, rushing to his side.

"I probably shouldn't talk to you about it."

"Don't be silly. It's obvious something that has upset you."

"I'm okay," he said, taking a deep breath. "I'm in a state of shock more than anything. Just not too sure how to react."

"We have to talk. What happened?"

"I just got a call from Kerry. Bella passed away today."

Chapter Six

The next morning, John and I had our big meeting with Scott to finalize our plans for the lawsuit. We met in an impressive—and ludicrously expensive—reception area where we waited for him to finish up another meeting.

"You're surprisingly quiet this morning, considering you spent the night at Carter's," John remarked. "Usually you are all bubbly and annoyingly chipper."

"How do you even know I stayed at Carter's?" I asked. "Don't tell me you slept at my place last night?"

"No, I'm actually getting used to staying at my place now. The clothes were the giveaway. I've not seen them before, which means they must be the ones you bought to leave at Carter's."

Touché, I thought. "I did stay at Carter's, but we didn't have sex."

"Oh, is it… you know…?"

"No, it's not my time of the month."

I told John about Bella passing away and how Carter and I spent the night in bed together, but he just held me in his arms as we both drifted off to sleep.

"How do you feel about all this?" John asked. "I know it sounds a bit heartless, but this must be difficult for you, what with the whole 'she was married to your boyfriend' thing."

"Honestly, I have no idea how I feel. On the one hand, she was partly responsible for killing my brother and obviously shouldn't have been drinking and driving, but on the other hand, that drug by PharmaTech messed her up, so they have to share the blame."

"What about Carter's reaction to it all? You aren't mad at him for missing dinner and for being so upset?"

I shook my head. "Not at all. Given how important she once was to him, I think he's handling it remarkably well. And he's not reacting like he is still in love with her. I believe him more than ever about that. I know he loved her once, but I don't think he has for quite some time."

"This is just going to make Kerry even more determined to get her revenge on PharmaTech."

"I know. We're going to have to make sure we retain control of all this. In fact, I'm going to ask Carter to have her back off a little bit. She can be involved when she needs to be, but for the most part, he should be the one to pass information on to her. That way, she won't to be able to put pressure on us."

"Good idea." Something behind me caught John's attention. "My God, is that him? I hope it's him."

I turned around and looked at the man walking our way. Carter had spoiled me, so other men did not easily impress me now, but even I had to admit that this lawyer was easy on the eyes.

"Hi," he said, extending his hand to me. "You must be Emily and John. I'm Scott. So nice to meet you in person.

"Hi, Scott," I said, shaking his hand firmly. John muttered something that I couldn't understand, and judging by Scott's confused expression, I didn't think he could either.

"I've got a meeting room reserved. Follow me."

Scott was more slender than Carter, so he didn't bulge muscle through the suit in quite the same way Carter managed, but he did have a nice physique and was no stranger to the gym. I couldn't deny being attracted to him, but it was more a feeling of wanting to go home and jump on Carter as opposed to actually wanting Scott.

"Calm down," I whispered to John. "He might not be gay, and he might not be single."

"I don't care if he's single; I can work on that. And if he's even the least bit curious I'm going to try my luck."

Scott showed us into a small meeting room with a table in the middle and four chairs. Despite the room being small, it didn't feel overly cramped thanks in part to the glass walls letting in an abundance of light. Another young and attractive attorney was already sitting down at the table.

"Emily, John, please let me introduce you to Bethany."

John and I shook hands with her and we all sat down at the table. Bethany screamed "junior attorney." She looked like she was in her early twenties and had a soft, timid way about her. She was probably here for the experience of meeting clients, and perhaps she would end up doing some of the research on our case. I knew enough about how law firms worked to know that senior associates didn't do the research if they didn't have to. That was fine with me. It usually ended up being cheaper that way.

"I'm here because I will be helping Scott with your case," Bethany said, confirming my suspicions.

"From what you told me so far," Scott said, "there will be a lot of litigation involved, and that's not really my area of expertise. Bethany is a senior litigator at the firm, and she has an excellent record at settling cases and winning them if they end up going to court."

Senior litigator? Bethany didn't look like she was a senior anything, except maybe a senior in college. In addition to looking a little young, I had always imagined that litigators were tougher and more hard-nosed. I had trouble imagining Bethany scaring the expensive lawyers at PharmaTech.

"I always settle cases, if possible," she added. "Going to court is so expensive for clients, so if we can get a good deal without going to trial, I always recommend to the client that they accept it. But I am more than willing to go to bat for you in court, if necessary."

"We'd rather avoid court, as well," John said. "Has Emily explained the motivation behind this case?"

"This isn't just about the patent and military contract," I said. "Those are the things we know they have done wrong, but we really want to expose them for something else."

Scott frowned and looked confused, but Bethany didn't seem so surprised. Many cases were probably about petty revenge as opposed to legal issues, so she was probably used to it.

"From what Scott has told me," she said, "PharmaTech has done a lot wrong, and in different areas of the law. That gives us a lot of flexibility here. The best approach is probably for you to tell me what you want to achieve and I will figure out a way to do it. I hate to spoil any illusions you may have at the justice system, but the fact of the matter is that we have a lot of power to do harm without even getting into a courtroom. I'm sure we can help with your objectives, so tell me what you want to do."

I explained everything we knew about PharmaTech and how they had bribed government officials to get their faulty drugs on the market. If Bethany was skeptical about our claims, she didn't show it. At the end of the meeting, she explained that we had a good case but that the tricky bit would be getting PharmaTech to talk about the drug. She promised to come up with a plan, yet warned us that the process would take a while and we shouldn't expect miracles. Unfortunately, Bethany would need a large retainer fee, but she promised to discuss the possibility of a contingency fee with a partner.

"That went about as well as can be expected," I said as we left the law firm.

"I don't agree," John said. "I'm disappointed. Scott is clearly not gay."

"How do you know that?"

"Didn't you see the way he and Bethany were looking at each other? There's definitely something going on between those two. I guess he could swing both ways, but the odds of that are not in my favor, and I don't fancy getting in the middle of those two. I mean that literally and figuratively."

"I couldn't really picture you with a lawyer, anyway. Part of the problem with Tom was that he had a more boring job than you did. You need someone with exotic lifestyle like yourself."

"I suppose I had better get out on the town tonight, then. Fancy joining me for a drink?"

"Sure, why not? I know Carter could do with a drink."

"No, don't bring him. I want to pick up a guy, and I can hardly do that with him around soaking up all the attention."

"Just make sure we go to an actual gay bar this time."

"Don't worry. I won't be making that mistake again. This place will be all gay males and their girlfriends."

"I'm leaving as soon as you pick up a guy."

"With any luck, you won't even finish your first drink."

Chapter Seven

The day of Bella's funeral arrived quickly. I had assumed her death had been a shock to all concerned like it was to me, but her parents had known it was coming and made the choice to switch off the life-support machine. Carter asked me to accompany him to the burial, but I had to refuse. I wanted to be by his side, but I couldn't bring myself to go. The whole thought of it seemed more than a little weird, but he insisted it would be okay and that he wanted me there with him. In the end, we compromised and I agreed to go to the reception that took place afterwards. He came by and picked me up on the way there.

"I'm still not sure this is a good idea," I said as I stepped into the car. "What will her family think of you bringing me?"

"I told you, they are completely fine with it. In fact, they want you to be there. You have to remember that they still feel a great deal of guilt that their daughter was to blame for your brother's death. And they are happy I have moved on. They're really nice people, and they aren't naïve. They know Bella and I were young at the time and we weren't destined to be together."

"I just don't want to upset anyone."

"The only way you will upset people is by not being there," Carter insisted. "Now, tell me how you got on the other night going for drinks with John."

"It was fun, I guess, while it lasted. I finished my first drink and then went to the bar to buy the next round while John talked to some guy he met. When I came back, the two of them were already... hooking up, so I was left holding two drinks with no one to talk to."

Carter couldn't contain his laughter. "Only in a gay bar could an attractive woman like you be left standing alone."

"It was quite depressing. I even had a free drink for anyone who would come speak to me. I suppose it's better than being harassed all the time in the normal bars."

Carter seemed in relatively good spirits, considering the occasion. He probably felt as awkward as I no doubt would at this thing. After all, he was technically bringing his new girlfriend to his wife's funeral reception. Despite what he said about the family being happy for him, the circumstances were no doubt uncomfortable for him, too.

The reception was being held at Bella's parents' house. Given how rich I knew Bella's family was, I was surprised to see that they lived in a relatively modest house. It was probably the family home they grew up in before making it big. That said, the cars in the driveway cost more than some people's houses and more than made up for the lack of value in the house itself.

I half-expected the room to go quiet and for everyone to turn and look at us as we walked in, but it was filled with the sound of ten different conversations taking place at once. No one even noticed us arrive.

"Come on," Carter said, "let's go get the difficult bit done first."

Carter took me by the hand and led me to the kitchen where we found Bella's mom preparing food for her guests. I took a deep breath and stood up straight, hoping to make a positive first impression on my boyfriend's former mother-in-law.

"Teresa, this is Emily. Emily, this is Teresa, Bella's mom."

"Pleased to meet you," I said, offering out my hand. She ignored it, instead kissing me on the cheek and putting her arms around me for a quick, but intense, hug. "I'm so sorry," I whispered into her ear. "About Bella. I never met her, but Carter made her sound like an incredible person."

That wasn't exactly true, but I could hardly have said otherwise under the circumstances.

"It's very sweet of you to say so, dear. I can't speak ill of my daughter, especially not now, but I want you to know how bad we feel about the accident. We knew she was drinking more than she should have been at the time, but we had no idea she would drink and drive. I thought we brought her up better than that. After what happened... We just didn't know what to do. I wonder whether we could have been more strict with her, but—"

"It's not your fault," I said, placing a hand on her shoulder. Teresa was on the verge of tears and probably would have already been crying if she were not all cried out from the funeral. "Carter explained about the drugs. I know she made a mistake by drinking, but people make mistakes when they're young. I would do anything to get my brother back, but I'm going to focus my anger on those who are truly responsible."

"If I ever get my hands on those involved, you can be sure they will pay." Theresa had quickly moved from being upset to being angry, but I could hardly blame her for not being in control of her emotions on a day like today. "If you ever find out who they are, just tell me where they live. I'll see to the rest"

I nodded and promised to get revenge for Bella and William. But even if I did find out where they lived, there was no way I would tell Teresa about it. I believed her when she said she would go and take out her anger and grief on them, and that didn't seem like it would help our case. I would make them pay, but my idea of punishment would be to strip them of all their money and let them spend their days rotting in prison.

We didn't stay too long at the reception, but I made sure to meet Bella's father and speak to Kerry. She must have told her father about the lawsuit, because he asked a lot of questions and wanted to know how it was proceeding. We didn't have a lot to tell him, but he was pleased to know it was moving forward. To my surprise, Kerry didn't ask too many questions and seemed more preoccupied keeping various family members from fighting. Bella had had a big family with lots of cousins and aunts and uncles, and it was clear they didn't all get along. Not everyone looked like they were as rich as Kerry's family, and I suspected the money had caused a lot of tension between them.

The most surprising news of the day was that Bella had a brother. Neither Carter nor Kerry had ever mentioned a brother. Carter did go and speak to him at one point, but I was never introduced to him.

"See, that wasn't too bad, was it?" Carter said once we were back in the car.

"No. I'm glad we went. I think I have a better understanding now of what Bella went through and what the family meant to you. I can see that you were close to all of them and not just to Bella. That makes this all a little easier to understand."

"I'm so glad to hear you say that. I hope you don't mind, but I'd like a couple of days to myself, just to get a few things in order."

"Sure. Take as long as you need."

"Thanks. I'm ready to put this whole thing behind me now. I know we still have the lawsuit to deal with, but as far as I'm concerned, that is now completely separate. My previous relationship with Bella is a thing of the past. Let's focus on us, okay?"

"You read my mind," I said, putting my hand on his thigh and leaning back my head back on the headrest where I drifted off to sleep for the rest of the journey home.

Chapter Eight

Without wanting to get too carried away, it did seem like John had met the perfect man for him. The guy he picked up in the bar, Michael, was casual and laid-back, and he worked as a waiter in one of the trendy bars in San Francisco. This meant he had an erratic schedule, so now John was the one complaining that he was never able to see his boyfriend. It was an interesting switch up, which I took great pleasure in teasing him about.

John had resorted to eating most of his meals at the restaurant where Michael worked just so that he could see him. This worked out well for me, because John often wanted company and meant I got a table without standing outside in the hour-long line. They didn't take reservations—that seemed to be a common trait for the hipster places in San Francisco—so usually you had to go and write your name on a list and then wait. John and I got to walk right past all that and sit down at a table. I knew John was using me just so that he had someone to talk to, but there were plenty of benefits for me too, so I looked past it.

Unless I was eating at one of Carter's restaurants, I found it impossible to go out in San Francisco in the evening without feeling overdressed.

Even in just a simple pair of jeans and skimpy top, I seemed to look like I had put in more effort than everyone else. Of course, I had actually put in less effort, because while the locals liked to pretend they didn't care how they looked, the opposite was usually true. It took effort to squeeze into those skinny jeans and the weird clothing combos were actually coordinated with a great deal of thought put into them.

While I felt slightly out of place, it was nothing compared to the man in a suit sitting at a table by himself in the corner of the room. He could have been a poor relation of Carter's, but fell just short in every department. He was good-looking, but you wouldn't stop and stare at him. The suit looked expensive, but wasn't made to measure like Carter's were. He had an air of confidence or perhaps arrogance about him, though, and might also have been in a similar line of work.

"See that man over there?" I asked John with a subtle nod toward the corner of the room.

"Yeah. Why?"

"I'm going to guess he is only in town for a conference. He looks like he's from the East Coast, judging by the suit and tie he's wearing. Probably saw that this place is highly rated on one of those review apps and figured he would pop in. I bet he had quite a shock when he walked into a place like this."

John smiled. "Yeah, this doesn't look like it's that kind of place, does it? But then, I guess we shouldn't judge by appearances. Carter seems to have gotten the hang of places like this now."

"I'm not sure I would go that far, but I am trying to get him to broaden his horizons a little bit. I'm not sure whether it's the food, the people, or both, but he's getting used to it. Anyway, I'm not giving him much choice in the matter. I love the expensive restaurants he's taking me to, but I can't eat at them all the time. I find it kind of exhausting being on such good behavior in public. It's like you can't really be yourself, you know?"

"Unfortunately not," John said. "I don't have as much experience eating in lah-de-dah restaurants as you do."

"How about next time, you come with us? Actually, why don't we make it a double date— Carter, me, you, and your new man?"

"We may have to save up a bit first, unless—"

"Hello, John. Emily. How are you?"

I hadn't even noticed anyone approach, but the man in the suit was now standing at our table looking down at us with a cheerful grin. He knew our names, so my instant reaction was to think that I had met him somewhere and forgotten him, but as I stared up at his face I was sure I did not recognize him.

"Um, hi," John said. "Can we help you?"

"Oh, it's more about how I can help you. Mind if I take a seat?" The man didn't wait for an answer. He pulled over a chair from another table that no one seemed to be using—although he didn't ask—and sat down with us.

"Do we know you?" I asked, inching my seat ever so slightly away from him. There was something about him that I didn't feel comfortable with, not to mention that it seemed incredibly inappropriate to sit down with people before introducing yourself.

"No, you don't, but I think we will get to know each other quite well over the next couple of months. My name is Brian Smithson. Not ringing any bells? I'm the CEO of a little company called PharmaTech."

For all intents and purposes, the CEO was in charge of the company, and in theory, dictated company policy. In other words, if PharmaTech had been bribing people to push its drugs onto markets, this guy would know about it. Hell, he was probably the guy who came up with the idea. I had no clue what to say to him; I wasn't sure if we even could talk to him. Did he know about the lawsuit? It would be one heck of a coincidence if he were here otherwise.

"I've just come from having a nice little chat with our lawyers," Brian said. He retained a smile on his face, as if he was giving good news. It freaked me out no end. "We get sued all the time. It comes with the territory. But usually, those lawsuits are just against the company, so you can imagine my surprise when the lawyers said that I had been named personally in the suit."

"I don't think we should be talking to you," John said. "Whatever is happening, our lawyers are dealing with it. Let's not make this personal."

"Listen, you little shit," Brian said, the smile on his face replaced by a snarl. "You made this personal when you fucking sued me. This is most certainly—"

"How did you know we would be here?" I asked, interrupting his little rant. "I really hope you aren't spying on us. We'd have to add that to the lawsuit."

"You have your stupid boyfriend to thank for that," Brian said.

Shit. What had Carter done? I was about to speak when I noticed Brian was looking at John.

"Your little waiter friend couldn't resist talking on Twitter about how his perfect new man was coming to the restaurant just to spend time with him. It doesn't matter, anyway. What matters is that I am giving you an opportunity. An opportunity I recommend you think long and hard about."

"Or what?" I asked. "You've already tried to take us down at every opportunity. If you could do anything else, you would have done it already, so don't think we are scared of you."

Brian leaned toward me. "We have plenty more options here, and many ways to make your lives miserable in both legal and illegal ways. In case you haven't noticed, I don't play nice, and I'm certainly not going to start doing so for you. Don't think I'm going to make exceptions just because one of you is a fag and the other a cripple."

I took a few moments to let his words sink in, but I refused to let myself react to them. John let it wash over him as he always did. He once explained to me that he now found homophobic abuse more funny than frightening these days, because homophobes were the ones in the minority, at least in San Francisco anyway.

"You're scared," I said. "That's why you're here. You're scared of us and what we can do. If this were just another lawsuit, then you'd assume it would go away. I bet that's what usually happens, isn't it—your lawyers just deal with it and you never get involved? Well, this time, you should be scared. You should be worried. Because we know what you've done. And not just that—we have proof. That lawsuit isn't the half of it. You just wait for the rest of it to hit you. All those stock options you have won't be worth jack shit by the time we're through with you."

Brian stood up, sending his chair to the floor as he did so and attracting the attention of those around him. "You're going to spend thousands on legal fees and end up losing your company. Don't say I didn't warn you."

"Wow, Emily," John said, once Brian was gone and out of earshot. "Where did that come from? You kicked ass."

"Honestly, I have no idea. But I could do with a drink now."

"Let me buy you one," said a voice from behind me. This time, I recognized the speaker. It was Carter, and boy, was I glad to see him.

Chapter Nine

"My, my, what an attractive table this is," Michael said as he approached to take our order.

I sensed his eyes linger a little too long on Carter instead of John.

"Oh, don't worry. You're the best looking of the bunch, sweetie," Michael added when he noticed the look on John's face.

I liked Michael already. He was a little more camp than the men John usually dated, but he seemed sweet and a lot more fun than Tom ever was. Lately, John seemed to be taking my place as the serious one. Michael would do him good, although it was hard to say if it would last.

"Emily and I aren't eating," Carter said. "So just drinks for us, please."

"Why not?" I said. I was starting to get a little hungry, and as good as his cooking was, I really didn't want to wait for Carter to cook us a meal at his place.

"We're leaving soon and heading back to my place."

"But—"

"Emily," John said slowly, "you're going back to his place. Take the hint, dear."

"Oh," I muttered, looking down at the table to try and hide the redness blossoming on my cheeks.

John ordered enough to eat for the three of us, so Carter and I snacked at his appetizers a bit. That is, when Carter didn't have his hands full of my thigh. Every time John looked away for even a second, Carter would place his hand on my leg and give it a light squeeze. Each time he reached down his fingers would be further up my thigh than the time before, and I knew that soon he would graze against my lower lips.

Without realizing it, I was holding my breath in anticipation, waiting for his hand to creep up toward my sex. Finally I felt his little finger flick against my increasingly wet panties. I inhaled sharply and bit down on my lower lip. Fortunately, John was too preoccupied sucking up his food to notice.

"Do you want some more drinks?" Michael asked when he came by and saw we were nearly finished.

"No," I replied much too quickly. "No, that's it for us. We have to leave soon."

Carter threw some money down on the table and I practically dragged him out of the restaurant.

"Where's your driver?" I asked. "He had better be here soon. I'm not sure I can hold out much longer."

"He'll be a while. I only just asked him to pick us up and he mentioned that there is traffic. We may have to wait twenty minutes or so."

"I can't wait that long," I said.

"Emily Saunders, are you suggesting what I think you're suggesting?"

"I need you to fuck me, and I can't wait till we get home. Can you make it happen?"

Carter looked around, grabbed hold of my hand, and dragged me up some steps into a small park. I'd never had sex outdoors before. Hell, I'd never had sex outside the bedroom before. The evening was mild enough and the grass wouldn't be too damp, but being so close to the street and to people scared me stiff.

The park was right by the street, but slightly elevated. There was a brick wall, about waist-height, that went around the perimeter. It would offer some defense from prying eyes, but there were more than enough tall buildings around for people to get a good view if they looked out at the right time. The streetlights nearby meant that the dark would only offer so much protection.

"Are you sure this is okay? What if we get caught?"

"The risk is half the fun," Carter said.

He dragged me over to the far end of the park that had the advantage of not looking out directly over the streets, although it was still far too close for my liking. He grabbed my blouse and pulled me close to him while at the same time pressing me back against the wall. I gripped the cold bricks as Carter clawed at my blouse, practically ripping off the buttons.

Once my chest was exposed to the cool air, his fingers wandered between my legs and quickly worked their way under the thin cotton of my underwear before slipping inside my wet slit. I needed to moan but wanted to keep as quiet as possible, so I pressed my lips hard against his and sighed into his mouth.

My hands went to work opening his pants and freeing his growing member. I pulled down his boxers as I went down onto my knees, reluctantly forcing his fingers out of me before opening wide and taking him inside my eager mouth.

Carter moaned and held the back of my head as I sucked hard, feeling him stiffen between my thirsty lips. I clamped my hands on his ass and used the support to push my mouth down hard onto his cock, taking as much of its inside me as I could manage before my gag reflex kicked in. Carter's fingers massaged my head as his legs started to tremble from my efforts to suck him dry.

Just as he was close to finishing, he gripped me under my shoulder and pulled me up, then flipped me around and bent me over. I rested my hands on the wall and stuck my ass out behind me. Carter stuck a thumb under my knickers and pulled them to one side, exposing my arousal to anyone who happened to walk past. He quickly thrust himself inside me, forcing the air from my lungs as I tossed my head back and moaned, forgoing all attempts to remain quiet.

Carter slammed himself inside me while his fingers dug hard into my hips. The sound of his balls slapping against my sex echoed around the park and probably gave away our secret passion to half the city.

My attempts to remain quiet just made me need to scream all the more. I found myself trying to resist the orgasm building rapidly inside me, but that just brought it on quicker. When Carter grabbed my hair and pulled my head back, simultaneously thrusting himself even deeper inside me, I lost all control and came wildly. The sound would have been unmistakable. Carter's orgasm followed soon after, and he shook violently inside me until every last drop was out.

I collapsed onto my knees, utterly exhausted, and sucked the last drops from his pulsating shaft.

"I can't believe we just did that," I said. "I've never even dreamt of doing anything like that."

"Incredible," he said, slightly out of breath. "You're incredible. The car will be here soon. Let's go, I want to get you back to my place to do that again."

He pulled me up to my feet and we walked back to the street, trying to look innocent. We didn't even make it back to his apartment. Carter grabbed me as soon as we were in the car and I came again before we arrived at his place for a night I will never forget.

Chapter Ten

"Should we be worried about this meeting?" John asked. "It would have been easier to have just sent us an update via an email, or even a phone call, wouldn't it? Why do we have to go meet the lawyers in person?"

"John, are you scared of lawyers?" I teased.

"No, although Bethany does weird me out a little."

"She's sweet."

"Exactly. She looks like she wouldn't hurt a fly, but based on her reputation—which I looked up online—she's a demon in the courtroom. Anyway, I was more talking about the money this is all going to cost. With Scott and Bethany in the room, there's at least a thousand dollars an hour's worth of attorneys on the clock—and that's assuming they don't rope in any junior associates to sit in, as well."

"They agreed to the contingency fee, remember?" I said, reminding John of the email we'd received from Bethany a few days ago. "It means we only pay if we win, and the amount we pay is a fixed percentage of the proceeds. It doesn't matter if they have the owner of the law firm or a trained chimp in there. We still pay the same."

"Oh. Good."

I didn't tell John, but I was rather excited about the law firm agreeing to the contingency fee. Not only did it mean we could avoid forking over cash now, but it might also be a sign that they had confidence in our case. Otherwise, why would they agree to risk not getting paid at all?

The case had been active for a few weeks now, which didn't seem like long enough for there to be any developments of note, but Scott had insisted on a meeting. If I had read between the lines correctly, that meant there was major news.

This time, there was no waiting in reception. Scott and Bethany were ready for us and we were taken straight to a meeting room. This one was much bigger than the last one we were in and could have fit twelve people around the table easily. The extra space was needed for all the documents piled high and spread out around the table. Scott and Bethany had made some effort to clean the place, but the empty cans of soft drinks and the pizza boxes in the trash made it clear this was a war room of sorts.

"Hi, Emily. John," Scott said, beaming. "So glad you could come and see us in person. Please, take a seat."

John and I sat down at the part of the table with the least mess on it. I pushed some paperwork out of the way to make room for my laptop in case I needed to take notes. Bethany finished debriefing a junior attorney about something and sat down next to Scott.

"As you know, we're still in the early parts of the process," Bethany said, "but we have had an incredibly productive few weeks. I've never seen a case move so quickly. I think PharmaTech is hoping they can shut it down before the media gets wind of it."

"Can they?" I asked. "Shut it down?"

"God, no," Bethany replied. "Not now. This train is well and truly in motion and it's heading to its destination without delay. You're going to win your case easily. We have a confession on record from one of the employees we deposed. My God, you should have seen the look on her attorney's face when she started talking about things they had clearly not rehearsed."

"It's that easy?" John asked. "We're going to win, just like that?"

"Yes," Scott replied, "but that's not the interesting part. Sorry Bethany—you run with it. I'm just excited."

Bethany smiled at Scott in a way that screamed sexual chemistry. "You can tell he doesn't work in litigation much, can't you? Scott's right, though. You will win your case, but we also have them on the faulty drug issue you mentioned."

"You're kidding!" I said, although Bethany didn't look like someone who would kid about her cases.

"Nope. We deposed the CEO, a Mr. Brian Smithson, and he cracked. At first he was cocky and arrogant, but then I mentioned that we had another employee on record talking about bribes. I kept asking questions about that and his lawyer kept shutting me down for asking irrelevant questions. The lawyer was completely right; I shouldn't have been asking those questions, and I was about to quit when Mr. Smithson lost his cool."

"It was like something out of a movie," Scott said. "Mr. Smithson referenced the drug by name, even though we hadn't mentioned it. Bethany said something like, 'How did you know what drug we were talking about?' and that was the end of it. His lawyer shut down the deposition instantly, but it was too late. We have them, and they know it."

"These depositions are official documents," Bethany said. "There was a court reporter present who recorded every word, and they can be filed with the court and become part of the record."

"So, we could make it public?" I asked. That was the most important bit. PharmaTech could pay any fine the court threw at them, but if this became public knowledge, then they would have a whole other problem. Their reputation would be ruined, and there would probably be official investigations for them to contend with.

"Oh, yes," Bethany confirmed. "These two employees—and probably many others—are going to jail for a long time for the parts they played in all this."

"Who was the other person?" John asked. "We know the CEO—unfortunately—but who else is involved?"

"The other person was a bit lower down the food chain," Bethany said. "She was the one who committed most of the offenses against you. I don't think she did any of the bribery stuff herself, but she admitted to knowing about it. I can't remember her name—hang on." Bethany rooted through all the paperwork until she came across the piece she was looking for. "Here it is. Miss Kerry Woodson."

"Kerry," I remarked, turning to John.

"Shit," John muttered.

We hadn't given a second thought to what would happen to her in all this. Had she known all along what price she might have to pay to catch those responsible for her sister's death? Either way, she was now looking at a hefty prison sentence for something she didn't even do.

Chapter Eleven

John and I never wanted to lease office space. At first, that decision was made for us because we had no money. Now we could afford it, but just didn't see the need. We both worked from home most of the time and made the occasional trip to the café when we felt the need for a change of scenery, and that had always been enough. Recently, however, I had started giving more thought to all those "office available to rent" signs I saw all over San Francisco.

When we'd first started up the company, no one cared about whether we had an office or not. In fact, it was kind of expected that startup companies would not have office space. Now, though, we were trying to portray ourselves as a serious business and not one still short on cash. The desire to look important was more pronounced than ever today, because it was my first-ever interview with a journalist.

"Sorry about this," I said as the journalist, Amanda, squeezed herself in to one of the last seats in the café. "It isn't usually this busy at this time of day."

"Oh, don't worry about it," Amanda said. "I interview founders in places like this all the time. It's part of the scene in this area. Besides, I'm a freelance journalist, so it's not like I have an office myself."

"I've never done this before," I said. "How does this work? Do I have to say 'off the record' when I want something to be confidential?"

I wished John was there to provide a bit of support, but Michael had the afternoon off and they wanted to spend some time together. John had always been incredibly supportive about Carter, so I could hardly say no. Besides, as John himself was only too quick to point out, he would have been far more likely to say something stupid than me.

"I guess, but we don't have to be that formal about it. I plan to show you the article before I publish it, so you can always let me know if you're not comfortable with something in there. I'm not trying to catch you out—your business sounds like one I can get behind, so I'm just hoping to get you a bit of extra publicity."

I slumped back in my seat and relaxed a bit. I tried not to take her comments completely at face value, even though they did seem sincere. She would hardly be the first journalist to lie in order to get a good story, but that was probably being arrogant. Few people had even heard of us at this point, so a scandal involving LimbAnalytics would hardly make the front page. A scandal about PharmaTech, on the other hand...

"I take it this interview is all about our lawsuit against PharmaTech?" I asked.

"That was certainly what brought you to my attention, yes. I will need to include details about that in my story, otherwise no one will want to publish it. But, like I said, I'm hoping to bring some good publicity to your business."

"What do you want to know? I'm afraid there might not be a lot I can tell you. My lawyer has told me only to talk about what is already public record, and I expect you have seen that."

"I thought you might say that," Amanda said with a knowing smile. "And yes, I have read the claim you filed against PharmaTech. It's... interesting, to say the least. I understand that you cannot give me any new information or facts, but can you perhaps clarify the legal procedure that is underway. I have no legal background or experience writing about it, and quite frankly, I'm sure I will make a complete mess out of it."

"Well, as you can see from the complaint, we've made a number of allegations against PharmaTech. Most of the legal issues relate to one simple set of facts: PharmaTech used an employee to get information on our business under the pretense of working with an investor. As you can imagine, we had no qualms about telling the investor our plans and updating them on our next steps. Sometimes we did this because we needed additional cash to put the plan in motion, but other times it was just because we felt obliged to keep them in the loop. Plus, John and I are inexperienced at all this, and it was good to get a second opinion on things."

"So, everything you said to the investor went straight back to PharmaTech?"

I nodded.

"Wow. I don't consider myself to be naïve, but I never would have thought a huge company like PharmaTech would stoop to those levels. They must be really interested in what your business is doing. They do say imitation is the sincerest form of flattery."

I laughed. "Yeah, I guess they do. And we are flattered, but I don't think that excuse will wash with the judge. At least, I hope not."

"I checked the court records yesterday and saw that PharmaTech responded by denying the allegations. It has even accused your company of doing something similar. How do you respond to that?"

Bethany had given me a rehearsed answer to use to this exact question. "We expected them to deny the claims, but we are confident that we have enough evidence already—even before commencing discovery—to prove the truth of our claims. We were disappointed, but not at all surprised, to see that PharmaTech brought counterclaims. Of course, we will be denying all those allegations, and they have no evidence to support such claims."

Amanda couldn't help but laugh. "Excellent response."

"Did I do okay?"

"You were perfect. Anyone would think you had rehearsed the answer. Seriously, though—thank you. This is all great stuff. I'm surprised no one else has picked up on this lawsuit."

"Apparently, big companies like that—especially pharmaceutical companies—get sued over time. Most of the suits are just people trying their luck, so I suppose it's tough to weed out the good ones."

"I can believe that," Amanda said. "I only looked twice at this one, because I recognized the name of your company."

"You did? I thought we were still flying under the radar."

"Maybe, but I take an interest in any tech startups that are trying to make the world a better place, as opposed to the ones making billions from messaging apps."

"I wish more people did that," I said.

"My motivations are somewhat selfish, if I'm honest. My mom suffers from reduced mobility, and it might be hereditary. I'm hoping a company like yours will come up with a solution before it hits me."

"I can hardly criticize you for being selfish," I said, pulling up my pant leg and gesturing to my artificial limb. "I'm using my own company for personal gain."

She smiled and nodded. "True, although I recommend you don't word it quite like that if you end up in the courtroom."

"Don't worry. I'll have my lawyer come up with something."

Amanda turned off her recorder and we chatted about other startups. She spilled some juicy gossip on some founders that I knew. The information was all technically public, but in many cases it had been well hidden by expensive lawyers threatening to sue any newspaper who published it. Amanda herself had a few great stories she'd had to squash for that very reason.

She left once she had finished her coffee and promised me a copy of the article within a few days. I messaged John and pretended that the whole thing had been a huge ordeal and very stressful—that way, he would feel like he owed me one. He didn't respond immediately as he usually did, so I took that as a sign that his date was going well.

His date with Michael made me realize that I hadn't gone out for a proper date with Carter in a while. I sent him a message and told him to meet me by Pier 40 tonight. I was going to take Carter on a date he would never forget.

Chapter Twelve

Carter popped up in front of me as I waited near the pier. He'd been hidden among a throng of baseball fans making their way to the stadium, so I hadn't seen him approach. I'd warned him that we would be outside all evening, but had neglected to mention that he could dress casual. His sweater and pants would have let him fit in at any exclusive golf club, but he was going to stand out like a sore thumb at a baseball game dressed like that.

"Where are we eating?" he asked, planting a kiss that sent warmth shooting through my cold cheeks.

"Over there," I answered, pointing to the stadium. "The food isn't up to snuff, I'm afraid, but the entertainment is good."

"Baseball?" he asked incredulously. "Are you taking me to watch a baseball game?"

"Yes. It's the Giants versus the Dodgers, so it's a big one and the tickets were not easy to come by." Not for cheap, anyway. "I know you think it's a boring sport, but I'm going to try and convince you otherwise."

"All right, but you realize what this means? When you come to England with me, you have to go watch a game of cricket."

"Don't cricket games last five days, or something stupid like that?" I asked. At least I was only putting him through a few hours of torture.

"The good ones do, yes."

I rolled my eyes, grabbed his hand, and pulled him toward the stadium. "Come on. We need to get a move on. I want to buy you a hoodie and cap to put on—you can't sit in the bleachers dressed like that."

"I can go with the hoodie, but there's no way you're getting me in a baseball cap."

"Scared of messing up your hair?" I asked, quickly ruffling my fingers through it in a fruitless attempt to dishevel him.

"I just can't stand baseball caps. I've never really understood the point of them."

I looked up at the sun that was still about an hour away from going below the level of the stadium. Carter would soon want a cap when we were sat facing the sunset and he couldn't see the game, but I'd let him find that out for himself.

There was a long line to get past security. I could have sworn that when I first started going to baseball games with my brother, there had been no security to walk past when you came in. Now you had to have your bag checked and go through a metal detector.

"Do people actually try to bring guns into the stadium?" Carter asked. "I assume that's what the metal detectors are for."

"Welcome to America, dear," I said before setting off the metal detector. I always showed my leg to security before walking through, but that made no difference. They still had to scan my entire body, just in case.

"I felt safer in prison," Carter remarked as they finally waved us through.

We went straight to one of the overpriced gift stores and bought Carter a hoodie, which he wore instead of his sweater, and a cap, which he left in the bag. We made it to our seats after missing the Dodgers' first two hitters, but they hadn't scored or got any men on the bases.

"I'm going to go grab some drinks," Carter said. "I've a feeling I'm going to need some libations to get me through this."

Most fans hadn't got settled into their seats yet, but even with all the commotion, I caught a few people look twice at Carter. Whether that was because of his insanely good looks or his English accent, I couldn't tell. It was probably a combination of the two.

He didn't return until the second inning, but he still hadn't missed anything of note. The Giants got the first hitter on base, but then the next three struck out in quick succession.

"This beer had better be damned good," he said, handing me a plastic cup. "I've never paid so much for beer in my life. I've bought rounds of drinks in London for less."

"Good thing you're a millionaire, then, huh?" I whispered, not wanting to broadcast his wealth to everyone around us.

"I might not be if I have to buy many more of those beers."

"Oh, hush up. Let me explain the rules to you."

I talked Carter through the basic objective—score more than the other team—and how to score runs. After just a couple of minutes he seemed utterly confused, but to his credit, baseball was a tricky concept to explain to a newbie. I remembered that when William had first started teaching me, it'd seemed like the game was based entirely on statistics, which wasn't exactly how I enjoyed spending my spare time. It had taken months of the games playing on the TV in the background before I had finally started picking it up enough to enjoy it.

"Okay, so why did the bowler just throw it to the guy on first base?" Carter asked.

"Pitcher. The guy throwing the ball is the pitcher, and he did that to stop the guy on first base running to second."

A girl in front of us glanced at Carter. She thought she was being subtle by pretending to look at something in the distance, but it was obvious where she was looking. The girl nudged her friend, and even though I couldn't hear them or see their faces, I had a pretty good idea of what they were saying. The constant attention women showed Carter was equal parts infuriating and flattering. As much as I hated it, I couldn't help but feel pleased to be the one girl he loved.

"Is the batter out if the wicket-keeper catches the ball?" Carter continued. If he was embarrassed at asking all these questions, then he did a good job of hiding it.

"What the hell is a wicket-keeper?" I asked him.

"The guy behind the batter."

"Oh you mean the catcher. No, that's not a way to get them out. Well, sometimes. I'm actually not sure how that works…"

The loud clunk of ball on bat reverberated around the stadium. I missed the hit, but my head snapped back to the field where I saw the ball fly into the stands for a Giants home run.

"Wow, finally, someone hit it for six," Carter said, using another term that was completely unfamiliar with me.

"Carter, that's a home—"

"—run. Yes, I know, I'm just playing with you now."

After the home run, the game went back to being rather dull, so I took the opportunity to teach Carter a few more of the common terms that were being thrown around by the crowd.

"That's called a 'backdoor slider,'" I said after a Giants' pitcher threw a ball that curved into the strike zone.

"It's called a what?" Carter replied with a smirk.

"A backdoor slider. Why are you laughing?"

"Just sounds like a euphemism for something else, that's all. Do you like backdoor sliders?"

I had a feeling I knew what he was referring to, but had no idea whether I liked it or not. "Stop being rude."

Carter wouldn't admit it, but he had changed a lot since opening up about working with Kerry against PharmaTech. All those secrets he had been keeping from me must have weighed him down, and now he was finally able to be himself around me.

The real Carter was fun and a lot less moody than the one that kept secrets. He no longer carried that air of mystery around with him—in some ways, mystery was exciting, but after a while I craved this kind of openness and honesty from him. That was what long-term relationships were made of.

Chapter Thirteen

"Ready to hear another settlement offer?" John asked.

"After the insultingly low offer they came up with last time, I'm tempted to just ignore it," I answered.

PharmaTech's lawyers had contacted ours soon after the case was filed and offered us $300,000 to settle. Our lawyers were obliged to ask us whether we wanted to accept it, but it didn't take long for John and I to make up our minds on that. We hadn't come up with a number that would be acceptable yet. To be honest, the money was far from our only priority at this stage. In addition, we also wanted to see the people involved get punished, issue a public apology, and institute a withdrawal of the faulty drug from the market. Our problems with PharmaTech went way beyond what they did to our business, and any settlement offer would need to reflect that.

"I certainly don't think we need to go down to Bethany's office this time. I am not going all that way again just to leave five minutes later. Let's just give her a call."

John called Bethany and put her on speaker.

"Hi, John," she said as she answered the phone. "Thanks for calling. I assume Emily is there with you?"

"Hi, Bethany," I said. "I'm here."

"Good. I'm glad you both called—I think you're going to like what I have to say. As you know, PharmaTech has come up with another offer. I was expecting them to try to lowball us again, but in the last couple of weeks, they have conducted an independent and internal investigation into some of the facts we alleged in our complaint. I'm guessing they found some interesting stuff, because this offer is many multiples of the last one."

John and I shared a look. Was this going to be the big moment? Bethany, Scott, and Carter had all been telling us that our lives may change soon, but John and I never took that too seriously. It was like how when you bought lottery tickets you knew you could win, but you never really expected to. Now I felt like we had all six of the main numbers and we were just waiting to hear the Powerball number. We still hadn't won, but our chances were a lot better than usual.

"First of all," Bethany continued, "the money is a heck of a lot bigger. PharmaTech has offered to pay the company twenty million for this case to go away."

Simultaneously, John and I both looked at each other. That was more than enough money to keep the company going for the foreseeable future. Even in our wildest dreams, I don't think we could have imagined spending that kind of money. We could even get into manufacturing our own products, something that had seemed impossible before.

"The only real catch on that is that you would have to maintain a degree of confidentiality about the whole thing. You could tell people you settled the case, but wouldn't be able to mention the money involved. Other than that, your business can continue and spend the money however it chooses."

Shit. I knew it couldn't be that perfect. I wanted the money, obviously, and I wanted to punish PharmaTech financially, but John and I had both agreed that it had to be more than money involved. The faulty drug was still on the market, and that had to change.

"I'm not sure we can do that, Bethany," I said. "I'm sorry, I know it's a really good deal, but we agreed to get more than just money."

"And you're about to," Bethany said. "There's more to come. You can't tell people about the settlement, but that's just dealing with the corporate espionage issues. I don't know exactly what the internal investigation showed up—God, I would love to see that report—but it was obviously drastic. In addition to paying you money, they are also going to withdraw the faulty drug and two others that turned up during the investigation and go public about them. Anyone who comes forward and claims to have been

415

harmed by the drugs will get to discuss a separate settlement. That includes the family of this girl you know."

"Wow," John said. "That's incredible. I thought that would have taken years to achieve. I assume you are happy with this?" he asked me.

"Oh, I'm happy. Very happy. Bethany, I assume you recommend accepting this offer?"

"Definitely. In my career I have seen very few offers as good as this one. It helps that they are a public company. They have to comply with all sorts of rules about reporting things like this, and allegations of bribery of government officials are enough to wipe a company off the map. Apparently, the CEO and a few others involved have already been terminated from their employment and should end up being prosecuted. They didn't tell us how many people were involved, but it may not have been that many. The more people that know, the more chance someone will leak the information. The fact that this stayed a secret for so long suggests only a handful of people knew about it."

I didn't take too much pleasure in the CEO losing his job. Not because I felt sorry for him, but because I knew he would likely bounce back quickly. Someone with a resume like that will easily pick up another job, even if the allegations of his bribery got out. Still, I couldn't in good conscience refuse such an offer just to take some sort of petty revenge against one person. We had got what we set out to achieve, and a hell of a lot more.

"What about Kerry?" John asked me, although he said it loud enough that Bethany picked it up on the other end.

"Who's Kerry?" Bethany asked.

"Never mind. Just a friend," I said. "But while I'm thinking about it, do you know if criminal charges will be filed against the employees involved? Or does that somehow go against the agreement to keep all this private?"

"I expect charges will be filed," Bethany said. "I imagine PharmaTech will try to keep this in-house, if possible, but the Department of Justice will want to get ahold of those who did the bribing. There will be lawsuits and prosecutions for years to come, although I'm guessing the whole thing will be settled with as little publicity as possible. That's the US justice system for you."

I had no idea what that meant for Kerry. She hadn't done any of the bribing herself, but she had gone on record as having known about it. Maybe the Department of Justice would consider her an accomplice? Kerry was the one who planned all this, so she would either accept the consequences or had planned around them. Either way, we couldn't let that affect our decision now.

We gave Bethany the go-ahead to accept the offer, and she told us to expect paperwork in the next few days. The money would be paid to the company, but given that John and I were the only shareholders now—Bethany assured us that the investor's shares were not valid—we were effectively millionaires ourselves.

John made plans to see Michael, and I made plans to see Carter, but first we both went to dinner, just the two of us, to properly celebrate what we had achieved. We may have had some help along the way, but most of the credit belonged to us, and we treated ourselves to more than one cocktail in our own honor.

Chapter Fourteen

As much as John and I enjoyed each other's company, after a couple of hours we were both a little eager to go our separate ways to see our boyfriends. I arrived at Carter's apartment about half an hour before I said I would be there and found it empty. Although the effects of the cocktails were starting to wear off, I still felt a little giddy and more confident than usual.

My attempt at finding something to watch on TV was fruitless, so I went into Carter's bedroom and decided that now would be a good time to take a closer look at some of the toys I knew he kept in the lower drawers. John had already seen them from when we were looking for information on his hospital visits, but I was still in the dark about what he had. There had been many nights I could have looked or even asked Carter to show me, but I had never quite had the courage until now. Maybe it was liquid courage, but people were brave in different ways.

A few months ago I would have been shocked, and honestly, a little disgusted at what I found, but having now been in a sex shop and explored some previously hidden recesses of my sexuality with Carter, I was now more intrigued than appalled. Most of the stuff seemed to be in one drawer, and I recognized a few pieces from our trip to the adult boutique.

If there were one word to describe Carter's taste in this kind of "equipment," then it would have been "leather." The more adventurous—and in some cases, confusing—items remained in the drawer, but I took out a corset with a matching thong, a leather choker with stainless steel spikes, and finally, a leather whip with nine tails.

The clothing items looked a lot more intimidating than they really were. I'd worn corsets and thongs before, and while the choker looked kinky, I had similar things at home—albeit not in leather—from when they were in fashion.

I got undressed, and with no small degree of difficulty tied myself into the leather corset. The thong and choker were much easier to get on. I held the whip in my hand and gave myself a few gentle lashings across my upper thighs to get a feel for it. The impact stung, but there was a definite appeal in thinking of Carter punishing me with it. *If only my ex-boyfriend could see me now*, I thought. I'd changed drastically in the past few months, and not just from having more sex. The changes were more in the mental approach I took to thinking about my body and what I wanted Carter to do with it and to it.

I checked the time on my phone and realized that Carter would be home any minute. My first thought was to hop into bed and have him find me there waiting for him, but I'd done that before, and it seemed rather ill-fitting with what I was wearing and holding in my hand.

Instead, I went back into the living room and turned off all the lights before taking a seat on the sofa. When he arrived, he was going to get one hell of a surprise.

Carter ran a little late, but just as I was about to get my phone out, I heard the elevator stop and the doors start to open. He strolled out and threw his keys down on a small table before turning on the lamp. Instead of looking at me, though, he walked straight into the kitchen, turned on the light there, and opened the fridge. It wasn't quite the effect I was going for.

"I've been waiting," I said in my best slow and sexy voice.

"Holy shit," Carter said, turning and looking in the direction of the living room. "Why were you sitting in the dark?"

He could still barely make me out, so I stood up, whip in hand, and walked toward the kitchen, stopping once I was in the light.

"Oh, my God," he said under his breath as he looked up and down my body. His gaze finally came to rest on what I held in my hand. "What's all this? Not that I'm complaining, but wow, I was not expecting to come home to you like this."

"I've been going through your things and trying them on. I've been a very bad girl, Carter."

"Well, then," he said, taking a couple of steps toward me, "I guess you need to be punished. Bad girls should always be punished."

He took me by the hand and walked me over to the sofa. He sat down and pulled me next to him.

"Say 'orange' if you feel uncomfortable, and say 'red' if you want me to stop," he whispered in my ear.

He took the whip from my hand and planted a firm kiss on my lips. Then he placed a palm on my back and pushed me over his legs. I let out a gasp as I fell forward onto the sofa cushions on the other side of his thighs. My ass immediately stuck up into the air as if eagerly awaiting its punishment.

Carter let the soft tails of the whip trickle all over my bare ass cheeks and the backs of my legs. I already knew this was going to be something I enjoyed. My heart was racing in anticipation, and I could already feel my sex pulsating with raw desire.

He hauled the whip up into the air and I felt the leather tails leave my skin. I held my breath and dug my nails into my palms, waiting for him to punish me.

I heard the leather move through the air just before I felt the impact of it on my skin. The sting of leather on my ass was only mildly painful, but the tension had built up inside me so much that I expelled all the air from my lungs in one violent breath and moaned as if I were already experiencing the orgasm that was surely going to hit me before much longer.

"Did that hurt?" Carter asked.

"Only a little."

"I guess I will have to go harder next time, then."

This time, I didn't have time to hold my breath before he brought the whip up and down again in one smooth motion. I yelped and winced at the pain on my skin. My breath was as heavy and fast as my beating heart, but I soon found myself ready for more.

"Again," I commanded. "I've been a very bad girl, Carter. I need more punishment than that."

Carter didn't need to be told twice. He snapped the whip down again on my ass, and then again and again in quick succession. I let out a deep, guttural scream as the pain worsened each time he brought the leather down. The whip had now touched every part of my rear that wasn't covered by the leather thong.

He grabbed hold of my right ass cheek and dug his fingers in hard. "God, you have such a nice, pert ass. Just looking at this ass and not being able to fuck you is torture for me." He untied the straps holding up my thong and pulled the whole thing off. "Judging by how wet these are, it looks like you enjoyed your punishment rather more than you were supposed to."

He lifted me up so that he could get undressed. Then he stood, completely naked before me, and pushed me back down onto the sofa before climbing on top of me. He spread my legs and pushed his shaft into my wet, eager slit. He grabbed hold of my hair with one hand and pulled my head back.

"I love you," he whispered into my ear. "But now I'm going to have my way with you."

He let go of my hair and grabbed a hold of my waist in his strong hands, lifting my ass up before thrusting his entire member inside me. Each time he slammed against me I moaned into the soft cushions of the sofa. My pussy was so wet he could barely stay inside me, and I came twice before he pulled out and sprayed his passion all over my back. Thankfully, leather was quite easy to wipe clean.

Chapter Fifteen

A few days passed, during which John and I were able to live relatively normal lives. The lawyers took a while to draw up the settlement agreement, and it was another day or so before the business world noticed that the lawsuit had been dropped. We were not allowed to talk about it, but the local community seemed to have a strong intuition that we had won. Once a couple of the local tech websites ran with the story, it became news. That was when our lives really changed.

John and I were inundated with calls offering us jobs, consulting positions, investments, and interviews. I ignored most of those calls and emails, but I did respond to a few where people who had written to thank us for taking on PharmaTech. It seemed that the company had pissed off a fair few people over the last couple of years, and usually, they got away with it.

Whereas before only one journalist had wanted to speak to me, now they all wanted to get fifteen minutes with me and John. We rejected all the offers for the time being. Neither of us really saw the benefit in speaking to the press at this point, and we were both concerned we might slip up and say something we shouldn't about the settlement. One day soon we would sit down with Bethany and get a better idea of what we could and couldn't say, but for now, we intended to keep our mouths shut.

I took some satisfaction in knowing that Amanda's article was the only one out there of its kind, and that it must therefore be getting a lot of hits. I had approved her article just before the settlement and it should have now been online. But when I ran a quick search, nothing came up. I went back to my email to make sure I had responded to her confirming I was happy with the article. The email was there, but she had also replied with a further comment that I had missed. The email lay dormant amongst the other 649 unread emails.

I noticed an issue with the story. Can we talk? I think it's important.

Amanda had done enough to earn my trust, so I replied, asking if she could meet at the coffee shop again. She emailed me back immediately and we agreed to meet.

With all the attention I had been getting recently, I half-expected to walk into the coffee shop and need to sign autographs. I was pleasantly surprised to find that not one person seem to recognize me. Even Jane, the waitress I knew, wasn't working today. Amanda was already at a table and had bought me a coffee, so I walked over and joined her. She looked a lot less relaxed than she'd been last time we met, and that had me a little worried.

"Sorry it took me a long time to reply to your email," I said. "Things have been crazy recently."

"That's okay," Amanda said, and then went quiet.

"I couldn't find the article online. Does that mean you weren't able to sell it? I don't want to sound big-headed, but I would have thought the article would be in high demand right now."

"I never showed it to my editor."

"You holding out for a better price?" Amanda was a freelance journalist, and she had every right to sell her stories to the highest bidder—although as I understood it, the correct practice was usually to offer it to a preferred editor and give them first right of refusal. Still, I could hardly blame her for trying to cash in a bit. After all, she was the one clever enough to ask for the interview in the first place.

"No, no, it's not that. I'm not going to publish it because I don't want to draw any additional attention to you personally, and to the lawsuit."

"What do you mean? There already seems to be a lots of attention on the lawsuit, so I wouldn't worry too much about that. Besides, we won!"

Amanda forced a smile, but it soon disappeared from her face. "Congratulations. I know you are the talk of the tech industry at the moment, but they aren't looking too closely at the case. Fortunately, most of them don't want to look directly at the court filings. But someone is bound to do that sooner rather than later, and when they do, they will put the pieces together. You don't want that, so I thought it best to not publish the article."

"We don't have anything to hide," I said, frowning. "There are certain things I can't say, but everything we filed with the court is public information and I don't have a problem with it."

"The thing is, I did a bit more digging after the interview. I'd been so pleased with how it went that I forgot to ask one of the questions on my list."

"What question?"

"You didn't just sue PharmaTech. You also sued another company—an LLC that I had never heard of. I went back to the court documents and reread them. The LLC you are suing was the investor—or an investment vehicle for an investor, anyway"

My stomach tightened as I realized where Amanda was going. I had never looked at the official documents filed with the court, but it only made sense that our lawyers would have sued the investment company as well as PharmaTech. The investment company was likely an empty shell, so we'd get no money from them, but that LLC did have one very important secret that I wished would stay hidden.

"I want you to know that I was trying to help," Amanda said. "And I still will help, if I can. Anyway, I did some digging and found out who was listed as the founder of the LLC. That information isn't easy to come by—fortunately I have a, uh, contact at the Secretary of State who was very helpful—but someone else might do the same."

If it were any other journalist in front of me right now, I might have played dumb and pretended to have no idea what she was talking about. But Amanda had earned my respect, and it was quite clear she knew what was going on.

"You know about Carter?" I asked.

She nodded. "I got lucky. When I found his address of record, I went snooping and saw the two of you come out of the building together. Listen, I don't fully understand what is going on here, but you seem like a really genuine person, so I don't believe the two of you were up to anything shady."

"We weren't. The whole thing is a complete mess, but those claims against PharmaTech were true. Still, Carter and I are an item."

"I figured as much. I have no right to tell you what to do, but if you do want my advice, here it is: you and Carter should not be seen together for the foreseeable future. In fact, I would recommend Carter go underground, if at all possible."

"Why? The case is closed now, so he's out of the woods, isn't he?"

"Legally? I don't know, maybe. But that's not the point. Once PharmaTech comes clean about this drug, then some very powerful people are going to get involved, and powerful people want to become even more powerful. They do that by seeing people get punished. Emily, everyone involved in this affair will end up sued within an inch of his or her life. They may even end up in jail. It may take a while, but it will happen."

"What can we do?" I asked. I had assumed that Carter had covered his tracks, but if Amanda could find him, then others would, as well. Carter had nothing to do with the bribery, of course, but once the lies started flying, then who knew what would stick? He already had a criminal record so that wouldn't help his case.

"His best chance is just to stay under the radar. I know it sounds a little drastic, but maybe have him change his name or leave the country. He doesn't have to hide, as such, but he should make it harder for people to find him."

"We can do that," I said immediately, not thinking through the consequences of such a big step.

"No, Emily. You don't understand. It's not something the two of you can do—Carter has to do this by himself. If you stay with him, then he will be found out. I'm sorry, Emily, but if you want Carter to

430

stay out of this mess, then I recommend you don't spend any more time with him."

"Are you sure?" I asked. It was a stupid question. She was sure, and so was I.

"Yes. I'm really very sorry. Let me know if I can help."

Amanda got up and left, leaving me to wonder how on earth I could ever end the best relationship of my life.

Chapter Sixteen

Lots of words could describe what I was about to do, but I had no idea which one was correct. Was I being brave? Sometimes I thought so. I was taking a huge risk that could easily backfire on me, and the knots in my stomach made it clear I was nervous. I couldn't believe I was giving up a man who made me happy, happier than I had ever been in my life.

Or was I just being stupid? I was giving up everything because there was a chance something bad might happen. Just that—a chance. I wasn't afraid to take risks in life—if I was, then I would never have started my business—but this wasn't a risk I was taking. It was a risk Carter was taking.

When I told John what I was going to do, I had assumed he would try to talk me out of it. I was hoping he would succeed. After he got over the shock of what I was saying, he actually seemed to agree with what I was about to do.

"Is there really a chance he could go to jail?" he asked.

"I spoke to Bethany about it, although I was a little vague on the details. I know she is our lawyer, but I still don't want her to know all that kind of stuff. Anyway, she said that he probably wouldn't go to jail because the government wouldn't get involved in that part of the case. If the FDA did start digging around, they would focus on the bribery allegations involving the drugs. Carter's role as the owner of the LLC only touched on the corporate espionage stuff, and that is something to be sorted out between private parties."

"So, what's the problem, then?"

"The problem is that Carter will be hounded for the next five years or so by every person who wants to sue PharmaTech because of the faulty drug. Think about it: there are going to be hundreds or thousands of legitimate cases, and even some where people just sense some easy money. Bethany said that lawyers would sue every party they think could be responsible. In all those hundreds or thousands of cases, Carter will be sued. Plus, desperate people like that scumbag CEO will tell lies about everything. If someone so much as thinks Carter was involved in the bribery, then you can bet prison will be back on the table."

"I'm sure Bella's family will pay for an expensive lawyer to protect him."

"I'm sure they will, but would you want to be associated with all those lawsuits? That will follow him around for the rest of his life. I'm just not sure I can do that to him. Every day, he will wake up wondering if today is the day he goes back to prison for something he didn't do. He's already done that once."

"Wow," John said, shaking his head. "This is a tough decision."

"You don't think I'm being stupid?"

"You're definitely not being stupid. I'm not one hundred percent sure I would make the same decision, but I can see why you are thinking about it. I still think Carter would survive all this—he's a pretty tough guy, after all—but I admire you for not wanting to put him through it."

"He's already spent five years of his life in prison sticking up for a girlfriend. I can't ask him to do something similar for me. He deserves to live his life."

"It won't be easy. You do realize that, don't you? He's going to do everything in his power to keep you."

"I'm hoping that by the time I'm finished with him, he won't think I'm worth fighting for. It's the only way. Will you help me do this?"

John sighed and pinched the bridge of his nose as if trying to fight off a sneeze. "I can't quite believe I'm going to say this, but yes, I will help you get rid of the best man either of us will probably ever know."

In the end, we came up with a plan of sorts. It wasn't a great one, but it would have to do. I had considered inventing a pretend boyfriend or lying about having an affair, but John had talked me out of it. That would be far too out of character for me, not to mention no other man could hold a torch to Carter. He would see through that lie in a second.

First, I had to ignore Carter for a week or so. I still responded to messages, but tried to avoid speaking to him on the phone and didn't see him once, despite him constantly asking me to dinner. I needed to look like I was far too busy with work to spend time with him. Finally I caved and agreed to meet him, but I made it clear I was somewhat reluctant to see him. I already felt like a bitch, and I hadn't even broken up with him yet.

"Is everything okay?" he asked as soon as I sat down at the table. I had considered doing this in public because I knew Carter didn't like to make a scene, but that just felt far too cruel.

"I'm just really busy," I said, not apologizing for being unresponsive.

"That's a shame, because I was hoping you might consider taking a holiday for a week with me. I have to leave the country and come back in again to move on to this new visa. I could just go to Canada, but it makes more sense to pop back to the homeland

and see family. How about it? Do you want to come to England with me for a week?"

"Carter, I'm way too busy for a vacation. Actually, I'm way too busy for this at all. Ever since the settlement became public, I've been inundated with work and requests to help people. There are conferences I've been invited to all over the country, so I'm going to need to travel a lot."

"That's great," Carter said, looking pleased for me. "Those sorts of conferences are a great place to meet people—you'll make loads of connections in the industry."

"We won't have time to see each other."

"Don't be silly," Carter said, looking a little confused. "I don't know if you have forgotten, but I am rich and my job is basically fake. I will just travel everywhere with you. We can stay in expensive hotels and live a life of luxury. I'm kind of looking forward to it."

"No, Carter, you don't understand. I've worked really hard to get where I am now, and I want to do this by myself."

"All right," he said, definitely looking a little hurt now. "I guess I will just see you when you are back in San Francisco."

"Please listen to me, Carter. I want to be by myself now. The last few weeks and months with you have been fantastic, and I will always remember them, but I don't see a future for us now. I'm not the girl you first met. I've changed a lot, and I have you to thank for that, but now I want to find myself and my place in the world."

"Emily, what the hell? Are you saying you don't want to be with me anymore?"

I tried to force out the word "yes," but it wouldn't come, so instead I just nodded firmly.

"Where the hell has this come from?" He was shocked, angry, and upset. I couldn't bring myself to look at him.

"This was always going to happen," I said, standing up from the table and raising my voice. "We must have been stupid to think this would ever work. For God's sakes Carter, your ex-wife killed my fucking brother. Do you really think I can spend the rest of my life with you, knowing that?"

John and I had agreed that I would act like a bitch when ending it was Carter, but by bringing up my brother's death as an excuse, I wasn't *acting* like a bitch—I was *being* a bitch, and I hated myself for it.

"We can get past that, Emily. I know it's fucked up, but I love you, and I know you love me too. Us being apart is not going to bring your brother back."

In desperation, I swung my arm and slapped Carter had on the cheek. It felt so wrong, but he barely seemed to register it anyway. I quickly scampered over to the elevator and pressed the call button. It was still on the ground floor and would take precious seconds to arrive. I wasn't sure I could last that long without bursting into tears.

Carter grabbed my arm. "You're not leaving, Emily. I can't just let you leave like that. I have no idea what the hell is going on right now, but I'm not letting you go. You are the best thing that has ever happened to me."

I tried to pull free of his grasp, but his grip was too strong and my desire to pull away was too weak.

"Did you mean it's when you said you loved me?" I asked.

"Of course I did."

"Then you will let me go."

The elevator doors pinged open, but Carter kept hold of my arm. I stared into his eyes and noticed that he was as close to tears as me. I heard the elevator doors begin to close again and a part of me hoped he would keep hold of me. Instead, just a second before the doors shut, he reluctantly let go of my arm.

I stuck it between the closing doors to open them again and stepped into the elevator. I turned to face

Carter and just about managed to contain my tears until the elevator doors were closed. By the time they opened again on the ground floor, so much water was streaming from my eyes I could barely see where I was walking. I had no idea where I wanted to go, anyway. For the second time in a few weeks, my life had changed irreversibly. This time, it was not for the better.

Chapter Seventeen

I spent the next week living at John's just in case Carter decided to visit my apartment in a final attempt to change my mind. I needn't have bothered. After a few attempts at contacting me on my phone, Carter gave up trying. Technically, he was out of my life, although mentally he was still very much a part of me. How could someone be out of your life when you spend every waking moment, and most of the sleeping ones, thinking about them?

John didn't once give me any grief over my decision. I still don't think he completely agreed with what I did, but he could see I did it for sensible reasons. He was on his best behavior around me at all times, which was slightly unsettling, but between the two of us we managed to continue working effectively. We both knew I was not pulling my weight at the moment, but John was kind enough to overlook that.

He spent enough time in my apartment that I did not feel guilty for being at his, but I knew I would have to leave soon. He had a great place, but Michael was coming around more often now, and because of his erratic schedule, they ended up having sex during the day while I was awake in the next room. Every time I heard the bed bang against the wall or the mattress squeaking, I would think back to what Carter and I used to do in the bedroom. He was the only man I had truly given myself to, and I couldn't imagine being that way with another man.

One afternoon, shortly after John and Michael had left the apartment to go for a walk, there was a loud banging from the front door. The security on John's building was not quite as good as mine, so I was a little nervous as I tiptoed to the peephole. I moved my head close enough to see who was on the other side, but without covering it up to give away my presence. Standing in John's hallway was Kerry, and she looked pissed.

When I left the Carter, I made sure he thought part of the reason I was leaving him was because of his history with Bella and her family, so it seemed unlikely he would send Kerry over to fight his battles. She banged again on the door, making me gasp.

"Come on, Emily," Kerry yelled. "I know you're there. I can hear you on the other side of the door. Open up. I need to talk to you about Carter."

I still didn't want to open it, but I could hardly leave an angry woman shouting in John's hallway. I undid the latch and opened the door a couple of inches, enough that Kerry could open it herself and come in. I quickly retreated to the sofa to keep some distance between us.

"I assume you've spoken to Carter?" I asked.

441

"Yes, although he didn't say a lot. He didn't have to. Can I sit down?" she asked.

She was no longer outwardly angry, but I could tell from the tone of her voice that she was frustrated with me and I was about to get a lecture. I motioned for her to sit down next to me.

"I'm not going to change my mind," I said. "I want to spend some time by myself now. I think the whole thing with Carter was just me getting whisked away in the romance of it all. Let's be honest—at times, our relationship was more like a soap opera."

"Carter is blind where you're concerned. He thinks you're completely truthful all the time, but I know you lied to him. You're ending it with Carter to protect him. Let me guess: you think that if he leaves the country he can escape the fallout of everything that is going to happen around the PharmaTech lawsuit?"

"That has nothing to do with it."

"Nonsense. Carter and I both knew the risks before we did this. I'm going to prison for sure, because I had to admit knowledge of the bribery during my deposition in order to open up the case. Carter did what he could to hide his identity behind shell companies, but he always knew he might get caught."

"Then you have to see that this is the best thing for him. After all he has done to help you and your

442

family, don't you want to see him get on with his life?"

"That's why I'm here. Whatever may happen to him if he sticks around here, he will get through it if you are by his side. One thing I know for sure is that he will *not* be able to get on with his life without you in it."

"He could end up in prison."

"Carter went to prison for five years for my sister, and I can tell you that he did not love her a fraction of how much he loves you. He would spend the rest of his life in prison just to spend one day with you."

I shook my head, not sure if I was disagreeing with what she was saying or just trying to convince myself that I had made the right decision. " You're probably right, but I can't let him do that."

"Don't you think it's his decision to make?" she asked me. When I didn't answer, she sighed, bowed her head, and then took a deep breath. "I shouldn't say what I'm about to say. I've tried, Emily. I've tried to convince you, but you can be as stubborn as Carter sometimes. You would never have made the decision you made if you knew the whole truth."

"If you are about to tell me he's been keeping more secrets, then let me tell you that will not make me change my mind. He's kept enough secrets from me already. If I find out he was lying about other things, then that just makes the decision easier." Surely there couldn't be more secrets? Every time I found something out he promised me that nothing else was hidden.

"You didn't go to his trial, did you?" Kerry asked.

I shook my head. "My dad went to most of it."

"Even if you had gone, I suppose it wouldn't have made any difference. Most of the information was kept out of evidence because they feared it would prejudice the jury. That's a load of crap, in my opinion. Rules like that are why an innocent man can end up spending five years in prison."

"Kerry, what is it? If you have something to say, then hurry up and say it. Otherwise, please leave."

She dug around for something in her handbag. "You owe Carter more than a quick goodbye." She pulled some paper out of her bag and handed it to me. "Read this. If you still want Carter out of your life afterward, then that is your decision. But first you owe it to him and to yourself to know everything. Carter saved your life."

Chapter Eighteen

Kerry dropped another bombshell on me before leaving. Not only did she leave me with a piece of paper that completely changed everything, but she also told me that Carter had returned to England and had made no plans to return. I read those few pieces of paper over and over again until the words were practically seared onto my eyeballs.

Dad had always said there was something strange about Carter's trial. He mentioned that Carter got caught lying a couple of times and there were definite inconsistencies in his story. If the jury had seen what I now held in my hands, then he would never have gone to prison at all.

I could not understand why this evidence was not shown in court. I asked Amanda to do a bit of digging since she seemed to be so good at discovering this kind of information. She reported back a few days later to tell me that it was never brought to light because Carter's attorney had excluded it at his request.

Not only did he take the blame for the accident, but he also ensured that he would go to prison for it, presumably out of some misguided desire to see someone get punished for William's death.

I felt largely responsible. I never asked enough questions. When I woke up in the hospital, my thoughts were consumed with William and I never asked about what had happened to me. Maybe if I had been more curious or if I had gone to the trial I would have been able to keep Carter out of prison.

Kerry had been right. I did I owe Carter. I owed him my life.

I picked up the paper she had given me and read it one more time. It was a copy of a police report. The police had been first on the scene the night of the accident. There were lots of bars nearby and the police had been responding to a disturbance when the call came through. Most of the details had been recorded by the two officers who arrived on the scene and questioned Carter before he had time to weave all the lies into his story.

Reading the statement had been utterly surreal at first. It was like reading a movie script, except I was the star. Well, maybe not the star—probably more like the damsel in distress. Either way, I was part of the action, yet I had no recollection of any of the events.

The way Carter had described the accident, he had merely swapped places with Bella in the car and waited for the ambulance to arrive. He didn't say much more than that. The police statement revealed the whole truth. Bella's car had hit ours on the driver's side, which was why William took the worst of it, but our car ended up sliding up against a guard rail designed to stop cars going over the edge of the hill. The railing has done its job, but parts of the frame of the car had crumpled on the impact and left me with a piece of metal protruding from my calf.

When the police arrived on the scene, Carter was trying to get the passenger side door open, but the car was wedged against the metal rail and there was no way to make it budge. At first the officers pulled him away from the wreck and insisted on waiting for a rescue team to free me from the vehicle. At this stage, it seemed Carter admitted to driving while Bella just stayed in the car. He told the officer that the driver was already dead but that the girl in the passenger seat was still alive. Either five or ten minutes lapsed, depending on which officer you believed, and the ambulance had still not arrived. Then the car started slipping.

The metal rail was not strong enough to support its weight any longer. Inch by inch, the car started slipping over the side of the hill. The two police officers and Carter quickly leapt into action. Between the three of them they were able to keep it on the road, but they knew it was only a matter of time before their strength gave out. After a couple of minutes, one of the police officers lost his footing and the car nearly went over the edge. At that point, Carter decided to act.

He opened the back door, climbed in, and leaned into the front of the car. According to the police report I was still conscious at this point but mumbling incoherently. With Carter's weight now in the car as well, the police were struggling more and more to keep it on the road. With little time to act, Carter pulled the metal from my leg, at which point I lost consciousness. He somehow dragged me out of the car and onto the side of the road.

Once we were both out of the car, the two police officers gave up any attempt to keep it on the road and focused on radioing in for medical assistance. With no one to support the car, it started slipping again and was about to go over the edge, taking William's body with it. Both police officers described Carter's next actions as stupid. He placed me down on the road and then ran back to the car. He opened the driver side door and pulled my brother's dead body out just seconds before the car went over the hill where it ended up as a crumpled wreck.

I don't know what had more emotional impact on me, that Carter had risked his life to save mine, or that he had risked his life just so that my brother's body didn't go off the side of a cliff.

It would be another ten minutes before the emergency crews arrived, but that was enough time for Carter to save my life again. The metal that had pierced my leg had also ruptured an artery. He stayed by my side and applied pressure to the wound, using his shirt to soak up the blood. The police statement even mentioned that he was holding my hand and begging me to make it through the entire time while I lapsed in and out of consciousness.

The entire time this was going on, Bella was sitting in the passenger seat of her car pretending that she had nothing to do with the accident. Carter had little choice but to admit to being the driver. The faulty birth control pills supplied by PharmaTech were probably the reason Bella crashed the car, but that didn't excuse the rest of her behavior. She still chose to drink and drive. I would never have gone to prison for someone like that. Carter was a much better person than me.

The police statement didn't change the uncertain future Carter would have with me, but he had earned the right to make that decision for himself. If he still wanted to be with me, then I was damn sure not going to argue.

I heard a ping over the speaker system that snapped me out of my thoughts.

"Ladies and gentlemen, this is your captain speaking. Please ensure your seatbelts are fastened and your chairs are in the upright position. We are now beginning our descent to London Heathrow airport."

Chapter Nineteen

England looked so small on the map. California was about twice that size, so I had, perhaps a little naïvely, assumed that I would catch up with Carter in no time at all. He could have been staying in any of the most expensive hotels in London and living a life of luxury, but I had a feeling he would be at home with his parents. I certainly hoped so, because otherwise, finding him would be impossible. Thankfully, Kerry had given me their address, so I could at least give it a shot.

I had never heard of the town in which he lived and didn't even know how to pronounce it, but it wasn't far from London and I didn't anticipate a long journey. The first thing I did after the plane landed was take the train into London. This involved going in the opposite direction from where I needed to go, but a taxi from Heathrow would have been far too expensive and there were no direct trains.

From King's Cross train station I was just a short underground train ride away from all the infamous sights of London. There was still plenty of daylight left and I could have made a trip to Buckingham Palace, the Tower of London, or just taken in Big Ben. I'd wanted to see these sights since I was a little girl and my dad had started buying me progressively bigger and bigger jigsaw puzzles of foreign cities. The London puzzle had been one thousand pieces and had taken me weeks to complete, although that was partly because William had hidden three of the pieces and taken great pleasure in watching me struggle. Big brothers were like that sometimes.

The puzzle looked like a photograph, but after getting thoroughly confused a few times when watching movies set in London, I realized it had been somewhat exaggerated. Big Ben, Buckingham Palace, and the Tower of London were *not* all next to each other on the River Thames.

Even if all those attractions were right outside the train station, I still wouldn't have gone to take a photo. None of them would have looked as impressive as Carter standing before me.

After ten minutes of fiddling around with the ticket machine, I finally found the correct ticket to take me to Salisbury, which was the nearest station to Carter, but the machine wouldn't take my American bank card. I dashed over to a ticket booth to buy one the old-fashioned way. The train wouldn't depart for another thirty minutes, but I couldn't concentrate on anything else, so I went to wait for it on the platform.

By my standards, I had packed light, but British trains—or at least the one I got on—were not meant for people with suitcases. I clambered on board and ended up having to squeeze the small suitcase between my legs when someone complained that it was taking up a seat. The train journey was going to be at least two hours, and there was no way I could sit like this the entire way. Much to the utter bemusement and horror of the businessman next to me, I hitched up my trouser leg and pulled off the artificial limb, giving my one remaining leg a bit more space. It says a lot about rush hour commuters that the man next to me never said a thing and no one else seemed to even notice that a girl had pulled a leg off and sat with it on her lap.

There was no room to get any work done on my laptop and I couldn't focus on reading. Instead, I stared out of the window, first at the increasingly suburban areas of London, then at some smaller English towns, and finally just the countryside. It looked beautiful with the sun beaming down on the grass that was full of cows and sheep. Unfortunately, after about an hour and a half, the sun disappeared behind the clouds and the weather looked increasingly gloomy with every minute.

With a frustrating predictability, the rain started to fall just minutes before my train pulled into the station. I was one of the first people off and I made it to the taxi rank before a queue formed, which was quite an accomplishment, considering. I pulled up Carter's address on my phone and read it out loud to the taxi driver. His reaction was to pull out a small GPS device from the glove compartment, which didn't exactly fill me with confidence.

As the taxi left the shelter of the train station, any illusions I had that the storm might pass were soon shattered by the noise of rain hammering down on the car. In my haste, I'd never even thought to bring an umbrella on my trip to England.

The app I was using on my phone estimated that the journey would take around twenty minutes, but it had barely been fifteen when the taxi driver pulled to the side of the road and totaled up the fare. The sun had set in astonishingly quick time and it was now dark outside.

"Are you sure this is it?" I asked, looking out of the window even though I could barely see through it for the rain.

"Yes, yes, it's just down there," the man said, pointing down the road. "I can't drive any further because it is a one-way street, but it's just a one minute walk, at most."

The map on my phone was not showing the road as being a one-way street, but I wasn't in the mood to argue. I threw money at him, and despite his unhelpful demeanor, I gave him a generous tip.

I struggled forward in the rain, trying to pull my light jacket up to cover my head with my free hand while the other dragged my suitcase along the concrete. After a couple of minutes I realized there was no one-way street, but the taxi was long gone at this point. I ducked under a nearby tree, thinking that might offer some temporary protection from the rain, but instead the rain just collected into large drips on the ends of leaves before falling down my back.

The map on my phone showed that Carter's house was nearby. I just had to keep going down the same street and then take a left. It was a four-minute walk, but I would be drenched to the bone in less than twenty seconds, anyway, so the distance hardly mattered.

With the map committed to memory, I picked up my suitcase—dragging it along the ground would only slow me down—and left the quasi-shelter of the tree. The rain made short work of my thin Californian clothing, and as predicted, I was soon soaked through.

I moved as fast as my artificial leg and the wet road would allow as I turned onto Carter's street. He was number twenty-one. My eyes strained to make out the house numbers, but the streetlights merely lit up the rain in front of my eyes, making it even harder to see what lay in the distance.

I managed to see what I thought was a number seventeen on a door, but then the next house was apparently number twenty-nine so I must have been wrong. At least I knew what side of the road his house was on. I retraced my steps, but the next number I could pick out was number fifteen. The suitcase started to weigh down on my arm, so I resorted to dragging it until a wheel got stuck in a drain. I tried to pull the suitcase free, but it was wedged tight. I knew it was only a suitcase, but right now it seemed to perfectly sum up how I felt: stuck in the road and going nowhere.

I closed my eyes and took a deep breath in through my nose. To an onlooker I would have looked strangely calm and serene standing there in the rain. What I did next took me by surprise.

"Carter!" I yelled. I took another deep breath. "Carter!" I screamed, louder and stronger this time. Lights turned on in living rooms all around me, and I saw curtains open as people looked out at the crazy lady.

I felt stupid, but what the hell—I'd come this far already. I threw my arms open and screamed his name one last time. "Carter!"

"Emily?"

I spun around to confront the voice from behind me. The street lamp shone down on Carter, who stood there in the rain wearing an increasingly wet sweater and khakis.

For a moment I just stood there, looking at him. I'd spent most of the trip here thinking about what I would say to him, but now that he stood right in front of me, I had no idea what to say.

"Emily, what are you doing here?" he asked, taking a step toward me.

"You saved my life."

"I don't under—"

"Kerry explained everything. You saved my life the day of the crash. I'm so sorry, Carter. I didn't mean to push you away. I just wanted to keep you safe and away from this whole mess. I... I..."

I had no words left in me. Warm tears streamed from my eyes and mixed with the cold rain dripping down my cheeks. Carter snapped out of his malaise and closed the distance between us in two quick paces.

"You have nothing to be sorry for," he said, pulling my soaking wet body in toward him. "God, you're freezing."

"I want to be with you," I said. "Will you forgive me?"

He released me from his embrace and put his hands on my shoulders. "I told you Emily, there is nothing to forgive. Do you have any idea how much I love you?"

I looked into his eyes and a smile started to form on my lips. "I love you, too."

Carter effortlessly picked up my suitcase from the road and took hold of my hand. We were both drenched now, and I could see at least three people staring at us through the nearby windows.

He laughed and shook his head. "I still can't believe you're here. You came all this way for me?"

I nodded. "Yes. That, and I want to see Big Ben."

He laughed again. "Come on, let's get out of the cold and rain. The house is warm and we have the fire on."

"You have no idea how appealing that sounds right now. Throw in a hot bath, and I will owe you big time."

"I think that can be arranged. I need you nice and relaxed."

"Why's that?" I asked.

"Because it's time for you to meet my parents. I've spent the last week talking about how amazing you are. They'll be home soon and would love to meet you."

Carter opened the door to his parents' quaint, cozy home. I'd never been introduced to a man's parents before, but then I'd had a lot of firsts with Carter, and I was sure there would be plenty more in store for me in the future.

We stripped on our way up the stairs, leaving a trail of wet clothes behind us, and sank into a hot bath together. There was no room to do anything in the tub other than bathe—and there was barely room for that—but we were happy just talking. We'd only been apart a week, but we had a lot of catching up to do.

Author's Note

Thank you so much for reading my book and for supporting an independent publisher. I really hope you enjoyed it—I know I loved writing it.

If I may be so bold, I would like to ask a favor of you. Most people do not leave reviews, but if you enjoyed the book (or even if you didn't and have some feedback for me) please do consider writing a review. Independent publishers like myself are entirely dependent on reviews—we cannot sell books without them.

Thank you!

About the Author

Miranda Dawson is a 25-year-old Californian who can't find the man of her dreams and so writes about him instead. She likes reading romance novels and watching scandalous television shows. Her writing is influenced by both!

You can contact me at miranda.dawson@sfpublishingllc.com or check out my Facebook page.

Printed in Great Britain
by Amazon

A
PEACOC
ON THE LAWN

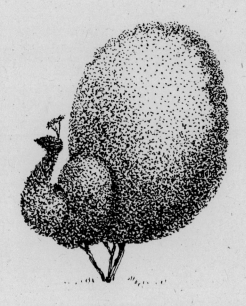

A Kitchen Garden Book

Text © Francine Raymond
Illustrations © Gabrielle Stoddart

By the same Author.
In the same series:
Keeping a few Hens
Food from the Kitchen Garden
Beekeeping for Beginners (with P. Hands)
Keeping a few Ducks in your Garden
A Goose on the Green
Also:
The Big Book of Garden Hens
A Henkeeper's Journal
A Christmas Journal
All my Eggs in one Basket

Published by the Kitchen Garden 2005
Troston
Suffolk 1P31 1EX
Tel 01359 268 322
Email: francine@jfraymond.demon.co.uk
www.kitchen-garden-hens.co.uk
www.henkeepersassociation.co.uk

ISBN 0-9532857-6-6

Printed in England

Many thanks to Quinton Spratt, Jo Kendall and
Simon Hansford.

'Remember that the most beautiful things in the world are the most useless; peacocks and lilies for instance'.
John Ruskin: The Stones of Venice

Introduction

In Italy they say peafowl have 'the feathers of an angel, the cry of the Devil and the appetite of a thief'. And the Romans were responsible for introducing them to Britain.

Certainly, if tidy flowerbeds are a source of pride and joy, peacocks are not for you. They have an uncanny knack of heading straight for your favourite plant, nipping it in the bud or levelling it to the ground. And if your male is dressed in summer finery complete with five-foot train, he can wipe out an entire border with one swipe. I'll suggest ways of avoiding these disasters anon, but you can't prevent them altogether.

Then, of course there's the noise. The paean call can send shivers down your spine or leave you reaching for a shotgun. One book I researched devoted an entire chapter (with gruesome snip-by-snip illustrations) to an operation to de-voice a peacock: a remedy that has obviously exercised many a frantic mind at 4.30 on a spring morning. If *you* feel you might be tempted, *put this book aside now*. Once mated though, in his defence, the cock will stay largely silent, only firing warning honks if threatened - a noise always worth investigating. But in truth, you need plenty of space between you and your nearest neighbours. Or preferably no near neighbours at all.

Peacocks are birds for the great outdoors. Confine them at night for your own peace of mind; in Springtime perhaps, to protect the shoots in your garden, and definitely when broody or with chicks to give them a good start in life, but they can survive on their own and must be allowed to range free in open spaces.

Why keep peafowl? There will be no delicious boiled eggs for family breakfasts – peahens only lay during the mating season; and as an alternative Christmas dinner (roast peacock once graced tables at the New York Waldorf Astoria) the meat is tough and you just won't want to. To be honest, they do little except sit around looking incredibly beautiful, especially in Spring and Summer when they are in full fig.

To me though, the glory of those feathers, iridescent in the morning sun, and the pride I feel when my gentle peahen brings her brood onto the lawn, is worth every flattened flower and dawn alarm call. So, if you are prepared to be captivated by these aristocratic creatures and count tolerance and an overriding love of beauty among your virtues, read on.

Where to begin

Have you enough room for peafowl? These are not birds for a *pied-à-terre*. A fully-grown male measures around six foot from coronet to train, and needs plenty of room to turn round. Your flock will need access to grass and soil: modern, minimalist gravel and concrete won't do. You'll need a garden of at least ½ acre plus a few tall trees for them to roost in. It is possible to keep a pair as caged birds, but they'll get bored, stressed and prone to disease. It's best to give them free range.

You will, however need a large aviary to house them for the first couple of months, or your affair with peacocks will almost certainly be short-lived. They will wander off, back in the general direction they came from. Though unhappy with their first few days caged; pacing back and forth in a way that will have you reaching for the door, resist that urge. After a few weeks they'll accept their pen as home.

How many birds should you have? If you are an experienced poultry-person with rolling acres, your flock (or collective term – muster) can be as large as your pocket. At time of going to print, a Blue peacock sells for £45.00 and a hen for £35.00. I would start with a trio of Blues - a cock and two hens. Any more and you will need an aviary as big as the one at London Zoo. Later you can breed from them to augment your flock. You could keep just one, but peafowl are sociable birds who like an accomplice with whom to destroy your garden. My boy hangs out with the chickens while his mate is away broody.

Most experts are against the idea of keeping peacocks with other poultry. A disease, called Blackhead, to which peafowl are vulnerable, is carried by chickens and turkeys. Friends' experiences seem to contradict this, especially if both are kept free-range within reasonable numbers (see p28 for remedial action). Other pets must be trained not to chase your flock, but peacocks are less vulnerable because they can fly.

There are accounts of rogue peacocks damaging cars, perhaps mistaking their reflections in shiny bodywork as rivals. Our birds never show the slightest interest in any vehicle parked in the drive, perhaps our cars need washing more regularly. However, they do trumpet the arrival of visitors, which is useful, and they spend hours admiring themselves in our French windows, though they don't attack. Maybe it depends on the individual bird and perhaps we should put a garage on the list of compulsory equipment.

Shopping for peafowl: ours were a generous donation from someone whose flock had grown too large. There are advertisements in the poultry and smallholding press, but always visit before buying and check your purchases are healthy and happy. Breeders will help with packing, because a 2 metre long bird is not an easily transportable parcel. If you live in, or can visit East Anglia, Quinton Spratt, who helped us with this book, breeds and transports peafowl all over the world. He can supply and advise, (see p31).

Where to keep your peafowl

Hopefully, the pen where your new arrivals spend their first 6 to 8 weeks will be the one they use as their regular bedroom. Site your aviary in a sheltered spot against a wall or fence that offers a view of the garden, so your newcomers can survey and get to know their surroundings before they are released.

The minimum sized pen for a trio is 20sq ft, but the larger, the better. You could use a strong fruit cage with weld mesh sides. The roof should be covered to stop the birds escaping and part boarded with corrugated iron, board or Onduline to offer shelter over the perch (see p31 for netting and cage-makers). Despite their delicate beauty, peacocks are hardy birds. Left to their own devices they will roost in trees. Pathetic when wet - a full tail is heavy when saturated - but rugged enough to hop down in the morning with frost on their backs, peafowl thrive in snowy parts of the world.

You can offer a series of ladder perches – the lower ones will be useful for chicks and provide access to the highest one (at least 5ft off the ground to accommodate the longest train). The roosting poles should be 4" x 4" timber (*never* metal, their feet might freeze) with the upper surface bevelled for comfortable roosting. You could place a sliding droppings board for easy cleaning under the highest perch, and the dry spot underneath can be encouraged for use as a dustbath by adding wood ash, sandpit-grade sand and anti-louse powder.

However beautiful your *palais de paons*, your new arrivals will be ungrateful lodgers in the beginning. Young birds used to being

9

caged will settle in quickly. My peacocks grew up on a large and beautiful estate and I suspect they were unimpressed with their forced downsizing.

Encourage your birds to roost in their pen every evening by feeding their last meal inside, and shut them in. But, they will probably head for the tallest tree in your garden as soon as they're released. Mine have various perches depending on wind direction. Spartacus, the cock, is a more reliable forecaster than the Met Office, often roosting a good hour before it rains and predicting the ferocity of the weather in his choice of tree.

Use the time your birds spend caged to tame them. I say this ruefully, as I never took the opportunity, and though my peacocks trust me, they won't feed out of my hand, unlike their offspring, who are very friendly and blissfully ignore warning looks from their mum.

What to feed your peacocks

Like most poultry, peafowl are omnivores and need a basic diet of mixed grain (available from the feed merchant) to which I add peas, leftover potato, pasta, rice and fruit. I was told to offer protein in the form of tinned catfood or cooked sausage. Conscious that I might be neglecting their diet, I tried petfood, but they studiously ignored this and helped themselves to live fodder from our seven-acre, partly wild garden. Imprinted on my memory is the day Spartacus – the hunter-gatherer - swooped across the lawn, a macabre silhouette with a frog speared in his beak, its poor feet waving wildly.

Ornamental birds drink surprisingly copiously - about two to three cups a day, especially if they are caged and fed mostly dried food. I leave galvanized drinkers around the garden, and take care to refresh them in hot weather and when it is icy.

All birds need grit to help them digest their food. Most will find it within the confines of an average-sized garden. For those in cages, grit must be supplied from your feed merchant. Also available is a range of high protein game and ornamental poultry feed (with Omega 3 oils for glossy plumage) from Allen & Page, as well as peanuts and sunflower seeds. Scatter a handful of feed per bird per day directly onto the ground. The evening meal should be served in the pen on a flat dish, and removed later to deter uninvited guests. The flock is then secured for the night.

Left to their own devices, peafowl will also eat plenty of grass and other greenery. In Winter, I supplement with finely shredded lettuce or brassicas. On their strolls round my vegetable garden Spartacus and his wife Juno will happily peck at the rhubarb leaves and beetroot tops, which are only left uncloched because they can't get at the bits I want. If only they could open the fruitcage and reach the strawberries, they would be in peacock paradise. The best I can offer are bruised and damaged leftovers and raisins as a special treat. They seem particularly fond of yellow, orange and red coloured berries, flowers and vegetables. Bad news for your nasturtiums – good news *vis-à-vis* dandelions.

Like every other bird in the garden, the peacock is up at dawn and wants you to get up too, to feed and admire him. Spartacus stands and calls on the wall directly opposite our bedroom window, just outside strangling distance. When absolutely sure I'm awake, he will saunter off to the spot where he habitually has breakfast and wait. I don't get up at this point and neither should you– it's just a game we play. But, you should feed your flock at about the same time every day, in roughly the same place. Peacocks, like most animals, are creatures of habit and like a routine that you (and whoever looks after them while you're away) will have to stick to. Start as you mean to go on.

Your aviary built, and with a range of foodstuffs and drinkers to the ready, it is time to choose a breed and welcome your birds.

Which breed

The noble Peafowl (male peacock, female peahen) is the most spectacular member of the pheasant family. There are two species kept commonly – *Pavo Cristatus* – the Indian or Blue Peacock, the one that springs to mind when imagining a peacock; and *Pavo Muticus* - the Java or Green Peacock - indigenous to South East Asia. Mutations including the Black Winged and the ethereal White peafowl are described overleaf.

Different breeds and mutations can be kept together, but consequent offspring, especially those with white splashes are poor, and White females will predictably always prefer the gaudier Blue or Green males.

Juno's companions and Hera's symbol, long valued for their ornament, peacocks were introduced to Europe by Alexander the Great. The Romans used peacock feathers to induce vomiting after over-indulging at orgies. To Buddists the peacock is a sign of wisdom, and Persian Shahs sat on Peacock thrones. Courtiers admired them at Versailles; in India, where it is the national bird, peafowl bile is a cure for snake venom, and in Asia the meat is said to restore virility. Even today their feathers are thought to evoke the Evil Eye, though in early Christian times the peacock was a sign of immortality. I feel the more eyes I have watching over me the better, and can't resist collecting them to bring into the house for decoration. Apparently, white peacock feathers are in great demand for bridal bouquets.

Roast peacock was a visual feast at mediaeval banquets. With head and coronet gilded, flesh basted with beaten egg, and tail feathers fanned out, the meat is said to be so tough it doesn't decay, and was later superseded by turkey as the festive choice.

The Blue Indian Peafowl *(India)*

Popular and easy to keep, adapting well to the British climate, the male has a dark green metallic head and a brilliant peacock blue neck and shoulders, merging to a purply-blue on the breast and green on the abdomen. The back and rump are bronze. The tail feathers in season almost defy description, each terminating in the legendary 'eye'. The peahen is elegantly understated in shades of brown, with a green neck and pale blue eye shadow.

The Green Peafowl *(South East Asia)*

A slimmer, taller, spectacularly elegant bird, beautifully shaped, with metallic blue green head, a bronze neck with blue markings and an emerald green back. The female has similar colouring. Rather expensive (£200 per pair) and not for beginners because they are more susceptible to the cold and need permanent penning to stop them flying off. Though known as the Mute peacock, they are not soundless, just slightly less strident.

Black Winged Peafowl

Of the many mutations bred from the Blue, the most successful is
the Black Winged or Black Shouldered Peacock. With shiny
black shoulders, wings and thighs, but other features similar to
the Blue, this cross was first developed over two centuries ago.
Pairs will breed true and the chicks are yellow at birth. Females
are buff/cream with brown markings. Peahens are always duller
to be better camouflaged for successful sitting.

White Peafowl

The most striking mutation. To see a white male display is like watching a piece of lace being fluttered in the sunshine. Whites are sports of the Blue and occur naturally in the wild, though would probably not survive. The yellow chicks can be delicate and need special care. Hens and cocks must be caged together during the breeding season or she will elope with a blue or green suitor. Whites need shelter to keep their plumage at its best.

Augmenting your flock

Introducing newcomers to your flock will involve penning them in 'quarantine' for 6-8 weeks. Probably the easiest solution is to build an annexe at one end of your pen with its own perch and shelter. Give the new occupants full range of the whole aviary once the rest of the flock has decamped in the morning and return the new birds to their own quarters at bedtime. A long thin whippy stick is useful when herding.

The flock will be used to each other by the time the period of confinement is completed and provided there is plenty of space for them all, there should be no problems. Keep an eye on them all at feeding time though and make sure your newcomers are getting enough to eat.

The easiest way to increase your flock is to breed your own, but you will need new blood every other generation or so. Peacocks are mature at three years, peahens at two. The peacock is a perfect gentleman compared to most cockerels. My Buff Orpington is ever rampant, and mounts his wives whenever he can. I suppose that's the price paid for constant eggs.

Spartacus on the other hand, must woo his wife Juno. This lengthy procedure starts in early April. Heralded by the first of his famous shrieks and accompanied by much rattling of tail quills, painstakingly grown all winter, he does a drumroll turn to show off his *derrière* - a slightly ridiculous but nonetheless charming powder puff of the softest feathers.

For at least a month, the whole display is completely ignored. Even the chickens are more impressed than Juno. As time goes by, he will often back her into a corner while displaying, and she has become adept at ducking out at the last minute. Windy weather can play havoc with his courtship, sometimes spinning him round completely to display to all and sundry.

Finally, after six weeks, when even *he* is beginning to seem a trifle bored with the whole palaver and has learned to eat while displaying, (demonstrating, I feel, a rather poor level of commitment), Spartacus conquers Juno, balancing himself by grabbing her corona. The whole brutish business is over in a matter of seconds. Shaking herself, she moves on with dignity intact, as though nothing has happened.

Then, after almost daily mating and just when I'm beginning to think he is wasting his time, Juno disappears and simultaneously, Spartacus shuts up. No more 4.30 alarm calls. Hurrah. From then on, he will only call out if we approach the nest.

Peahens choose the silliest places to nest. Large tinted eggs are laid in shallow hollows on the ground and the hens are vulnerable during the whole 26 day incubation period to foxes and dogs. If possible, pop an open-bottomed cage over the broody once she has settled and camouflage with branches. Let her out once a day at the same time to eat, drink and perform her *toilette*. Non-stop chatter from a nearby portable radio also deters predators, as does Renardine or regularly applied human pee.

Most textbooks insist peahens make bad mothers. This hasn't been my experience. Possibly they don't wait to hatch out all their eggs and that would be a disadvantage if you were breeding for profit. Don't let them sit on more than four eggs - though this seems the norm for free range clutches in this country. Many of these breeders/writers suggest brooding under chickens or even Muscovy ducks, but I believe chicks learn most from their own mothers. If you intend to incubate mechanically, 'Incubation at Home' by Michael Roberts is instructive.

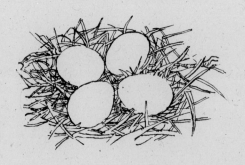

Peachicks

During the nesting period, Spartacus is usually at a loss. He and the Buff Orpington, whose wives are perpetually broody, hunch together like a pair of expectant fathers, resigned and rather fed up. Juno sits well, though is often agitated by squirrels who will take eggs and chicks.

Then, exactly 28 days from the time she started brooding, she appears on the lawn, elegantly side-stepping her chicks. Peachicks are yellow and brown and slightly larger than chicken chicks. Their little wings are well developed with proper feathers. They are *very* vulnerable to predators and have no body fat to keep them warm, but mum will brood them. Corral them back into the main pen with treats for the hen and judicious herding, so they don't fall prey to cats, crows, rats or hedgehogs. The peacock will stand guard, but keep an eye on him: some don't make good fathers and may have to be excluded from the pen. He'll probably roost nearby or on top of the cage.

After a week or so, the chicks should be able to flutter onto the lowest roosting pole with their mum and will sometimes appear alien-like from the middle of her chest, brooded and protected from the cold and wet. Over the following weeks they will make their way up to the higher roosting poles. In the wild they would hop from the lowest branches upwards encouraged by their parents and will do this in your garden as well, but it is safer to encourage them into the pen. Fewer sleepless nights for you, too.

Peachicks should be fed little and often on turkey starter crumbs from your feed merchant. They will probably show little interest

22

in food for the first couple of days, having ingested the yolk sac inside the egg. Their mum will teach them what to do. Incubated chicks may need to be taught to peck – use your finger to make pecking jabs at the food. Water should be offered in a fountain drinker or shallow dish with an upturned flowerpot in the middle to prevent the chicks falling in and getting chilled. Gradually introduce whatever the rest of the flock eats, chopped or shredded to size, including hard-boiled egg and shredded lettuce.

The peahen will continue to brood and look after her offspring until they are three months old. They can then be let out of the pen with the rest of the flock, but will need supervision from you. Length of leg seems to be the most accurate way of predicting sex. At three months the cocks are evident by the barring on their backs, and then they start to strut, just like their dad.

Gardening with peafowl

This could be a short chapter because, unless you are prepared to take precautions, you won't have much of a garden. A formal garden with sturdy box and yew survives well, once established, but if your peacocks are free-range – and I hope they are - you can't stop them from wandering, (unlike hens, which can be confined and in the case of my Orpingtons, need rocket power to get them aloft, peafowl can fly). Your flock will amble around the vegetable garden - at dawn - carefree, pecking their way through whatever takes their fancy.

In short, everything you hope to eat must be covered: in cages, beak-proof tunnels and cloches made of bamboo, glass, wire or bent willow. Flowers will need extra staking to keep them upright when you-know-who sweeps by. A walled, fenced or netted kitchen garden with a roof is a must. The same companies that provide netting for pens can be called upon to supply large gauge netting to cover a cage to protect your crops, (see p31).

Apparently, peacocks are put off by a single strand of wire stretched across the top of a wall and beds can be protected with a low wire or woven willow surround because they try to avoid entanglement. The gardeners at Houghton Hall in Norfolk tell me that flapping and shouting will eventually train birds to eschew the flower garden for the acres of rolling lawn beyond.

Your flock will eat a lot of grass, but they don't rake it like hens. Evidence of their presence on the lawn is minimal, apart from their soft, smelly excrement, which is good for the soil - not pleasant to step in though. Guano from the dropping board can be layered in the compost heap as an activator. All bird manure is rich in nitrogen. Terraces and stonework can be hosed down with a high-powered blast. Pens that are in constant use should be dressed and raked with peat, sand or dried leaves to keep the floor sweet and the sweepings make good compost.

Peafowl do not differentiate between weeds and other plants. It's all grist to their mill and they'll spear slugs and snap flies on their daily circuit, cocking their heads to one side as they consider what to demolish next. In India, peacocks are venerated because they enjoy the odd snake and fearlessly keep the cobra population down. In our more mundane climes they'll take frogs, worms, slugs, weevils and butterflies, especially cabbage whites.

Infrequent dust bathers, preferring to preen and sunbathe, the whole flock tend to pick just one bathing site, queuing to use it like a large household with a single bathroom. Encourage them to use the space under the dropping board in their pen with frequent toppings of wood ash and you'll avoid unsightly craters in the rest of the garden.

Despite my dire warning, gardening with peacocks is not a problem if you protect the things you care about and are indulgent to your birds. Less tenacious than other poultry, peacocks are easily put off and will move on to something more accessible.

Problems

Peafowl are hardy birds who can manage on their own with little help from you, as they do on many a large estate. But, given space to roam, some extra food and a pen for shelter, they will thrive.

All birds moult annually in late summer and shed their feathers, but none as obviously as the peacock. All his carefully acquired, meticulously preened and beautifully displayed finery will be discarded carelessly round the garden. It is a low point of the year, and birds are more prone to disease. A little crushed garlic or rescue remedy in their drinking water can give them a boost.

It is possible to keep several males in the same large garden. Each will stick to his own territory or lec, and call to attract females to his harem during the mating season. But each will try and out-call the other, so it's your eardrums that will suffer. Henfriends get on well together, unless they are protecting young. Tame your birds early to prevent rogue males developing anti-social behaviour towards humans. Male peafowl often go roaming after the business of raising a family is over. They may wander off for days but usually return (worth a warning to neighbours though). You could snip the ends of the primary flight feathers on one wing to discourage escape, but this would leave your birds vulnerable to predators. Never clip wings during the moult, because immature feather shafts contain veins.

Wherever poultry is fed there is a likelihood of rat infestation. Don't overfeed your birds or leave food lying about, especially at night. Store sacks of mixed corn and pellets in galvanized dustbins with metal lids to deter unwelcome diners. If vermin are a problem, I can recommend the Wide Piper, a clever rat-diameter piece of pipe with a see-through bait dispenser (available from agricultural suppliers), which will keep the poison out of reach of your flock and other family pets.

Even if you make every effort to provide your flock with all they need, occasionally one will fall ill or become injured. Generally, when a bird is unwell she'll stand dejectedly with head and tail down. Catch her with a long-handled fisherman's landing net and isolate her immediately with drinking water and observe. Usually she will perk up of her own accord. If not, contact the vet. Often the trauma of capture and transportation to the surgery is the last straw, so a call-out may be in order. Sometimes an experienced avian vet will advise over the phone. Ask your breeder or a peacock-owning neighbour to recommend someone.

If a trip in the car is inevitable, place the patient in a large well-ventilated cardboard box. Pop the lid on, and she'll calm down. Few birds can see in the dark, which is why they roost at night to escape danger. On long journeys make sure the box is placed on newspaper on the back seat of your car, rather than in an airless boot. In the wild peacocks can go for eighteen hours without food or water.

There is a disease known as Blackhead that can affect peafowl. It comes from an intestinal parasite carried by wild birds and chickens. Blackhead affects the liver and symptoms include listlessness and yellow diarrhoea. Your vet will prescribe, but *it is important to act promptly and treat within two days*, so keep a remedy to hand.

28

Peafowl suffer from a variety of parasites, none of which require routine prevention in a small free-range flock, but need to be kept an eye on to check they don't overpower their host who is perhaps already suffering from illness or old age. Broody peahens are sometimes put off sitting by fleas or mites, and should be treated in early summer, before they nest. Your vet will advise. Occasionally, birds can damage a leg or foot flying down awkwardly from a height and will need treatment.

Your beautiful peacock and his hens can live for 25 years, so adopting a flock is quite a commitment. But though you may sometimes rue their presence in your garden on sleepless early mornings in springtime, feel honoured by their company and you'll be sustained by endless visions of loveliness throughout the rest of the year.

Notes

Directory

Eltex - feeders & drinkers	01384 898 911
Allen & Page - for feed	01362 822 900
Gridfeed Thornber - broody cages	01706 815 131
Gamekeeper Feeds - supply catalogue	01789 772 429
Knowle Nets - cages/netting catalogue	01308 458 186
Agriframes - fruit cage catalogue	01983 209 209
Anthony de Grey - designs to order trellis/cages	0207 738 8866
Stonebank Ironcraft - metal pergolas/cages	01285 720 737
Quinton Spratt - breeder	01508 489 471
@ Forncett St Mary, Norwich, Norfolk	07730 883 115

The World Pheasant Association
PO Box 5, Lower Basildon, Reading, RG8 9PF

For up-to-date poultry health information
www.henkeepersassociation.co.uk

Incubation at Home - Michael Roberts	Gold Cockerel Books
Diseases of Free Range Poultry - V. Roberts	Whittet Books
The Pheasants of the World - J. Delacour	Spur Publications

Places to see Peafowl:

Houghton Hall, Houghton, Norfolk	01485 528 569
Leeds Castle, Kent	01622 765 400
Warwick Castle	0870 442 2000
Kentwell Hall, Long Melford, Suffolk	01787 310 207
Wyken Vineyards, Stanton, Suffolk	01359 250 287

This book, and others in the range, on keeping hens, ducks, bees and cooking with vegetables and eggs are available by mail order and from our shop, The Kitchen Garden, Church Lane, Troston, Bury St Edmunds, Suffolk IP31 1EX   01359 268 322
Come and see us on Fridays and Saturdays during the season or visit our website   www.kitchen-garden-hens.co.uk